One Hundred Views of NW3

Pat Jourdan

Copyright © Pat Jourdan 2020

The right of Pat Jourdan to be identified as the author of this work has been asserted by her in accordance Copyright, Designs and Patents Act 1988. All rights reserved. No part of this book may be reproduced, stored in a retrieval system or transmitted in any form or by any means (electronic, mechanical, photocopying, recording or otherwise) without the prior written consent of the author, except in cases of brief quotations embodied in with reviews or articles. It may not be edited, amended, lent, resold, hired out, distributed or otherwise circulated without the author's written permission.

patjourdan.wordpress.com

Relevant focussed images and sensual detail draw the reader in.
Carol Thistlethwaite
Determination to find fresh uses for language, not ordinary description.
William Oxley
Her excellent pamphlet, The Cast-Iron Shore, erbacce press, Liverpool, does indeed have a painterly quality.
Carol Ann Duffy
The prose (of *Grounded*) is immaculate and enigmatic from beginning to end. The observation of detail is uncannily good.
Eugene Mc Cabe
She has an exquisite sensibility and a rare quality of empathetic resonance. Pat Jourdan has an absolute way with words – she conveys her own feelings with an immediacy which resonates with her adopted Irishness. She describes life with a stunning suddenness – a painter as well as a poet.
Barry Tebb
Little-known but gifted poet of the Liverpool School.
Ian McEwan, *Saturday*

Ever a canny observer.
Mark Lewisohn, *All These Years*

One Hundred Views
of NW3

Pat Jourdan

Also by Pat Jourdan

Novels
> Finding Out
> A Small Inheritance
> Maryland Street

Poetry
> The Bedsit Girl
> The Bedsit
> Ainnir Anthology
> Turpentine
> The Cast-Iron Shore
> Liverpool Poets 2008
> Citizeness

Short Stories
> Average Sunday Afternoon
> Taking the Field
> Rainy Pavements
> The Fog Index

Cover picture,
Room over Prompt Corner, Pond Street,
January 1960, Pat Jourdan

For
Amelia Hull-Hewitt, Hunter Jourdan & Inigo Jourdan

1 Painters' Instructions. On starting a picture always remember, clouds need clean brushes.

So how does it start? You never truly know. It muscles in from nowhere, you find yourself in a new place with no real recipe. Tomorrow will be different, there's no real plan except to simply survive, which takes a lot of effort. Another cigarette, another Nescafé, make it stronger, darker, get that extra energy, try more sugar, an extra spoonful, that'll work, perhaps.

As far as Stella was concerned, Dot was magic. A friend of one of the Art College students, Dot had somehow kept cropping up in every café or pub nearby and had become a friend although she was a good seven years older than Stella. A force of nature, she managed to persuade Stella's suspicious parents that a visit to Hampstead would be perfect, she could stay at Dot's flat. They needed help at some big New Years party and Dot had been asked to bring someone else as a waitress.

"I really wanted us to get the Chelsea Arts Ball, but that was already fixed up ages ago. This is a big party at the Hampstead Sports Club, it's quite important. You've got a black dress? That's all you'll need. We'll get the early train from Lime Street, I'll collect you." It was amazing how Stella's parents got on so well with Dot, but that was her gift, an easy 'everything is possible' confidence.

"It'll be some of the people I was telling you about," Dot said. "You know, the poets, the ones that do readings round each others' flats and so on. The other week they got a golfing handbook and the instructions for using a hoover and they were reading them in tandem, it was really surreal - it worked, apart from being hilarious as well. They are clubbing together to buy a tape recorder and get it all recorded. Perhaps issue tapes and all that." It was like waving sweets in front of a kid. It was everything Stella would dream of, the kindest cruelty.

Having to change trains, they waited at Crewe station at the end of the platform, sitting on the edge of an empty luggage cart. A middle-aged man approached them. Pointing at the hatbox, he asked if they were models. 'Models' was code for prostitutes.

"No, I'm a secretary and Stella's an art student," Dot told him. That made matters worse.

"Art? You do that life drawing, then, with the models posing?" Stella said yes, it was part of their training.

He warmed up.

"I used to go to an art class, evenings, we had one of those girls to pose for us, like, but she left and the class closed down. No other girl wanted to do it." He looked profoundly sad. "You can't get models in Crewe," he said poignantly as he wandered off. It became one of their catchphrases for ages afterwards.

8

They arrived at the Sports Club early, dressed in immaculate black. There was no one around yet. Dot had collected the keys from the barman at the Cartaret Club. As far as Stella was concerned, this was the height of sophistication, a private London drinking club full of well-dressed business men. Dot seemed to know several of them. As she stood by a table, a fair-haired man approached Stella.

"You are a friend of Dot's? I am Carlos the Latvian You are very lucky to meet me. There are only four million of us." He said this as though it was his own achievement, with no explanation of what he was doing here with all these wheelers and dealers in their sharp suits. Stella was glad to get out of the place and into the late afternoon gloom.

Stella and Dave met at the sink at that party, where they were both working as bar staff. If you could fall in love at a sink washing wine glasses, then anything vaguely romantic was possible.

"Look, can you hurry up? I need more clean glasses right now!" she had said, and then really stopped and looked at the classic tall dark and handsome lad next to her. A Buddy Holly lookalike. He pulled a face and then grinned,

"OK, if you insist, that's as soon as the next tray of empties appears." After that they started to work in harmony, pacing each other while strains of bright music reached them from the dance floor. The party went on until two in the morning when the special drinks licence ended. During the tidying up, after draping the wet towels across the taps and sorting out the broken glass into the bins, Dave turned to Stella and said,

"Do you know the wild feeling where you can have anything you want, and then you give up the belief and you can't have it?" It was nonsense but she deciphered that he was talking about herself and himself leaving the place together.

So after tidying up, Stella searched around the crowd and said a rushed goodbye to Dot. She went off into the New Year's Day pre-dawn cold wind with Dave. They walked past Dot's flat over the chess players' café at South End Green, the café windows empty now in the grey light.

They woke to a warm January morning.
"It's like spring," Stella said contentedly.
"No wonder! This thing's been on all night" Dave said, standing next to the arty oil stove with its black casing and decorative legs. He switched it off and wriggled into his clothes, "You want some tea?" Yes, she did. He shambled off to the kitchen, empty now as the others in the flat had gone off to work already. It was New Year's Day now, still a work day for most people. Only the unemployed and students were left, and that covered both of them. Dave and Stella had spent the night in a combination of reading T.S. Eliot's *The Wasteland* and making love. The sex was easy but the poetry was more of an effort. That was as much as she could remember, it was rather a blur. The book was still there, shoved under the pillow of his single bed. Her black waitress dress was

slung over the bottom of the bed along with the rest of her scattered underclothes.

He brought the two mugs of tea, well sugared. Dave stood looking out of the window watching a man next door walking down the garden path eating an orange, and started scratching his arms. Stella said she had noticed it last night, what was the matter - some allergy?

"Yes, this rash, don't know what's caused it, it's changed to really annoying and I've run out of cream, got to go to the doctors as soon as they open. It's not a crisis, just irritating, in both senses of the word."

The white house they were in was near the corner of South End Road and from this top floor window there was a clear view of Keats Grove. The room was small, with a single bed, a desk, chair, a wardrobe and a shelf of books taking up most of the white space. Even the floor was pale unvarnished wood. A trumpet nestled against the wardrobe. They had more tea and toast, then wandered along the edge of the Heath before getting some foodstuff from the small Co-op and cooking sausages and omelettes in the shared kitchen before the other three flat sharers came back.

"It works, most of the time, except when we have rows about jazz and I have different opinions from them. They like the sterilised stuff like Dave Brubeck, but I say it's the blues and blues-inspired stuff that's the real thing. It's got to come from emotion, not clever mutations of notes. But we all agree about The New Statesman, luckily. We share paying for it." It was such a ramshackle mix of sophistication and mess that Stella was intrigued.

They went off to a party that evening and that was the pattern of the next two days. The nights were a mixture of heartfelt talk, quotes from the under-pillow poetry and lovemaking that made the stars fall down. Dave was obviously well-experienced which made sex so much easier.

"But it's chemistry really," he whispered into her ear, as they squashed together on the one pillow. "We can't resist it, and even better, it can't be faked. We join together easily. Let's enjoy it as it is."

In that first morning Dave said the entrancing thing about being in bed with a girl was looking into their eyes the morning after.

"It's as if she's had her entire being cleaned, renewed, and it shines straight out of her eyes."

"So, it must be the same for you, it has to be. We're both new to each other each time. Polished and scoured."

They must have eaten something in those three days and nights - probably cheese on toast but food was incidental.

When Stella reached Dot's flat again on Monday afternoon, Dot was busy at the kitchen table typing out a report for her office on a portable typewriter.

"They let me have a day at home as long as I finish this lot off. Well, I didn't see that coming! Fancy you going off with Dave - you've not been seen for entire days! Come back to get your bag, then?" She was not concerned or offended at all. Dot was the ultimate in unruffled. Her life, switching between Liverpool and

London probably helped, as any problems in one place would be avoidable in the other. Her father, retired, had worked for British Rail and the family had free train allowance or something like that. Neither he nor his wife went anywhere so Dot could use the rail pass instead. Her parents kept a permanent home for her in the north and office work in Hampstead Town Hall paid for the flat. She spread a wild generosity in her wake, unconcerned with any results, good or bad. Stella crammed belongings into the hatbox and dashed down the stone stairs.

Dave was waiting for her down on the pavement.

"We can go somewhere on the way to your coach," Dave suggested. "I've got an idea of somewhere you'd like." Catching the tube they patched through the underground and got to the British Museum. Still in the aftermath of the New Year holiday, the place was almost deserted.

"I've got something to show you now you're here, there's one special gallery before you leave," he said. All London churned past outside; but now they were both walking through the still silence of the museum. He led her through galleries towards the showcases filled with clocks. The ticking of so many timepieces together made a clacking sound as if these hulking grandfather and grandmother clocks were chattering together over centuries while London traffic milled about outside in messy chaos.

Away from that outside world these clocks could be no witness to what had happened. Even through the war they had been hidden and safe. Their worth accrued more in this clockwork safety. Now, as if set free one clock was whirring, poised to strike its quarter hour and all the others clicked, ready to join in. Stella hoped Dave and herself could still be in the gallery when all the clocks would be chiming, but that would be in three-quarters of an hour's time and the coach back home to Liverpool left from Victoria at half-past five.

Dave wandered off behind a showcase stocked with the innards of early pendulum clocks. Their iron stanchions showed the structure, the inner workings with brass barrels, cat-gut, toothed wheels interlocking with a maze of other larger or smaller toothed wheels. His lanky figure drew her gaze through the showcases. Love could reach through glass easily, could reach through iron clocks' structures. It was shocking to see him now, out of bed, dressed, away from her in a public place, a separate public person He was changed in this elite atmosphere, surrounded by these timepieces.

One of these clocks was engraved, its face decorated with suns, moons, stars and as Stella drew nearer to it to inspect its workmanship, with Dave's face smiling at her through the glass opposite, they started to do a slow dance along the showcases.

How false all this construct was – these busy machines, whirring away, needing winding up, polishing, oiling - all to count the hours which these same machines had invented. Their last night had been outside this countable time, unpegged from these tight constraints. The wheels and their operations were false; how much better the candle clocks had been, the light of time instead, puncturing darkness.

Outside, the winter afternoon had already begun to close the day and the coach timetable was getting nearer. They would not wait for her. She walked round to where he was standing and gazed at the clocks with him, hoping to join both types of time, the mechanical and the unaccountable time of love.

The painted stars and moons, suns too, in all sizes and guises spread out in front of them as if the clockmakers had tried to capture every possible manifestation. Whatever today meant to her and him, however they could try to keep this instant hostage, the many clocks were indifferent witnesses and continued their manic ticking.

A rebel impulse to overthrow them and their conspiracy came and went quickly. Stella returned to the ordinary world outside of the world of love; back, being ruled by timetables.

"You know, I've got to get to Victoria Coach Station by half past five," she said, coming and round and slipping her arm through his.

"We can have a quick coffee, then, I know a place near here, I used to work round the corner in a bookshop." Dave had not much money so they went to a coffee bar where the new Gaggia's loud equipment drowned out conversation. They sold what appeared to be the sweepings of the machines in the cheapest drink, labelled *coffee dash* which tasted of old coffee grounds. Dave managed this treat with a sophisticated air, while telling Stella he had nothing to offer. He had been unemployed for several months already, he had told her so last night.

"That's why I have that small room, and lucky to get it too. Even more luckily, they're all jazz fiends, and I play the trumpet now and then, so they have to respect me now and again." On Saturday evenings the BBC had a special jazz programme and the four flatmates would congregate in the kitchen to listen and argue as different players were featured. Stella noticed that their girlfriends remained silent, it was a lads' thing entirely. They listened respectfully as if it was a religious broadcast. Miles Davis proved to be a real battleground. "Colder than ice, you could use him as an anaesthetic," Dave said to her smugly once they got back into his own room.

2

"I'll write to you" was the last thing he said to her through the coach window at Victoria station.

Wanting both calm and shoutings, we begin this epic thus – There is juris in my diction, contradiction all in fiction, oh please put me in the piction for the fingers taction ticktion. Lady; pause; insinuation.

He must have dashed back to write the minute after Stella left London on that Monday afternoon. His first letter arrived on the Tuesday morning. It was like a hand grenade delivered by Royal Mail. He blazed out of the pages, blue ink, fountain pen, with an almost italic script.

His love letters were a mix of Cézanne, Euripides, T.S. Eliot and an eclectic selection of other names, plus bits of Greek which he did not give translations of. This heady intellectual soup was interspersed with declarations of love, friendship and apology and admissions of deceit. He could not invite her to join him in Hampstead as firstly she would end up working as a waitress without finishing her art college course. That certificate was paramount. Plus he had promised to marry someone else and was not going to go back on his word. Although, he added, the girl was not on speaking terms with him right now (that explained their own tryst) and he might be free of his promise at some time soon.

O my God and a dream and a half crushed, crushed, destroyed, destroyed. And I who have been like a man missing an arm since parting brought such sweet sorrows suddenly dream no more. I have offered heart and home to Girl and I must fulfil all of my contract or my touch will only become a kiss of death O Kelly! O Kelly!

The next letter arrived a fortnight later and contradicted parts of the previous one. *Almost I might offer unconditional surrender but it is impossible. I have it not within me to be so cruel to her. Our three days haiku together were not just a pleasant interlude. Even so much more, so very much more. The pool will be my mecca if it breaks up. The two of you are THE two in my short span. I would love you both and shall but I can only live with one.*

We two soulmates outside time should still be able to enter time if this present very chancy arrangement should fail.

Her mother noticed the letters with a London address arriving and put two and two together.

"You better start having your letters sent to the college, if I were you," she said looking serious. Then, she broke ranks, a once in a lifetime lapse. "Your father goes up to your room the minute you go out and he goes through your things. He would read any papers you have in your bedroom, so do be careful." As soon as exams were over, Stella decided she would be off to London after all. This was no way to go on.

After that warning, Dave's letters appeared regularly on the college noticeboard. If Stella did not see any letters as they entered, someone would always dash up to the life room or one of the painting rooms,

"There's a letter for you!" and there it would be, wedged behind the crisscrossed tapes that spread across the green baize-covered board above the radiator. She was addicted; his letters brought energy.

Stop. Period. Stop. Don't save face. I love you, damn you. Terribly. It never was a one-night stand, never, never.

I don't think you realize how much you hit me, bang, just that. Bang! Long before we spoke, right from first focus. These things don't happen but it did.

So it hurts, so you reel, so I reeled before, so what, so what; better to have loved in vain than never have loved at all. With so much love, Dave.

Then the letters changed and the horizon tilted. Total bad news. Dave was still unemployed and in a mess.

Am in a bad way all things considered. Have just been to the quack who says that my skin rash is 'neurodermatitis' and the cold I have is a symptom and my insomnia likewise and it will have to be dealt with seriously, moderate sleeping draughts etc. And I have new glasses.

Well then I inflict on you my tortured self as the quack changes into a head shrinker. The outcome is that I'm neurotic to the point of being supported by the state

without working. The conclusion (at 21) of a magnificent career as a nut! Paraphrenia!. Accepting this as calmly as one might expect from a paraphrenic I am left speechless.

O.O. The half world of a partial resignation. While the cheerful voice sings failure.

A few more letters followed, full of crammed energy mixed with poetry.

As term ended and summer began Stella went off to North Wales as a chambermaid for the season. She still wrote to Dave but their link was trailing off.

His last letter advised her to read D.H. Lawrence's poem. *Read 'Last Words to Miriam' with my regrets although I'm afraid tiredness not misunderstandings failed me.*

Then there was silence and Dot brought the news from Hampstead that Dave had married Moira, a quick registry office wedding and they had moved to Tufnell Park. The discredited notion that the earth was flat was accurate; when people you loved went off into the distance, they actually did fall off the edge of the world. There was no round-earth consolation that if you started walking for long enough, you would re-encounter them on the other side of the sphere. No, they fell off the edge and were never seen again.

A year or so later even though all that initial vision was gone, Stella still felt drawn back to the dappled green of the trees at the edge of the Heath and the white and cream-painted houses of South End Road. It became a dream-place, too good to be true. The minute the summer chambermaid job in Llandudno ended, she moved and followed all the others who fled to the capital. Each time a student failed an exam, they went off to London; it became a different type of success.

But this London was cruel, its accountants had tied up everybody for centuries, starting with the robber barons. Going to work was paramount; without that Stella would sink into a well far worse than anything Alice in Wonderland had encountered. In long-ago infants' school, Miss Antrobus's class, just before taking the scholarship exam - for some strange reason, they had learnt it off by heart, the entire Mad Hatter's Tea Party scene, the part about

"But she was *in* the well, *well* in." What had been a bit of witty wordplay was now an actual fact.

3   London was complicated and yet a joke. Arriving on the Red Rose afternoon train from Lime Street and then transferring right onto the tube at Euston, hardly realising what she was doing, Stella watched the Northern Line southbound stations fly past. Everyone she knew lived in Hampstead but she would have to stay away, to keep from the family finding her. No use running away to the one place everyone would find her. Sticking to the Northern Line, though, meant it would be easy to visit friends on Sundays. But soon there would be few stations to choose from. The map of the underground system was set along the carriage ceiling showing the coloured twists

of the various lines. Northern Line was a sensible black. Morden, at the absolute end of the line sounded miserable, like a morgue. Tooting Bec sounded strange, like something in space travel. Balham did not sound too hopeful either.

Taking a gamble she got out at Clapham South and hoped for the best. Clapham Common sounded almost normal and a bit Victorian. It was a gentle summer afternoon by now, with the beginning of the rush hour. A Mars bar and a bottle of orange juice from a news-agents was enough to count as afternoon tea. Seeing a noticeboard for a B&B on Balham High Road, she walked into the small reception area and asked if a room was available. Paying the one night's bill of fifteen shillings in advance, she tumbled into bed, tired from the breakneck events of the day.

Breakfast was at eight and Stella had to move quickly now, desperate measures kicking in. There was only five pounds left to live on from now on. So, asking if they would keep her suitcase behind the counter, she went Up West, as they called it, to find an employment agency. Luckily the agencies did not charge the applicants, future employers paid the levy. Getting out of the tube at Piccadilly Circus she meandered around the streets, summoning up enough courage to apply at one of the employment agencies advertised above the shops. There were signs all along Regents Street; not noticeable until, like right now, you needed their help.

Trying out typing skills at the Alfred Marks agency the assistant politely pointed out that she was hopeless, speeds not up to any kind of scratch. The secretary in charge of the business section was merciful, however.

"What we can offer you, however, is a post as a shop assistant, how about that? You see, we also do commercial placements. It's a little grocer's shop in Mayfair, eight to half two, weekdays plus Saturday mornings. You could start on Monday. That's five pounds ten shillings a week." Monday was a few days away. Money was going to run out by then.

"But do you have anything that starts earlier than that? I need to find a job immediately." The secretary riffled through the cards.

"Hmm. There's a few days emergency fill-in at a West End restaurant, if that's any good for you. Someone ill, they need a temporary replacement. It's not far from here. Would you be interested? They were almost desperate." Stella brightened up at this. She was desperate too. After the receptionist's phone calls to both places, she was given cards with the addresses and told to phone back with the results. She dashed off to Ebury Square where they were glad to find she had a suitable black dress, food would be supplied, hours nine to three and payment cash in hand as an emergency.

"You do realise this is just for the three days, don't you? Our other waitress is off sick and we are very busy." The manageress phoned the agency to say it had all been settled. Then, off to the grocer's in Shepherd's Market, where the bluff manager was also glad to see her, start on next Monday, mornings early to half-past two in the afternoon.

"We're mainly a sandwich bar for the workers round about and that crowd's all gone by the afternoon. You can buy any groceries you want here, ten per cent off. And you can have any of what's left after lunchtime, the sandwiches and that, you can finish anything off. There's not much going on Saturday morning, it'll be your job to clean out the fridge and do general tidying up." He would start the application for her proper employment card too, she would be official now, a real member of society, not a student any longer.

With all that settled and with a few pounds left, she went back to Stockwell and picked out an advert in a Post Office window for a single room along Clapham Common South, paid a week's rent in advance to the landlady, rushed back to the B&B and retrieved the suitcase and collapsed asleep on the narrow bed in the new dispiriting room. Desperation was a major driver until you stopped moving. An entire new life, however patchy, had been assembled in two days, costing just under five pounds.

4 The restaurant session was an eyeopener. Crammed into what was obviously a basement, the customers had to enter via an outside set of worn stone steps. It was the nineteenth century servants' kitchens and the former coal cellar, revamped into a fashionable eatery. The many tables were crowded so near to each other that Stella could barely manage to walk between them. And the tables were so small, like card-tables, that there was only room enough for the main plate, side plate and a glass.

Serving anything was a miracle of balance. The red wines and the white wines were kept in different sides of the room, which added to the difficulty if customers changed their mind.

Meanwhile, the diners, sitting almost knee to knee, carried on as if they were eating totally alone in some romantic assignation. Others were pairs of businessmen who also discussed confidential arrangements as if no one could overhear them. Stella was exhausted but the tips jar on the counter already held some silver coins as anonymous thanks. Olive, the main waitress had a clientele who knew her well and her jam-jar was full to the brim. Her dark red nails hovered like talons ready to count the day's total.

There was, luckily, no evening session and after the lunchtime crowd left, the staff went into the kitchen to eat whatever was left. It was a generous move -

"You can have what you like," Geraldine the cook offered, while Bernard, the kitchen helper, showed Stella a place at the great farmhouse-type table.

"Rabbit in red wine? Or would you prefer pheasant? It's an acquired taste, as my mother used to say." They were friendly and inquisitive about her.

"Audrey's off sick, but you could stay on longer if you'd like, we need someone young here." It was an outpost of working-class safety, free luxury food forever and no questions asked. They could also take surplus stuff home to their families. But Stella knew it was not for her; the next job was already arranged.

It was everything that Dave's letters had warned against. *I can't advise you to leave college and even perhaps Liverpool. Indeed, I would suggest if anything that you stayed for the piece of paper they can give you. (This is a time of prosperity; it won't always be.)* She had the piece of paper and was starting off as a waitress anyhow.

Coming back from that proper full-time first real job – in the grocer's shop in Shepherd's Market, Stella decided to walk home all the way to South London. Work started early but the mornings were bright; now it was a balmy summer's afternoon, after all, and Regent's Park was loosely on the way home.

Being both a resident and a tourist had its up moments. Walking along one of the paths she had been no warning notice on this side of the field. They were not the jokey animals of cartoons nor noble romantic animals. Their dirty grey rumpled skin fell, almost in layers to their feet as they lumbered across the compound nearby. She looked up the steep hill of one elephant leg with distaste. They all looked so much better in the National Geographical magazine, striding through sun-drenched landscapes in Africa or India. The middle of London did not seem quite right for them.

Not far from that encounter, trying to get away from them as quickly as possible, Stella blundered into the Chimpanzees' Tea Party. This was more a folk-memory, surely; it was so bizarre that it was like another Pathé Pictorial film. The group of five chimpanzees wore dresses or trousers and sat at a table with a variety of cups, saucers and plates and a teapot set on the table before them. Sugar was sugar lumps and they ate them rapidly. One drank the tea direct from the spout of the teapot, so it could not have been real hot tea. Perhaps it was coloured water or a dandelion and burdock lemonade?

Another one put a cup on its head. There was no sharp cutlery, mercifully. Of course they made mistakes, it was only expected, and they reacted to the crowd's amusement by playing up to them even more so. Or perhaps it was hysteria, though as it was scheduled for most summer afternoons it must have been routine for the chimpanzees by now. Their summer clothes made a mockery of both themselves and the respectable older people who traditionally went in for proper afternoon tea at four o'clock. The male chimpanzees wore trousers with braces and the females wore flowery summer dresses. The entire theatrical production was highly embarrassing, with an undertow of cruelty. She vowed to avoid it from now on.

Zoos prevented animals from eating each other by placing them in decorative prisons. The chimpanzees were lucky to be let out like this while so many other breeds remained locked up their entire lives for their own safety, or that of the public. The public could stare, while other animals wanted to eat them.

Most days, though, Stella went by bus back to the new bedsit in Brixton. The one at Clapham Common, facing the Common itself, was too out of the way and deserted, no other lodgers were ever about and the landlady wanted the rent to be paid monthly now, which was impossible. The house was depressing. The room was gigantic, it was almost a day's walk across to the washbasin in the corner. The bed huddled in an opposite corner. Leapfrogging to another new place picked from yet another Post Office window advert was easy. The postcards made a hotch-potch of life. Babysitters wanted or offering services, cleaners wanted or offered, plus kittens, puppies, gardening, lost dogs, part-time jobs delivering leaflets or addressing envelopes. She slid out one evening with the packed suitcase, meeting nobody. The entire house was silent and the only living person was the landlady downstairs, with just a quick chat as the rent was paid each Friday evening. Every morning there were three bottles of milk left by the front door but whoever ordered them was invisible, it was as if the house was empty. The new place off Tulse Hill was a converted ordinary terrace house, with five other lodgers. They took turns at cleaning the hall and stairs, which made it more friendly.

Downstairs was mostly the flat of a couple from the West Indies. Joachim and Maria had come here to improve their prospects, they told Stella, as they showed her where the carpet sweeper and the brushes and dustbins were.

"We've got a daughter left with her Grandmother, yes, and we have two others, a boy and girl out with a foster-mother in Becontree," Joachim told her. "We go over and see them at the weekends. I am an engineer back home, here I study for proper qualifications, and my wife, she was a school cook, she works in a canteen now and she is also taking exams. When we go back, we will have proper jobs, much better prospects." The gamble was winnable, it seemed, but they were making great sacrifices right now.

Both of them were kindly and invited her into their front room and kitchen for tea immediately. They said she was to call in next week too, we were all friends now. Such friendliness was an oasis in the desert, it seemed. Their brother-in-law, Seth, appeared on that Thursday afternoon, a warehouse clerk, wearing the whitest shirt ever, it lit up the room. He was charming and cheerful, joking about his work and the mistakes wholesalers made with mixed-up orders.

"Things arrive boxed up and unlabelled so that we don't even know what they are – and we're supposed to price them up accurately and then send them to the right people!" Maria took Stella aside in the kitchen,

"My brother-in-law is searching for a wife and it looks as though he is really taken to you! We would be so happy if it works out like this!" Stella was amazed at the speed this had all moved at. She had only been in the house a fortnight. "See," Maria said, "Here is where we hide the key," showing where it was placed above the jamb of their door. Stella politely smiled. "You can just call in our flat whenever you like now, and you can help yourself to coffee, make yourself at home." Stella smiled as if she agreed that such open-hearted trust was normal. A pinprick of distrust broke the perfect picture though.

Why would she be going into their flat while they were at work, when her own room was on the floor above? What if they accused her of any pilfering if anything disappeared? And what was she going to do if Seth appeared and they were both alone in the flat? Anything could happen and the best thing would be to steer clear of the almost-trap. A friendly distance was sadly the only way of coping with this.

5 Afternoons getting back from work, upstairs on the bus where people could smoke on the way home became interesting. As the bus went along Stockwell Road the ceiling was startlingly patterned with shafts of red as they went past the length of a row of shops all painted red. Peoples' faces were transformed for moments into red phantoms. It was like spatters of blood, a nightmare, a horror film. The secret was that the entire street was made up of dozens of properties owned by Pride and Clarke, each shop selling new or second-hand motorcycles and motorbike spares. Each shop and the walls above were painted the same blood-red. On a hot afternoon the red ceiling made it seem an even more humid day.

Further along by Stockwell Green there was a sign over a business premises, "Puddefoot, Bowers & Simonett, Ivory Craftsmen, Restorers and Importers" and she often wondered how the three of them met – two proper stuffy business men and an exciting Italian; what would the connection be? Each afternoon she stared at that sign wondering at the story behind it.

In one week of shocks she had encountered elephants, chimpanzees and a nightmare red street. As a treat one morning she called into a Lyons Corner House for breakfast. It was a trip back into the nineteen forties. Upstairs, over a men's outfitters shop and a newsagents, the restaurant spread across such a large space that people in the far corners were almost in a mist. The subdued lighting did not help.

It was quiet, mostly middle-aged and older men sitting alone, many reading the morning paper. It was a sad pastiche of what they would be doing if they had real homes, she surmised. Here they sat with their bacon and eggs, followed by toast and marmalade. The wife, children and dog were all missing. It was a constrained form of suffering and she felt sorry for them all, as a passing tourist trying the place out for the first time. They poured out their tea carefully, not spilling a drop. Now and again the sound of a spoon stirring the sugar in a cup carried across the room. A paper ruffled as someone turned a page. An old man took out a pocket watch, wound it up, and checked the time. No one talked to anyone else.

If she stayed in the rented rooms world, this might well be her own future. But there were few women at the tables, and those women that were breakfasting alone looked like secretaries or other professional women who were quite well-dressed and successful. Perhaps ordinary women did not earn enough to have this as a daily habit, plus they tended to cope better alone anyway.

The new job meant learning strange skills. Mr Hunt had given her that week's copy of Shaw's List, a trade magazine which had all the latest prices of foodstuffs and household necessities. Prices had to be learnt every week as they changed inexplicably. Colman's mustard up a halfpenny, Batchelors garden peas on offer at a penny cheaper, on and on it went. Some firms went bust, some lines changed their titles, sizes changed, two in a pack, three in a box, and new food items were invented.

The shop had no labelling on any item; people took whatever they wanted from the shelves, brought their selection to the counter in their arms, and the assistant, knowing all the prices, totted them up on the pile of paper bags on the counter. Often the prices were partly guesswork, especially when they were busy. Mr Hunt said it was not worth labelling the tins and jars as the prices changed so often. The adding up was then announced and always accepted. The trick was never to give the customer the bag with their own adding-up written on it.

The cash register only registered the total amount paid into it. Any change given was not accounted for. Once Stella gave a woman change for a pound note, when the note tendered was only a ten-shilling note. The woman, a real lady, came back and politely gave her the proper change. Luckily there was no one around in the quiet interval after the lunchtime rush.

"I noticed this, and didn't want you to get into any trouble, my dear." There were no receipts given by the cash register either. It all worked on random honesty.

Stella could have translated passages from Molière or Caesar's Gallic wars, analysed the War of Jenkin's Ear, but could not give the correct change. Her education was useless in this new existence, this parallel world.

Bit by bit these new situations erased her past life. Only a few months ago at college they had spent an entire afternoon discussing Edouard Manet's *Les Paveurs de la Rue de Berne*. The lecturer said how Manet had to isolate the green oxide from other colours because the chemicals would interfere with each other. Artists of that era had to navigate this complicated mix of possibles and impossibles, poisons, fading and disintegration. The workmen in the painting continued in the Parisian sunshine, secure, it seemed, in an eternal summer afternoon. In reality it was painted not long after the Franco-Prussian war of 1871 but here was no trace of angst in the picture, it was no *Guernica.*

All this was getting lost in the midst of the cheeses, bacon, salmon and ice. The artist was no longer the observer, she was being changed into one of those workers now.

Cheese arrived in large wheels, Cheshire, Gloucester, Cheddar, Leicester Red. They stood like dumpy giants behind the glass counter screen. The skill soon learnt, was how to cut a proper quarter of cheese, using a simple wire and wood contraption.

"It's like a garotte really," Maisie, the main assistant cheerfully remarked. "You just get it straight, see, here, hold onto the wooden handle bit from the centre and then…pull, hard on the wire, like this." A few mistakes meant slithers of extra cheese being added to the customer's main slice, though real messes were used up in the sandwiches.

Soon Stella could measure a quarter, six ounces or half a pound accurately by sight. The highpoint, however, was cutting salmon for the most expensive sandwiches, that cost more than an hour's wage. Three entire salmon hung up on the wall behind them, with a selection of long rapier knives hanging alongside. The salmon was unhooked from the wall, (an instant's drama,) laid out along the counter on a marble slab and the swirling knife twirled an almost chiffon-thin slice of salmon. It was dangerous and precise. Then the salmon was hooked back on the wall and flies swooshed away as they could not use any sprays. When there was no one around on Saturdays the rapiers had to be sharpened on a whetstone to keep them trim.

There were also the sliding sides of bacon alongside the slicing machine. Cutting could be set to thick, medium or thin, depending on what the customer wanted. It was one of the first things Maisie or Stella did daily; cut up new slices. Dashing downstairs to the basement half a dozen slices were grilled, sometimes using up yesterday's leftovers, ready to be put into sandwiches. The click and slide of the machine was almost hypnotising and it was tempting to go on and on without stopping, especially when fulfilling weekly orders from the houses roundabout.

The grand houses took what they wanted and somehow did not bother to get round to paying. One, a famous Lord, had not paid for over six months and the shop was caught in an embarrassing trap. To antagonise him by demanding payment would be dangerous, but at the same time the bill was growing day by day. It might as well have been the Middle Ages in the direct effect of these class differences. Maisie, Bill the delivery man and Mr Hunt coped by gambling on horses daily, chasing up names and tips in the daily papers. A win would catapult them out of their working class and into luxury; the promise kept them quiet. Stella did not understand this waste of money and said so, to Maisie's disgust.

"You've never tried it? Take a chance - your mother did!" It was Stella's turn to be disgusted now at such vulgarity. They continued to assess the various horses as if they knew them personally.

Mr Hunt was affable and the place almost ran itself. He spent Saturdays doing paperwork in the small back room. The place was heaped with papers slithering off the desk, tables, shelves. Above his desk there was an official government notice about workers' rights – regulations re Bank Holidays, sick pay, accidents, hours for lunchtime and tea breaks, hours of employment, uniforms and bizarrely, a regulation that in any place of employment where a woman was working, a chair should be available. This would have been wonderful except that the one spare chair was piled high with more of Mr Hunt's random papers.

Saturdays were spent doing maintenance. Stella cleared out the life-sized fridge. She had to stand inside it, scraping ice off the walls. A strange experience, a white cave that became seductive, the outside world seemed too brightly coloured in contrast. It was frightening to be isolated in this small arctic and she had to get out every now and then to warm up at the little electric fire that Mr Hunt supplied for the time. The heaps of broken ice were taken outside and thrown in a gutter. Then she had to cut off the mould that had grown on the edges of the wheels of cheese. This had to be done carefully, not to waste cheese or deform the shape. The box of paper bags was opened and handfuls of bags were threaded on string to be hung behind the counter.

Then the oven downstairs in the cellar had to be cleaned, plus the white enamel trays that the sandwich fillings were daily displayed on. The leavings of these, a few cold sausages, cheese parings, sliced tomatoes, bacon ends and other scraps, were hers to take home, plus the crusts of stale bread. Few customers came in as the American Embassy office girls and any builders or local maintenance men were not working on Saturday afternoons.

6 Afterwards it was wonderful to be out in the sunshine and she strolled through Mayfair staring at the different prosperous buildings and then down Park Lane to Vauxhall Bridge Road and so to home. At that age she was unaware of how much energy all this was taking; the fascination with the new surroundings was enough distraction. Late summer afternoons in South London she walked through terraced streets where West Indian children played between the parked cars. The hidden River Effra was long gone under the Victorian building epidemic.

Other days she got back via the Tube. It was still with a pang of regret that she had to go to the southbound platform at Tottenham Court Road to connect with Stockwell on the Northern Line, while everyone she knew was up in Belsize Park. It was a form of exile.

There was still the remains of another packet of Basildon Bond notepaper and envelopes, bought to apply for teaching posts advertised in Teachers' World. As there had been no replies to the many self-addressed and stamped envelopes enclosed, as far as she knew the entire enterprise had withered on the vine. Leaving places abruptly without any forwarding address had its drawbacks. It had been immediately obvious in July that she had missed the September vacancies. And these present random temporary jobs did not, could not, give any possibility of going off to even one interview. The trap was perfect; there was no opportunity to desert any job without causing problems with the rest of the staff and no way of getting by after losing money by any absence.

Then, as the new pattern of friends, however temporary, formed it became unthinkable to break away from them to hike off and start all over again teaching in foreign parts like Buckinghamshire or even Epping and Ongar. It was obvious that many of the posts were in girls' boarding schools set in deepest countryside, something like prisons. She would be teaching girls only four years or so younger than herself. Gradually the idea of planning for the January term faded away as daily life got in the way.

Stella wrote to Dot, who had after all, brought her to London in the first place last year. Now it looked as though they had changed places.

Monday 13th November 1961
Tulse Hill
Brixton

Dear Dot,

You have no idea what I've done. Have moved to London without telling you. Doing various jobs and moving from place to place, not settled yet. But I haven't gone crazy, I just left the last place, well, job, and room, a while ago and am now a shop assistant. It's all so many changes that I have to keep a little diary to keep track of it all. There was something Will Mason was saying last year, you remember, we stayed in his flat in Camden Town once. Sally was talking about someone and then she was explaining their whole being and existence, and she said,

"He's writing a *book.*" And Will said, "Aren't we all?" But I think I'm living mine right now.

Enclosed is one letter for Brian, if he's around. He was the only sensible one of the beatniks. They were going to go off to Jersey, wasn't it, to pick tomatoes. Did you ever hear from them again? You will be pleased to know that I've bought an actual alarm clock, which has destroyed the delicate sense of time which I was acquiring. It's deafening me. It's like having Big Ben striking on the mantelpiece. But before, I always had to ask someone here to knock on the door as they went past, to wake me up. All to get off to work I don't want to do.

The little travel clock had to be sold off instead when I was short of money here between jobs. It was a man in Brixton who bought items for cash. He looked at me as if I'd stolen them! And I got rid of that gigantic suitcase at the same time. Still got the hat box, the one that was part of my grandmother's trousseau, probably. Getting by is tight at times. Sometimes it's as close to the bone as anything out of Dostoevsky. Still applying for teaching jobs, but art teachers aren't much needed. I get the Teachers World and spend a fortune on return postage. Nothing happens.

Changed my job from the grocer's in Mayfair to a department store in Brixton and just got an income tax rebate (I'd had my suspicions that I was paying super-tax on under six pounds a week, but apparently Baker Street HQ knows what it's doing. Sometimes.)

So as yet I'm still in Brixton, selling handbags, umbrellas and jewellery, depending on whose lunch hour it is. They are short of staff but will soon be shorter as I hope to shazam off north to Hampstead. Brixton is not much conducive to a social life. Almost everyone is straight off the boat from the West Indies, India, Poland, Ireland and a few from China. The native London population is sort of depressed Cockney – without much life or any real character. Their voices really do have a whine to them, nothing at all of the rough solidness of their Upper Parliament Street counterparts. One old lady at a bus stop told me off for moving here from the North of England and taking up a local job and their hospital beds and housing places. She said what was I doing here in Brixton, why didn't I stay home up North?

The girls are identical, all with straw coloured textured hair in a mop shape, pastel coloured coats and black patent accessories. A few different ones have dark hair and you may see the odd one with long hair (though the hairdressers don't like it.) The boys are mods (this year's edition of the teddy boys) or homosexuals, or both. Quite a few have their clothes and shoes made to their own designs – there's a large proportion of actors and show dancers.

The girl who serves on the same counter has more or less given me an entrée into this society. (Declined; I've had enough.) Her boyfriend is in prison for breaking into his father's house and stealing money and she is buying his trousseau for when he comes out of Stafford Prison. Apparently, he'd cut her bleedin' eyes out if she didn't, so I wonder if she is doing it for love. She laughs about it all, it's an adventure it seems. Her friends come into the shop and talk to us about the latest one out of jail. Apart from all that, it's all boring. So that's about it. Do call in to Harry and Gloria's, next time you visit, they'd be pleased to see you. They've got a new flat by the Heath.

Don't give anyone my address. Looking forward to seeing you, Best, Stella.

Gloria had met Harry on a weekend trip down from Liverpool and he had, amazingly, proposed to her. He worked in an advertising agency with a good income and was in need of a wife; Gloria provided the instant family he needed. An unmarried mother; he would take on her two boys and it was seen as a success on both sides. Stella met her in Hampstead by accident. They had planned on leaving for London together months ago, but Gloria had too much to attend to and they had drifted apart. It was a shock to bump into her along Willougby Road.

"You've got to come and meet my new husband. He's incredibly rude, but very funny, you'll soon get the hang of him. Come round now?" It was a bit awkward at first, but Gloria's enthusiasm helped it along and yes,

Harry was constantly making jokes that did not always work, of an "As the actress said to the bishop" variety.

"She's all right," he said in front of Stella, "She can come round again." Turning to her he added, "You know where we are, and don't stand on ceremony, just drop in. You're welcome, drunk or sober." Gloria's two sons were already at the local infants school and it was all settled. An entire new life. Done. Stella was mystified. He was not exactly attractive, in his forties and it looked as if Gloria had settled for a security that was going to be dullness itself. She was already expecting a baby.

"He's delighted. He went and said to a man in the pub, You just have to hold Gloria's hand and she's pregnant!"

At work in Morleys of Brixton there were other slight friendships – Molly, on the toy counter, insisted Stella should go after work for afternoon tea to the new council flat her family had just been moved into. It was one of the first high-rises built in Brixton. They walked across a wide tarmacked front area, cleared for deliveries and other cars. Molly proudly pressed an entry button by the grand front entrance to get into a featureless foyer, then pressed more buttons to summon a lift.

"You don't want to waste time climbing all the stairs," she said loftily. The lift was bright silver inside and out. Everything smelled of fresh paint and the builders' left-over concrete. In the silence there was hardly any trace of anyone ever using any of the lifts or anyone walking along the spruce corridors. The flat was immaculate, Molly's Mum was in heaven, she said. So glad to be away from that old street. The floor was set with new Marley-tiles throughout, a clean lino floor in dark brown. Up so many floors from the ground, being near to the sky was increasingly possible. The past was discarded, they even had some new furniture now, like a new identity.

"It was worth getting some new stuff on the H.P. to celebrate and I bought new nets for the windows, specially, when we moved in," Molly's Mum said. "But you can't open the windows if there's a breath of a breeze, it gets more like a gale up here."

Molly had to show off her new acquisition too, a tape recorder. She proudly produced a large black plastic recorder from her bedroom and switched it on. It was a moment of reverence. It played *"Hit the Road, Jack"* as Molly looked longingly at it. Ray Charles sang confidently and smoothly.

"It takes two batteries," she added. Her mother brought them both a cup of tea and some biscuits. Then Molly played it again. Stella could not understand why Molly was so proud of merely recording what was already a recording played on a broadcast on the radio. She was celebrating the transference of one electrical message on one machine onto another machine. It obviously made Molly feel powerful.

Stella was far more interested in the view from the window, looking down onto the roads around. She pushed the net curtains aside to look down. It gave her a mild vertigo. Probably you got used to it without realising how or why. It must change you. While it was intriguing as a quick view, the thought of living up here, isolated from any contact with the streets was startling. The planners had taken an entire terrace street of housing and turned it up on its end. The silver lift was now their only way of reaching the world outside. Of course there was the communal staircase down, but that was like a nightmare, concrete steps going on and on and on, an endurance test.

Teetering above reality, Molly turned on "*Hit the Road, Jack*" yet again, fascinated. After another half an hour Stella thanked them both profusely and Molly escorted her down in the lift.

"I really enjoyed doing this, you must come round again," Molly said happily, waving her goodbye. "See you in the shop tomorrow."

7   Sometimes dreams come true without any trying. Stella took the tube up to Belsize Park on a Sunday afternoon to visit Gordon and Sue, another couple from the Liverpool pubs and coffee bars. They had not been together for long, in fact Gordon had appeared like a white knight to see Sue through the beginnings of a disastrous pregnancy. So far, none of the crowd knew who the father of the child was. It would be due in the spring. Gordon was going to stay with her throughout the pregnancy and probably afterwards too. They were happy to see her.

"Look," Gordon said, "We're moving out this week, what a coincidence. We've got a place in Highgate. We wondered if you'd like to have this place, do a swap. There's the rent all paid until next Thursday, we'd be out before then. What do you think?" Stella was tempted. It was a chance to get north of the Thames and nearer to the exact part of London where all her friends lived. The time in Limbo had disappeared, she would be safe now.

"Yes! Why not! That's speeded up my long-term plan, thanks!" They gave her the spare key there and then.

"I'll tell Ali that you've taken over the rooms, so there won't be any change in the rent, and that's all he's interested in. He's always playing cards and doesn't want to lose any money from rents if he's losing at cards too," Gordon said. He showed Stella that there was an extra room, intended as a bedroom, but they had dragged the bed into the front room to be near the one gas fire in the cold weather.

On Monday evening Stella arrived at the Belsize Park house with some belongings in the circular hat-box that had belonged to her grandmother. She no longer had a large suitcase as it had been sold to a junk dealer when she had no money, along with the beautiful little travel clock and a dress ring that was a twenty-first birthday present. She remembered going to his semi-detached house near Tulse Hill and the man turning the items over and asking why she was selling them. The gigantic suitcase was brand new, bought with savings from last summer working as a chambermaid in an hotel in Wales. He looked seriously at her, summing up the situation and gave her two pounds for the lot. It was a week's food saved.

Starting that new job at Marks and Spencers on Camden High Street had meant waiting for the week's wage packet on Friday. You had to save up if you wanted to move from one job to another. Slaves were not supposed to move about. Now of course she had to find a new job this side of the Thames. The Labour Exchange provided a job for a few months, a quick filling-in for the Christmas trade. She would need another place after that, juggling employment dangerously. Keeping to some semblance of legality, Stella had left her rent on the mantelpiece of the back room in Tulse Hill, a silent goodbye to Joachim and Maria and the other tenants, as well as the landlady.

Stella rang the bell, but then tried the front door in Belsize Park Gardens and found it was already open. Walking up to the top floor she had to let herself into the flat, opening a lock and a large padlock which she had not noticed before. The padlock looked crude like something fastening a shed door. As Gordon and Sue were already gone, the rent book with its money was left on the table. The first snag was evident – they had left a kitten behind, with one tin of cat food. It looked at her listlessly. This was not a good beginning. Being more interested in human beings she had forgotten Gordon's attachment to cats.

"Oh, he always had four cats," Dot had told her ages ago. "They each had a food bowl in a separate corner of his room in Canning Street. It stank to high heaven." She had not paid attention and only now remembered there had been a large cat and some kittens in the room last time she visited.

There was also the fact that there was no window, just a skylight, which was somehow unsettling, rather like a trap. She went downstairs, knocked on a door at the end of the hall and asked for Ali, who appeared from a back room. Behind him in the dark room a group of men were sitting at a table spread with playing cards. A lithe young Indian, he seemed not to care as long as the money was right, just as Gordon had said. He was not angry at their leaving, probably relieved that there would be no baby on the premises. Some legal responsibilities might kick in once a baby was on site.

After Gordon and Sue had gone, the attic room looked even more grotty. Working at Marks and Spencers she had spent the last month selling thick winter coats in the children's department. The first week of working a week-in-hand had meant walking from Brixton and back from Camden Town in order to save money. It took nearly two hours either way and getting back to Tulse Hill she was so exhausted it was merely a case of eating something and collapsing into bed, then getting up before seven in order to walk all the way to work in Camden High Street again.

The one bright spot was a growing affair with Keith, one of the porters at the store. After the first week, the wage packet appeared and she could eat with the others, instead of having a homemade sandwich in secret in the cloakroom. That Friday they had been sitting together in the canteen, she had been reading the newly-bought Guardian and they had started talking about a fracas in Parliament.

"You're quite intelligent," he said, "What on earth are you up to, working in this place?"

"Paying the rent, I've just got to London -it's a long story. But food and rent are the main reasons." No telling him of the scandal with her brother and sister and the rapid move away from the family in Liverpool. When she told him about the previous days of making-do and walking to work and back, he was astounded and really sympathetic.

"You could have told me! I'd have given you something to live on! You shouldn't have been left like that!" After that lunchtime, Keith and Stella watched out for each other and snatched any chance to talk. Going to the stockroom for refills, a long chain of till-keys at her waist, Keith might be loading the shelves with a fresh delivery of jumpers, scarves, trousers, jackets, all folded and docketed and checked. They would have s snatched conversation and a kiss. Twice a day the porters came round the counters and collected the discarded wrapping papers and Keith would make an arrangement to meet outside.

Some lunchtimes they went off to the wine-by-the-glass pub nearby and drink sherry. It was a sophisticated and slightly wicked thing to do. Strolling into the mayhem of Camden High Street and the crowded store they would go back to work smelling slightly of Amontillado. Neither cared.

"We'll be gone soon enough. They can't sack us now, they'd never get extra staff this late," he smiled mischievously, "back at the Labour Exchange!"

"They don't call it that any more."

"No, but it's exactly the same. They should call it the Slave Bureau and be done with it."

"I'll have to go right after Christmas the minute they open up again and get another job." There would be nowhere to go for Christmas day. It would be spent alone and unemployed. As if reading her mind, Keith interrupted.

"You're going to come round to my brother's for Christmas dinner, now, don't forget that. I've left that place I had in Chalk Farm, so you couldn't come round there," he added. "I'm staying at a friend's place for a bit." He looked into her eyes. This is love, she thought, we're so lucky. "We'll meet outside after work and fix the details on the last day." Stella was amazed how much difference this made, a bright light for one day. They started to go back to her place in Tulse Hill, smuggling Keith into her room. It did not seem to bother him that there were no sheets, as she had not been able to afford them yet, and the blankets were scratchy. But being together blocked their surroundings. He used her body enthusiastically, as she wondered if this was normal. Some of it was disgusting, she had not encountered thrusting into her throat that made her almost gag.

"There's states in America where this is illegal," Keith said, as he went on with his gymnastics. She could see their need to control actions like this. It was impossible to control such a surge of action, lying there naked, with other lodgers able to hear any embarrassing arguments. No other girl had ever mentioned this and she had not encountered this from Jim, her only previous experience. Such secrets. Keith was her boyfriend; this seemed to be the contract, all set in private. They stole out of the house in the morning so no one would know.

Other times they had a bath together, again creeping along the corridor one after another and talking in whispers. It was the usual four pence for the hot water, though they paid an extra tuppence for the luxury of extra warm water. There was then the problem of each emerging from the bathroom and making a run for Stella's room without being discovered.

In the morning they sat on the top deck of the bus to town, having a smoke, another day in the big city together. It had snowed overnight and everything was new, like a fresh page. The red Stockwell street was muted in the pristine whiteness.

The cold snap pushed foreign families in to get warm coats ready for the stiff winter. Most of the time, an appealing six-year-old with dark eyes – Greek, Turkish, Arab, all sorts, would have to act as a translator. Only the child could speak halting English, while the mother or more often a grizzled grandmother spoke rapidly in a far-off language. These women always looked at Stella as though there was some kind of trick going on, until eventually they would produce a heap of loose coins from a well-hidden pocket in their long black skirts.

She had to lead them to the cash till to show it was not personal, no bartering, but a business transaction that Stella was as trapped in as they were. Often the coats were returned a few weeks after, obviously worn, and they would demand a refund with an international drama of angry syllables. The child would be standing in the middle, sheepishly. It was a new form of pawnbroking.

On Christmas Eve the assistants were the only ones left sober and part-time translators in a cosmopolitan world, while all the grandmothers were at home cooking.

Stella would not be there for any of the returned coats; her contract ended at half-past five.

In the thick of the ritual cash-change-wrap at the counter, or dashing through the aisles to bring back even more stock of coats, jackets and assorted woollens, Stella found that the afternoon sped away in mass confusion. Keith and the other porters must have called round while she was busy serving and today they were both on different meal breaks. By five-thirty all the assistants were complaining about their feet hurting while they changed shoes in the cloakroom. It was growing even colder outside. Stella went and stood outside the front door saying goodbye to the others, one by one, as they disappeared into the last-minute shopping crowds.

By six o'clock her feet were getting stiff and she could see the security guard checking inside the darkened empty store. He came out to ask what she was doing hanging about in such cold. Snowflakes were already floating onto her coat.

"Waiting for Keith," she said proudly, trying to stamp out pins and needles.

"Keith? One of the porters?"

"Yes," Stella smiled.

"But the porters all went home at four o'clock. He's gone long ago. You'd better get home yourself." He gave her a fatherly smile and began to lock the doors again. Embarrassed, Stella said mildly that it would be easier to phone. But she had no number, no way of finding Keith now. She had moved only a week ago herself, he had not called round yet. His new place was a mystery so far, no address. There was no connection. He had disappeared completely, paid over two hours ago and gone.

Hurrying, frantic shoppers crowded along the pavements, intricate neon decorations flashing through the falling snow. Stella felt apart from all their excitement now. A wild beat was thudding through her. There was no point to all this, none at all. The family did not want her back; she was son the run from them. The rooms she lived in were a slum; there was no pint in getting any more of these terrible life-consuming jobs. Now Keith was gone as well. She was stranded here in the snow, Christmas Eve, with nothing to look forward to.

Automatically she went down the escalator at Camden Town underground feeling neither living nor dead. I shall be an automaton forever now, she thought, just to pay the rent. After Christmas I have to go and get another tenth-rate job to buy food to struggle to get up at seven most mornings, Saturdays included, one afternoon off, to eat to be able to work to pay rent. This is no life. The adverts all over the station walls cheer it up but they are all abstract. Real life is this, dirty concrete and dirty escalator steps. It has no point. Keith had taken away any connection that had any warmth, however patchy.

The train rumbled towards the platform and Stella could feel the strength of the wind pushed before it. I could just jump in front of it, then there would be nothing to worry about. It would be a pity about the people watching, it might ruin their Christmas – while she stood back to think about this, the train doors opened and sucked passengers in, departing with its clatter northwards.

Stella remained on the platform deciding exactly how to jump into the way of the next train. It would have to be timed properly but at least, unlike school gym lessons it would not matter how she landed. It would be once only. She moved to the edge of the platform and looked across to the direction board. The next one was to Edgware. Over her shoulder she could see more people coming down the bright corridor. They would be an encouragement and an excuse in the crush to get pushed even nearer to the edge.

The light grew brighter, as like a scene from a film, Keith walked towards her, hands in pockets, sauntering along. He looked surprised to see her. She turned towards him, reaching out. Colour flooded back into their surroundings. They got onto the next northbound train together as if nothing had gone wrong.

"Yes, we got out earlier. I was going to phone you up. Give me your number again." He produced a biro and wrote it on the back of his hand. She thought it was such a romantic thing to do as they stood there in the packed compartment. He was calm and cheerful as though nothing had happened. "Right" he said as they were pressed against each other by other passengers' carrier bags in the crush. "I'll phone you up early this evening about the last minute arrangements for tomorrow."

"Marvellous." She kissed him, getting out at Belsize Park, leaving him to go on to Hampstead Heath station . Her room was freezing. A sock shoved into the wall where a brick was missing did not keep out the cold. It had probably been removed by Gordon, to give the cats a way of getting onto the decorative balcony to use it instead of a litter tray. Now she would not have to buy anything for Christmas dinner. It was all arranged. Keith phoned that evening at 8p.m.

"I'll come round to fetch you at 2 o'clock tomorrow. Got to go now, Bill's wife has got me decorating the tree and I'm drunk already." He was already at his brother's house, not that far away at Belsize Avenue.

It snowed even more overnight. Fresh Christmas morning snow blanked out the skylight. Voices echoed up from the street, car doors slamming as people arrived for celebrations in other houses and flats along the road. Stella waited, cup of tea in hand. The alarm clock said midday. Her week's wages would have to last a fortnight as even if a new job could be started on the 27th of December, probably in the January Sales of course, a week in hand would have to be worked first. She had only just learnt that the hard way. 'A week in hand' was a new phrase which she had never heard before. Mr Hunt at the Shepherd's Market grocers had paid her on the first Friday and so had all the others. So much for a successful convent grammar school education. It meant starvation while working in any new job. It was some time before anyone like Keith had told her about subs, asking about having an advance taken out. Such poverty was so frightening that it was too terrible to talk about; if any employer got a whiff of how desperate she was, they would not give her a job at all. Good situations went to those who were already O.K.; employers could trust them.

By two, Stella was ready, clean dress, new earrings, yet another layer of spit and mascara added, handbag checked for rubbish. She left the door slightly open, to hear the downstairs bell clearly. Ali was usually good at yelling up and there were definitely people downstairs in his flat, she could hear the noise from here. She sat in the scuffed leather armchair, waiting. There was nothing else to do. Staring at the gigantic old radio, she wondered if it actually worked at all. All previous tenants had left it behind, probably obsolete and too big to move. Its long wires led to a small plug, half hidden under the curled edge of the dirty carpet. She looked round for a socket and there was one, also unnoticed, behind a broken wardrobe door which stood against the wall to act as a mirror. The radio started to crackle and whizz as though it had not been used for several years. The kitten was startled and ran off into the opposite corner. A posh woman's voice was going on about standards. Of course, it was The Queen's Speech, which meant it was after three o'clock.

He's not coming now. He's not going to ring up. It's all happening again, just like yesterday, waiting outside the shop. I don't know where his brother lives, his phone number or anything. I've got nothing to eat and it's Christmas Day. It's even more like Charles Dickens all over again. I am really in the wrong century. She sat in the lumpy armchair and stared at the ancient wooden radio that looked like a small temple.

"In these difficult times, we must always try to keep our high standards…" the queen continued as if nothing was wrong. But Stella had just noticed the electricity meter beside the mirror. Something about it jelled. The little padlock swinging on it looked exactly the same as the one left over from her own suitcase, the one she had sold in Tulse Hill. Within a minute she had got the little silver key into the padlock, turned it easily, and the container slid out with a crash. A shower of silver coins fell onto the floor and she dropped some of the rest onto the armchair cushion. The Queen was still going on about people being tested and being noble and how the spirit would never give in and people would always triumph over disaster if they kept to their high standards.

Stella ran her hands through the coins and started to move some of them into piles, but there were so many that they kept sliding about. The meter had not been emptied as long as Gordon and Sue had lived there, obviously. She emptied her handbag, filling it up with the heavy silver shillings, locked her door and went downstairs into the silent white street. She left a scribbled note by the front-door bells for Keith, saying she would be right back in ten minutes, but when she returned there was no sign of it being touched.

Unknown to most of Hampstead, there was an open-all-hours shop along Fleet Road. Gordon had known about it and passed on the address.

"He's open all the time, you can go whenever you want. Looks like an ordinary house, almost disguised." It was shabby, well-hidden and the window was always shuttered. Stella gently tried the door-handle and found the place was lit inside. The old man stood there behind the counter as if it was an ordinary day, an atheist Welshman, glad to supply her with milk, jam and biscuits ("No bread today, of course,") tinned strawberries, cornflakes and cheese and Ryvita and chutney and cakes. A small box of chocolates, to celebrate and shampoo, to be sensible. He loaded it all into a cardboard box.

"You'll be all right now? Don't slip in the snow, now!" Stella paid him in silver handfuls. They both made silver towers of pounds all along the counter, but she didn't care and gave him some extra.

"For luck, it's Christmas, after all."

Back at the house, the landlord's lot were singing, it was beginning to be a rose-tinted four o'clock sunset and she sat down and ate near to bursting. The Queen would be proud of me, she thought, I used ingenuity and bravery in the face of adversity. There was enough to live on now until new wages came along, as she carefully shut the meter box and relocked it, still with some handfuls of shillings, promising to pay it all back on payday, whenever that might be.

She puzzled at what might have happened. The heavy snowfall would have made even a taxi journey not possible. (Could she remember any taxis at the rank that afternoon? Surely not.) He'd gone to a party and met someone else that hight. He'd had a row with his brother, Bill, or even worse, his sister-in-law. He'd had a massive hangover and missed everything. There were all sorts of plausible reasons why a man would not get in touch.

And then later it hit her, full face. He'd had to wash off her phone number from the back of his left hand. There would be slight traces the next day and the day after that. Biro was like a rehearsal for a tattoo.

She could remember walking back through the snow-silenced streets with the box of goodies via the meter money. Strawberry jam on top of cheese on butter on Ryvita. Real Nescafé with oodles of sugar. The little, silly strategies of getting by.

A week at C&A Modes for the January sales followed, as expected and after that, cleaning at old folks homes and New End nurses' home. Bits haphazardly joined together.

8 One Sunday afternoon, visiting the Tate Gallery she met Linda, also from Liverpool. They vaguely knew each other from evenings in Streates coffee bar in Mount Pleasant. Linda said now she was the wife of an artist.

"My husband Chester is an artist, yes, really, he paints every day, he has a studio in the basement," she announced. "I call in here because it's on the 24 bus route and it's warm enough for the baby in the cold weather," Linda said. "We've got a house in Hampstead, you must come round some time, do." Soon Stella was babysitting for them in a large house down Flask Walk.

Coming back at two in the morning after the evening's babysitting, Stella found her room broken into, the padlock prised open, hanging totally useless and the kitten gone. Her belongings were scattered about as if someone had searched through them rapidly. Mahesh, who had left the room next door had said before Christmas she could help herself to whatever he had not taken away.

Going into his empty room had been a shock. It was so damp that small white mites were already crawling across the bedclothes. A couple of wineglasses, a milk jug and some cutlery were the safest things to take, plus some stationery. She risked taking a small rug and washed it immediately. And now those few things were gone. Stella was utterly frightened. She stood by the door, and then dashed out into the night, looking for somewhere safe. The only place she could think of right then was to go back to Chester and Linda's as quickly as possible. There was still a light on somewhere along the hall.

"Look, I'm really sorry, but can I just sleep on the sofa? The landlord or someone has just broken into my room, and there's things thrown about and they seem to have taken the kitten too. It's disappeared." Actually, the disappearance of the kitten was not really a tragedy, but was a bit of a shock. It was all a mishmash of happenings.

Luckily Chester had stayed up, sitting in the living room, relishing a solo drink in front of a dying fire. He was surprisingly sympathetic and not too fazed about the crisis.

"That's nothing to worry about, you shouldn't take it seriously. We've got a spare room upstairs after all, you can move in here. You can come in useful doing babysitting too." He showed her into a bedroom at the back of the house. "It's not been aired or anything, you'll find some sheets along in the laundry cupboard, here, along the landing." He shoved some bedding at her and went off downstairs without another word.

The room had a washbasin in it, and was next to a toilet, Stella discovered. The basics of life were here. Luckily she wore a petticoat, which could serve as a nightdress and as long as there was a lipstick and comb in her handbag, life could go on. The uncurtained window would have to act as alarm clock for getting to work tomorrow. Sunday morning clocking in was a bind, but the afternoon was free and there were always Tuesdays off to look forward to.

When Stella went back to the Belsize Park house and knocked on the downstairs door to complain about the break-in, Ali was angry with her, accusing her of stealing the glasses and a rug and other items from Mahesh's empty flat and neglecting the kitten.

"We could hear the kitten howling from down here, we had to go up and see what was happening, you should not leave it alone like that. We noticed Mahesh's belongings too. And what were you doing with the things from Mahesh's room? You stole his belongings! You are not an honest girl at all! Cruel and dishonest!" His friends, sitting at a table playing cards, their game interrupted by this scene, watched with disapproval. These men were always sitting there playing cards at the round table under the dim lampshade. A mixed group, the front door was always clicking open, the downstairs bell ringing at all times. These men could all probably have gone upstairs and helped to break into her room.

Ali's girlfriend, a blonde girl from Bradford hovered at his side, like a gangster's moll. She had told Stella that she could only relate to Indians, no affairs with white boyfriends for her from now on.

"They don't have the same appeal any more, it doesn't work for me. Ali is lovely. He spoils me." He had the grace of a ballet dancer as he moved, sinuous and lithe like a cat.

Not wanting to have any more contact with Ali or any of the crowd downstairs, Stella crept off to work the next morning with half of her belongings in the hatbox. If challenged, she would say she was going to the launderette, but of course at seven in the morning, no one else in the house was up yet. The only other people she had ever seen was a strange family, a Mr & Mrs and grown-up son, who descended the staircase once, all together, staring at her in silence and not returning her smile. They looked scarily like the Adams Family.

Coming back from work at New End Hospital she repeated the same trip to Chester's, the last belongings crammed into a pillowcase. That would make the excuse of going off to do the washing more believable, but Ali had given up on her and there were only vague shadows behind the downstairs glass door. The afternoon gambling session was more important after all. It was as if the rented rooms were merely an adjunct to the group of intent men downstairs who were there all hours.

9 Chester was certainly living the life of a bohemian artist - this was his third wife. Linda said she was using the clothes that the previous wife had left behind in the wardrobe. Obviously they were of the same build; tall and slim, the dresses fitted perfectly. There was no mention of the wife before that one or if any of the clothes left behind were hers too.

It turned out that all the arty success was an illusion, in fact the house and all that was in it was rented.

There was an inventory, Chester told her, that went as far as each fork and spoon. Everything had to be accountable for, if they were ever to leave. There were, contrary to his claim, electricity meters installed in the rooms ready for lodgers. They had to share the basement kitchen if they wanted to cook a meal at various times, Chester pointed out there was a rota pinned up on one of the cupboards.

Stella realised how bad things were when she saw Linda lying in bed, clutching the baby, wearing an outdoors coat one cold day. Perhaps it was a post birth lethargy, but it looked more like depression. Linda had married Chester because she, in turn, had nothing else to do; it was a way of avoiding all the problems Stella faced. Work or not work; there were only so many variations of the theme. Chester needed a glamorous and much younger wife and Linda did not want to go out to work. The baby, Stanley, was caught in the middle, a sort of hostage.

Chester kept saying he wanted to rebuild Stella as an artist, after breaking her down first, which she resisted. There was an angry scene when she was invited to dinner down in the basement dining room. Spare rib and loads of rice, posh poverty. It was almost impossible to gnaw the meat from the thin bones and keep any dignity. The usual gimcrack melodrama started about establishing a true artist community. Chester was going to be the founding father, obviously. Stella grew afraid, this was too much experimentation, she was not going to be used as a practise run for some new cult.

"You would have to start from the beginning and I will show you the right way," he announced.

"But I've already done four years, that's not going to disappear," she pointed out, but Chester did not care.

"It's a challenge and an opportunity that you can't dismiss," he stated. Linda looked on as if hypnotised. Stella thought of the two previous wives and knew how they must have felt. He was good at dramatics and Stella was too tired to respond with the same level of energy.

A few weeks later Chester announced that next Sunday afternoon was going to be a Private View at home. Stella would be babysitting as soon as she got back from work. Tuesday was her only complete day off. While the child would look appealing, Stanley had to be kept off centre. He did add to the semi-begging scene, though, of the attractive wife and small baby and struggling artist. The group of patrons arrived, (primed with a couple of drinks,) from the Flask after two o'clock. Chester played his part wonderfully like a circus manager. Linda strayed around filling up peoples' glasses and looking frail and willowy. Stanley the baby managed not to cry. Three paintings were sold.

Chester said afterwards that in proper gallery Private Views, the artist or the gallery often had someone to make a real performance about buying a picture, on the lines of "I can't live without this painting! I must have it! Now, where is my chequebook!" And there would be another pseudo buyer planted too, who also bought a picture while making a fuss.

"And then, it runs through the room," he said, "The rest of the crowd wants to join in, you have created a pull and they all want to follow."

To celebrate the three sales there was a party on Saturday night. Stella went to bed to stay out of the way, but Chester sent up a good-looking young man to persuade her to get dressed and come downstairs. Because the house had not been designed or properly adapted for multiple use, there were no locks on any of the doors, in spite of the installation of electricity meters. Paul walked in and insisted she should join them. She gave in and threw on some clothes, joining the crowd downstairs, mostly in the front room. So far, the front room had no tenant and they were advertising it frantically in the Hampstead and Highgate News.

They used its double bed as an extra sofa and Stella ended up semi-lying between the young actor and his friend - another actor.

The young actor, Paul, lying next to her, legs stretched out, turned out to be brother of someone who was on TV the week before.

"Your brother! I saw him in that! I was babysitting!" They both laughed. Suddenly Maria Spring, an actress, was standing at her feet, shouting,

"How dare you make fun of my friend Peter! How dare you!"

"I was not making fun of anyone, we were both having a laugh." Stella was confused what this was about, why Maria was so het up. Paul was silent. Maria then leant forward, grabbed her shoulders and started to batter Stella's head against the wall. Because of being laid out on the bed, Stella had no traction and flailed about helplessly, trying to get her balance back again. Thump, thump, her head banged against the wall. It hurt. Maria was shouting out all the time,

"Tell us who you are! Tell us who you are! You were laughing, how dare you! Who are you?" She went on battering Stella's head against the wall.

Her head was beginning to hurt. Paul was being no help. Someone managed to draw Maria away, but she went on shouting. Then Chester approached, extremely angry, and began shouting at Stella,

"How dare you be rude to Maria! She is a classically trained actress!" Chester re-established the social order. Maria, nasty and rude and cruel was an established actress, therefore good. Whereas, Stella, failed artist, was a cleaner, therefore bad. In the ensuing row (others dragged Maria away to sit down, hysterical, still going on about cheap tarts,) Chester told Stella to get out of the house this minute, she should take her things with her, right now, she was not wanted here anymore. She ran upstairs, flung her coat on, snatched her handbag and dashed out into the road.

It was late, well past midnight, getting on for Sunday morning and she had nowhere to go. Luckily it was a clear April night. Wandering round the streets, she thought about going to Harry and Gloria's along by the Heath. The main door to the basement was never locked and, now she remembered it, there was a separate bathroom off their hall. It merely had a bath in it, nothing else. The toilet, shared with other tenants, was separate. She crept into the cold bathroom and climbed into the bath taking care the tap did not drip. Amazingly comfortable at first, feet under the taps, head cocooned in the curved end, using the handbag as a pillow; but by the early hours a deep implacable cold seeped through the coat, clothes and into her very bones. But by then tiredness took hold and she woke to find someone was rattling at the door, which she had carefully locked.

Embarrassed, or even beyond embarrassment by now, Stella opened the door to see two surprised children, Len and Paul, with Harry standing behind them.

"What on earth are you doing here? I was just going to have my weekly soak and then it's off for drinks at lunchtime. What's happened?" She burst into tears, more for being found out than about the scene with Maria and Chester. But she told Harry and an interested Gloria all about the night's happening and they were both a mixture of being cross and highly amused at the events.

"He's crazy. Sounds like they're all crazy up there," Harry said. "You better stay here, you can sleep on the sofa and then you can save the deposit for a better place." He told her later that Maria was an unemployed actress, they always made scenes, it kept them in practice.

"She's thirty-four if she's a day, and they say she's just had an affair with a seventeen year old, and had to have an abortion. So she's in a state." Gloria added more from her store of gossip, "They say she did the exact same to a young barmaid from the Flask, all that 'tell us who you are' stuff. She's in such a mess she goes for any young woman, sees them all as a threat. Bonkers, absolutely bonkers." So the studio couch in the living room became Stella's new home.

Sunday morning, however, was still a work day and Stella dashed up to New End Hospital and had to clock in late. The time lost would be subtracted from next week's wages. Maria's mad scene of the night before was having wider ramifications.

In the afternoon Stella crept back into Chester's house and collected her belongings in the hatbox and a bin liner. It was all too much to carry down the streets or stuff behind Harry and Gloria's couch and so she went down to the basement flat and asked Jenny if she could leave some things in the outside toilet.

"I don't think anyone would be interested in stealing a few things like this. I'll come back for them when I'm properly settled, I'll leave a note so you'll know it was me!" Jenny was a pleasant, bright person and it was a pity they could not be friends now because of the connection with Chester. As Jenny was a minor civil servant she was quite safe, far out of his arty range.

The new job was like a mousetrap, Tuesdays were the only real day off. And how had she ended up here? After the move across the river from Brixton, it was time to tidy up life yet again after the Christmas job at Marks and Spencers came to an end. Going to the Labour Exchange, traced via a phone directory, Stella walked to Camden Town in hope. It was free, open and near, after all; other, commercial employment agencies round Tottenham Court Road were too sophisticated to try yet again. The Labour Exchange had not entered the era of put you at your ease public decoration. The benches were only benches, the walls were council green, the lino was that sempiternal caramel brown used by governments. The grey metal filing cabinets were in no way disguised from their army surplus origin and the windows had no curtains. No one would be supposed to be doing anything needing lace curtains by daylight and only cleaners would be there at night. Logic therefore said no curtains, but a little frosted glass was allowed in strategic places.

All of this was perfectly acceptable. But Stella was overwhelmed by seeing a cliché come alive. In fact, this one incident probably determined her life for the next five years. (The length of Utrillo's White Period, or the Second World War.) The shock, the vibrant cliché, was a Scottish woman wearing a kilt and a brooch of a grouse's claw set in silver, worn on a dark green jumper. Her shoes were something like brogues and here she was, sitting ruffling through a collection of papers in the Camden Town Women's Division of the Labour Exchange. She looked too healthy and somehow too crude (in its best sense) to be leading a life so closely associated with paper.

"Good afternoon, can I help you?" The wonderful accent, the burr, the richness of it.

What I need, would like right now, is perhaps a nice walk along purple moors with some mountains in the distance. And then calling in on one of your many relatives in some little cottage for tea and scones. I've never been to Scotland. You must go there sometimes, annual leave, Christmas, New Year and all that. Aloud, Stella said,

"Good afternoon. I'm looking for a job," and produced the application form that had been filled in downstairs at the reception desk.

"Well, you've come to the right place." She talked in clichés too, quite an encounter. "Perhaps we can find you something to suit. Now, where have you been working?"

"I've been selling handbags in Morley's of Brixton. And Marks and Spencers for Christmas." Already the Scotswoman was reaching out for index cards and was definitely going to find her another handbag-selling job. They did not think imaginatively in these places. They only repeated what was told to them, or what was mentioned on the previous line on the application form.

"I'm not really a shop assistant though," Stella said.

"Oh? Not really? But it says here you have been selling handbags for four months, and before that you were a – let me see now - grocery assistant – and before that a waitress!" She put the form down with distaste. "This is not a very good record, you know. You can't go on like this. You say you are not a handbag counter assistant? Three different jobs in six months! What were you doing before that?"

Obviously, that was a bad thing. It had seemed a very good employment record to have, there were no gaps, not even a day between the three places. It had all been achieved in three panic leaps, helped by the Alfred Marks Employment Bureau. Mary weaving a seamless garment for Jesus could have done no better.

Another assistant appeared now and they both glared at her.

"This employment record of yours is incomplete. What were you doing last year?"

"I was a student for the past four years." This got them both irate, as though she had been swanning around in the South of France all that time. They looked at each other with a mixture of disapproval and anger. Both of them had started work soon after leaving school at the age of fourteen. The lower middle classes were implacable. Here was a breach in the castle walls.

"Well, well now, we must do something about all this and see if we can tidy you up." No healthy walks across the heather now. She would probably stick to the paths anyway. "What exact kind of employment was it you were seeking?" Seeking? They were probably instructed to use words like that. Questing after employment. There was going to be no seeking about here, may as well just tell her outright all about it. Take a deep breath.

"Well, I'm an artist."

"Oh, really?" She was very hostile now. (Dundee cakes, that's what I've been trying to think of. For having with the tea in the little cottage, instead of scones. But she probably doesn't come from Dundee and maybe the cakes don't either. Better play safe, not offend her any more. Next week's rent's got to be got.)

"Have you any *proof* of this? Have you taken any examinations?"

"I've got National Diploma in Design; Painting, that's four years of study." That cut her back a little, but hostilities were not over yet. The two assistants exchanged meaningful looks now.

"I'll just go and check. A diploma, you say." She almost sniffed at this and went off to another office for information and returned from the other room, with a swirl of pleats and carrying a leather-bound official inventory. "Yes, you are a classified artist, does have an entry number here for that qualification." It was very awkward for her. She could no longer be so openly hostile because the game, after all, was being played her way; and she had lost. But now it changed to a personal dislike, subtly disguised with smiles and flapping papers. "Now we must find you a job."

The other woman left, going back to a filing cabinet across the room.

Then, by some fantastic manoeuvre, sleight of hand (the knight's move?) the Scots lady won the game, board and all.

"Start on Monday then. Alexandra House Old Folks Home. Seven pounds a week. We'll send your card on. From seven thirty in the morning to two thirty in the afternoon." Like instructions to the damned. You may write to your dearest ones. The chaplain will call. The clock will begin to chime and at precisely...

With the true exhilaration of the condemned Stella went out towards the tatty green, an assistant cleaner in an old folks' home. With the hindsight of altered position (the fresh air, the traffic noise, seeing the office windows from the outside) she felt pity for the isolated Scottish woman so far from home, so bravely coping, so fixed in her routine. For some days afterwards or really for about a year, the words 'classified artist' gave deep comfort in some very mundane hours. The Scots lady, like the bad fairy at a christening, had fixed everything with those magic words.

10

The choice had been limited; either go back to waitressing or shop-assisting or be a cleaner or train to be a typist or a nurse; there was nothing else.

In the first week on the way back from work, Stella called in to the greengrocers on Fleet Road. They sold interesting cheap vegetables like cooking tomatoes (already going off) and mushroom stalks (the interesting bit already sliced off.) When the assistant asked how much weight of the real mushrooms she wanted, Stella, thinking big, asked for a pound and was landed with a mountain of mushrooms, her first lesson in good housekeeping. Remembering the stringent quarter of a pounds her mother always bought, it had obviously been more prudent. Now there were all these mushrooms to get through, on toast or otherwise.

London County Council by the Grace of God decided one Friday afternoon that Stella was not needed at Alexandra House any more, the real assistant had returned from sick leave, so it was goodbye to all the mad old ladies who she had grown quite fond of and off to another uncharted future. Luckily they needed an assistant at New End hospital so now she polished floors in the Nurses' Home together with an assortment of Spanish, Swedish, Italian and French girls. The Sister Housekeeper said,

"It's wonderful to have someone who naturally speaks English." English was the lingua franca as the nurses were of a four-corners-of-the-earth selection too,

Japanese, German, Persian (she brought her own carpet too, it was beautiful, like velvet.) So Stella's mind, if not her vocabulary was getting somewhat broader. The hours were eight to three, Tuesdays off, Sunday seven thirty to one, she wondered how long she could stand it. There was, though, a wonderful uniform, a version of the real nurses' outfits. It included a long swirling brown cape for wearing outside, with a light-green gingham dress, white apron and white cap. They looked like trainee nurses walking up the high street, though the magnificent outfits had to be left in their lockers near the kitchens at the end of their shift.

Each summer morning, as Stella was walking up from Harry and Gloria's after another night on their couch, a white cat sat waiting for her, on the wall of a house in Christchurch Hill. It sat by the gate in the silent street, coming towards her for a pet. Festooned in wisteria and only recently painted white, the house was the dream of gentle English prosperity. The daily welcome by the cat made a difference to the day, its friendly presence reassuring and a gift of beauty. The new morning belonged to both of them. There was no one else about in the goldenness.

There was no space to paint at present, so one Tuesday Stella went off to the Tate to the latest exhibition to keep up with art. She came out of the Tate thinking that Francis Bacon certainly had problems, poor man, how lucid was his madness. Rooms full of shrieking heads, naked businessmen and meat-like crucifixions and dogs, the underside of society exposed, the pain levels accurate. It was heaven to come out to trees stuck into pavements and the normality of rush hour crowds.

The Ecole de Paris exhibition was entirely different, its problems were aesthetic and essentially a working out of problems in the craft itself. It was like walking into a library and finding only the pages of dictionaries stuck over the shelves, but no books. The essence was of a Post Impressionist mosaic, of texture experiments, of shock use of colours (black with electric blue, mauve paint ridged with gilt stripes), oils used so delicately that they became like watercolour, concrete mixed with paint, cut paper applied like a relief map of islands, one black line on a five by four feet wide canvas and one sublime idiot who played with 1920s shapes, the kind that could be bought in any stationers, a selection of gummed paper figures for scrapbooks.

Of course Stella knew he might be struggling after balance without the distraction of surface illusions, but another voce said "Why?" Pierre Soulages came out trumps, his pictures held together with chunky masses of black with slashes of colour glowing through.

One disappointment was the only Nicholas de Staël that she could find, in sad blue and balancing ounce for ounce along a line was hung downstairs in the corridor that led to the gents' lavatories. But the main feeling she got was of the high priests forging ahead, creating new 'texture' which was useful for advertising, which was what Harry did all day after all at the advertising agency. He looked for trends like this to excavate new visuals and the agency turned them into useful styles to catch the eye.

She got back to their flat and found Gloria was still waiting for Harry to come home, his dinner had been in and out of the oven several times, she said.

"Another half an hour and it's going in the bin. A good bit of steak, too. Total waste."

Gloria had a few records which she played again and again. *'I Remember Clifford'* by Art Blakely and the Jazz Messengers became the song of that spring. It permeated the walls, spreading further and further.

"I'm pregnant. Don't see it makes much difference now, but Harry's delighted. The doctor said that's why I keep feeling a bit sick, it's the start. I should have known!"

Behind the scenes, Harry decided it would be a good idea if Stella would go out on Easter Monday with Frank, a friend of his and a regular from the Magdala. It was as if Harry owed a debt to Frank and Stella was going to be the payment. Without realising what was really going on she found it had all been arranged around her. Frank was going to pick her up; they were going to go out on Monday afternoon and he was going to drive her to Brighton. It was a real treat. What girl could refuse? She would be back from work after lunchtime after all. Hospital work did not adjust for Bank Holidays.

The entire enterprise circled round Frank's white sports car. No one else they knew had a car, Harry often used taxis to and from his ad agency and everyone else walked or got on the bus or tube. Frank lived at home with his mother although he was well into his forties, which was how he afforded the car. The white sports car was his image of success and he knew all the men envied him as a cheap James Bond. Who was Stella, homeless and carless, to refuse him? Remembering Kay Kendall and Kenneth Moore in *Genevieve*, going off to Brighton in a sports car, she got a scarf and they set off. Down Balham High Road (the original B&B must still be there) and past Streatham Ice Rink, they raced past people on the pavements, men noting the car's glamour whizzing past them. This was Frank's experience every day; it was ego-boosting. The wind blew the scarf glamorously, just like the film. Stella, focus of envious glances too, was eyeing the far more fanciable lads her own age walking along the pavement. She longed to jump out and join them,

"This is not real! I can't stand him! Quick, let's go and hide in a coffee bar!

They chuntered into Brighton and Frank parked on the promenade as near to the beach as possible. He produced a rug from the boot. She thought, *He's done this several times before.* They walked onto the shore and he spread out the large travel rug on the sand avoiding a stony area. He immediately laid down while she managed to sit upright, hugging her knees. While he lay back as if they were in a double bed facing the sea, she chattered brightly to keep from any kissing he might attempt.

"Come on now, why don't you lie down and relax!" He resented her lack of compliance, it was obvious. At an exceptionally awkward instant, just as he was reaching to grab her, Stella distracted him by jumping up and going off to buy ice creams for them both,

"Look! Over there! The ice cream van has arrived. My treat." Luckily it soon grew colder and they moved from the beach just in time as the tide turned. After a short stroll looking at the antique shops' windows Frank suggested it was time they went off for a meal. Yes, food would be a good idea.

"I know a really nice place," he said. "You'll like it."

So, on the way back they called into a country pub. Frank obviously knew it as part of his usual seduction set-up. Stone fireplace, a welcoming log fire in the cool spring evening, it was perfect. Low ceilings, no game machines or music, just the muted chat of men in tweed jackets drinking at the bar. She imagined the red setter which should be lying in front of the fireplace. Chicken in a basket, with chips. Perfect. The best part of the day so far. It was strange how food easily altered one's attitude towards someone. For an instant she almost liked him, but remembered that was why most dogs greeted their owners, because they symbolised food coming soon and the dogs could not operate a tin-opener on their own.

Leaving the pub at 8 p.m. they arrived back at Harry and Gloria's about 10 p.m. They got back to a suspiciously empty flat, all gone off to bed early. Time for Frank to make his move at last and for Stella to try and diffuse the situation. This was difficult as the sofa was the only place to sit. The rest were ordinary dining chairs. He was angry at her. When he lunged forwards for a kiss, she had backed away and said it was not feasible.

"Really, I don't really want this to go any further now, we'd better not. It's going to get too embarrassing."

"But I've taken you out, all that way to Brighton!"

"If you think about it, I didn't really ask for you to do that, if you remember. Harry and you went and arranged it between you both, first, and then I could hardly refuse." Perhaps all the other available girls had cried off or been through the similar experience and it had been her turn. "I did not think it up, you did and you took it all as done and dusted." She felt sorry for his ineptitude but this was not her responsibility. It was all the more awkward because Harry and Gloria could probably hear what was going on here from their bedroom, or at least catch the highlights.

Frank growled and got up off the couch and strode out of the door. The thrum of the sports car sounded extra loud as he drove away.

Frank obviously complained to his friends in the pubs about her uncooperative behaviour. She was put on some kind of blacklist. One evening that week, going to sit at the same table as James, a part-time model for knitwear adverts and knitting patterns, Stella was interrogated. There was, startlingly, no one she knew in the Magdala that evening, otherwise she would have avoided sitting with him.

"I can't quite make you out, what you're really up to here," James said. She looked closely into his good-looking but empty face. He had a craggy jawline and a sculptured chin. He had the permanently smug look of a man who smoked a pipe while balancing one suede shoe on a log and gazing into the distance, while also getting a hefty fee.

"Are you a lesbian, or are you just frigid? Not interested in men? I haven't ever seen you with a boyfriend here." He must have had a secret register, Stella thought. She could not tell him about the affair with Pete, who was standing over at the bar right now with his back to them. Pete, the artist who was having an affair with a rich married woman who he was indebted to, who had some hold over the lease of his studio.

"I'd be mortified if anything ever got out about you and me," Pete had said. "I'd have to pretend I didn't know you at all." End of that. And there was Ed, who she had encountered at a party in South Kensington, a girlfriend left somewhere in the crowd, him very drunk and insisting on going home with her. Too drunk to drive, she had persuaded him to take a taxi and he had collapsed to sleep, awakening on the Sunday morning annoyed they had not managed to have had sex together back in his Chalk Farm flat, and amazed to be waking up in Hampstead itself. Stella reminded him where the car was parked over in South Kensington and he had gone off to trace it and they had not rekindled the romance. But Ed might have walked in right now.

"Come on now, I don't have to justify my existence here, it's called a public house for a reason, you know," she smiled. "There's a lot going on in the background, and just because I don't fancy you doesn't mean there's something wrong with me." She was not going to name names. In no time it would all have been cheapened into pub gossip, which was what James really wanted as material. There had been a marvellous couple of months' relationship with Pepe, a Spanish boy who was working at The Coffee Cup, here to learn English. As he worked until eleven at night, Stella would go out and make sure to be back at home when he called in after his shift ended. They were completely happy together, he was a complex mixture of sweet yet strong.

But of course his six months came to an end and he could not have taken her back with him, plus she did not even have a passport or the money for a plane ticket. They were both upset, but could do nothing about it.

"I will never forget you," Pepe said and then disappeared. She was not going to betray him just to please John's cruel curiosity right now. "I would just leave it as a blank, if I were you," she added.

11
It was obvious that staying at Harry and Gloria's on their living-room couch had to come to an end soon, their kindness had its limits after all. Three adults and two children, with another on the way, were a crowd in such a small flat, even though Stella was out most of the time. At least she was able to meet the boys from school each day after work and walk home with them. And now Harry's brother was coming to visit, she would have to move. Time to find another room. Before that there were other places, all a jumble now. Keeping moving was the only way to escape the snags; otherwise she would still be in that gigantic back room in Clapham South or the other place in Brixton or the Indian gambling house in Belsize Park Gardens or the mad artist's one off Flask Walk.

Perhaps there were important letters left at all those places, an unravelled life of important documents. All those letters enquiring after posts for art teachers in the

Teachers' World and their stamped addressed envelopes all wasted. Even chasing up copies of the Teachers' World had been an achievement; branches of WH Smiths were the only ones who sold it. But those type of jobs were not the kind you walked into on any Monday morning expecting to be paid on the Friday. The better the job, the longer the way into it, the interview, and then a wait of a month or more. So the quick employments solved one lot of problems, while raising more; no time to go off for interviews, no spare money. And all the time your social standing fell, plummeted until the working-class life obscured the educated background and the CV blurred any past achievements.

All that time only one official message had reached her, via her National Insurance number, asking how she had benefited from a college education and what post she now held. As it had a stamped return envelope she had been able to tell the government that after four years of training to be an artist, she was now working for a cleaning agency and her knees were constantly dirty from scrubbing kitchen floors.

12
Right now she was standing above Belsize Park Underground station looking out at the unheeding commuters dashing into catch their early morning trains.

The nights in between, as somewhere for her to stay, Harry had asked a friend, a drinker at the nearby Tunnel Club, to put her up for a few nights. It turned out to be a draughtsman's studio set right over Belsize Park tube station. The doorway was down a side alley, totally inconspicuous. Alfie led her into the building.

"Here's a key, now, don't lose it. There's a sink here and a toilet on the landing, take care you don't lock yourself out. Make sure you slam the door shut when you leave in the mornings. And put the key through the letterbox when you move out. I'll be away for the rest of the week, so you've got that long to sort yourself out." He left just like that, kindly with no trace of taking any advantage. Stella looked round the stacks of paper, the large architect-sized drawing board like a shrunken art school.

She gazed down at the commuters, the worker bees that kept the hive working. No one looked up – why should they? It was like being God, looking into their faces and picking up their Monday morning thoughts.

Stella had spent the night asleep alongside the half-circular window. A couch along the front wall meant she woke up to see the commuters below like ants walking, hurrying towards the station ticket office. After a quick facewash and with fresh mascara and lipstick it was her turn to be off to work now, to blend in with the others and disappear into that London like everyone else. But she was walking in the opposite direction towards a block of flats in St John's Wood, that morning's cleaning job.

On the way back from the afternoon's placement in Arkwright Road after six that evening, she looked again in the estate agent's window at the corner of Pond Street and there it was. Now she really had moved out of Harry and Gloria's living room and off their sofa things must speed up. They had given her time to save up for a deposit on a new room after all. She could not stay living above Belsize Park Station for many more days.

Right there in the estate agency's window was another gamble to take. Stella went right away into the paper-strewn office but no one was about. It was closing time after all. After a moment, a young man with wispy light brown hair and a worried look shuffled into the office. He stood with a heap of papers in his hands from the mysterious back room. He looked surprised to see her.

"Can I help you?" he asked, as he dropped the files onto the littered desk. He did not look very helpful right now, more as if he needed a stiff black coffee.

"I saw the card in the window about a room to let near here, could you tell me more about it?" He thought it over for a second as though he did not know what she was talking about.

"Oh, sorry, that place is gone already, I didn't get round to changing the window yet, too much to do in here. But there's a room going almost next-door, you might be interested in that. It's three pounds a week, plus gas of course. I can let you see it now, if you like, the guy that's in it is just moving out, he can tell you all about it."

Laurence took her past a shabby white painted wall and up the steps to a Victorian stucco terrace house. They walked down a dark brown lino floored hall to an also brown painted door. Laurence knocked on the door and introduced her to Rick, who was moving out.

"I'll leave you two to discuss things, You can get back to me if you've decided anything." And off he went. Rick said he was moving out to a house even nearer the

Heath, in fact, into his girlfriend's place. He was an actor, used to getting parts usually as policemen or thieves mostly on TV, he told her, semi boasting, semi complaining.

"There's nothing in between for me, it seems, no roles except perhaps doing Shakespeare up in Stratford on Avon and I don't want to go there. I was told off by the supervisor at the dole office, he said that being out of work a couple of months a year was no good for me, why didn't I get a nice safe job like his?

And I told him that being employed ten months this year, for an actor, was a bloody miracle!" She made a snap decision there and then. It was better than nothing. Plus it was within walking distance of everywhere she wanted to go to. South End Green was just at the bottom of the hill, with the 24 bus that even stopped outside the Tate Gallery. Rick continued to pack his clothes and belongings randomly.

"You might like it here, there's no hassle at all, no rules, it's quite quiet too. Bathroom's upstairs and there's another toilet too as well as that one near the front door by the payphone." Rick continued to collect his minimum belongings. "My clothes and stuff are already gone. These are just the last bits. If there's anything left behind, it's yours! There's a bonus here though – you get the electricity free because it's only one lightbulb after all and there's no sockets to plug any items into. There's an old Ewbank cleaner in the hall somewhere to run over the carpet with."

When he had left, Stella found that the mattress consisted of four thinner mattresses, each of them lumpy and discoloured. Trying not to think of how they had got like that, she tucked her one sheet tightly over the lot of them and hoped for the best. Rick had left her with a heap of blankets and another sheet, plus some food and a couple of shillings for the meter. Unusually, the ancient gas meter was on a shelf in the alcove right above the bed. It worried Stella that the lot might come crashing down on her at once, though it looked like a sturdy piece of Victorian or Edwardian engineering.

On the other side of the fireplace, set on a small cabinet, was the usual two-ring gas Baby Belling with its inexplicable grill. The grill pan was missing. Then came the window, which stretched all the way up to the ceiling, about six yards high. Thin curtains that looked as though they had come with the building fluttered at the sides, faded blue of some thin material. The view was of the massed gardens of other houses and a disused coach-house attached to the pub in the next corner. In the distance the train to Richmond rattled through merrily. An Ascot heater over the sink, a wardrobe, a government- surplus cane wastepaper basket, office desk and chair, with an added fireside chair completed the set. She would take it.

Stella went back to the cluttered office and paid Laurence the three pounds with a week's rent as deposit and he gave her Rick's old rent book, with the name scribbled out. His own signature was also a scribble and Stella never found out his surname. She went outside the front door, scraping the previous name off the bells and the name list by the payphone in the lobby. She went back to Belsize Park Station and put the key through the letterbox with a note of thanks. Harry and Gloria were obviously pleased that she had got somewhere proper at last.

On Saturday afternoon her first call was at the launderette, as soon as she could transfer her paltry extra belongings from Chester's up the hill. Acquiring her own two sheets and pillow cases had been a great step forward.

Chester, in his turn, had been an escape from the place in Belsize Park Gardens that was a Dickensian slum which had become frightening. This new place was a more picturesque slum. The downstairs toilet basin had a blue-designed pattern of flowers and maybe shepherds and shepherdesses; the small washbasin matched. It was a Victorian sense of propriety and showed how the original building had once been middle class and fashionable.

The final settling-in bit here was when she put the latest painting up on the mantelpiece leaning in front of the mirror. It had been started in that Belsize Park attic with the miserable kitten for company. At last there was somewhere where she could paint in peace and get involved in the new great idea. *One Hundred Views of NW3*; that was going to be the grand theme. It had started when Stella had discovered *The Great Wave of Kanagawa*, done by Hokusai about 1834 and yet as bright as today, shining right through the centuries. Though perhaps trying to follow Hokusai in his Hundred Views of the Fujiyama was too much of a folly. Far too ambitious. Ando Hiroshige had later done the same, with his *One Hundred Famous Views of Edo*. She would never be able to produce so many, or even to afford the materials and definitely never afford the framing for a hundred pictures.

Chester, being an almost professional artist, had told her of artists ending up in debt after a gallery exhibition (her dream.) The gallery would frame the pictures wonderfully, but then, obviously, they charged the artist for the outlay. Not enough sales meant the artist was then trapped in debt. And stuffing a hundred pieces of hardboard would be too much to manage under the bed or behind the wardrobe. But Chester, after all, had said small pictures were popular, though she disbelieved him.

"People like to be able to hold a picture in their hands," he had said, demonstrating by picking up one of his own paintings off the living room wall and holding it in both hands like a winning lottery ticket. Stella thought of the Mona Lisa and every really famous painting and how heavy any of them would be to try and hold, but smiled at him like the idiot he thought she was.

Luckily she then found out that Hokusai had done another series, of only 36 pictures, views of Mount Fuji, and that seemed far more feasible. It was a distant hand to keep hold of. "The Japanese relished every unexpected and unconventional aspect of the world. Their master, Hokusai would represent the mountain Fujiyama seen as if by chance behind a scaffolding" it said in Gombrich's The *Story of Art*. There was also *Fuji Seen Behind a Cistern*, another colour woodcut. A pity that her latest painting, in discordant reds, was called *A Song for Nellie Bligh*, but it gave the room a focus. She moved the picture a bit to the left of the mantelpiece to clear enough of the mirror to put her make-up on.

Thirty six! That was it! A magic number, definitely. Yonks ago in Dot's Hampstead flat she had picked up a copy of *"The Thirty-six Dramatic Situations"* by Georges Polti. She had never got round to reading it as it was a quick visit to London over two years ago, a dress rehearsal for all this, as it turned out. She remembered walking up the concrete stairs with their echo of each footstep and the green-tiled walls set up the staircase like a public baths. Dot's flat was directly over the Prompt Corner café, so beneath them the constant chess players sat at the tables, each with their clockwork alarms timing their games. The men looked like refugees left over from the war, intently playing and replaying strategies without any chance of a permanent solution.

Above them, the toilet in the flat was totally blocked and as Dot did not have the money to get a plumber yet, they used the pub or the public toilets at South End Green. Meanwhile a couple of joss sticks did their best against the smell. *The Thirty-six Dramatic Situations* book paled in contrast with what they were going through right then, before Dot managed to borrow some money from a boyfriend.

"Something you'd love to know, by the way," Dot said. "Downstairs used to be a bookshop, and George Orwell worked there while he wrote *Keep the Aspidistra Flying.* And more than that, he lived over the shop, so he might have stayed in this very flat, there's only two others. Just think of that!"

"Probably the same old plumbing then, which is why we have to suffer," Stella said, unimpressed for the moment.

The new house had a payphone in the hall. The list of names soon became familiar. Anyone who rang up meant a loud shouting in the hall. They all got to know a new name in no time at all. So when Fiona came upstairs on the 24 bus one day she encountered Stella, smoking a Black Sobranie on the top deck. The smell was deeper than ordinary cigarettes.

"Do have one," she said, offering the impressive black and gold packet with its Imperial crest. "You're Fiona from the top floor, I'm Stella. I heard you on the phone this morning. I'm a cleaner at present, but really an artist. What are you?" Fiona, mystified at all this mixture said she was a product demonstrator for large firms and had to travel all over from city to city.

"I'm really a cabaret singer, but I have to keep doing something in the in-between times. The dresses cost so much to get made, they have to look expensive and I have to have proper hairdressers too. Another couple of years and it'll be too late."

"At least with painting and writing, you can do it at any age," Stella commiserated. "But just think, if we were both ballet dancers, it would already be all over!" They laughed at the thought of being old ballet dancers and so the friendship began as they both sailed into town.

There would obviously be a snag later, as to stand and paint using the mantelpiece would mean her legs being roasted by the gas fire, but it was still summer and she could paint flat on the desk when winter came.

13 February. Artist's sketchbook. *Snow on roofs like sky biting into tops of houses. Heathurst Road: coal man, black velvet coming towards her down the road, blacker than trees. Blue in green, black on white, white on black, white on white, coal in snow, snow in snow.*

It's easy enough to write it down, but painting takes more out of you. Translating those quick notes into coherent gestures of paint, giving colour and life to them, was exhausting at times. So quiet to do and yet so draining; it did not make sense.

She had not long settled in when Rutger, a sculpture student from the Slade called round to see if Sue's baby could be his. They had an affair soon after Sue had moved from Liverpool, one of the first of the group to arrive that spring like swifts or swallows. It already felt so long ago.

"It's really important to me you see, more than for most men, because I'm sterile, or supposed to be. This baby would be so wonderful, I'd be really more than happy to support her and the baby. Do you know any more about it at all?"

"How did you get to know about all this? And where to find me?" Stella was amazed at how he knew all the details.

"Sally told me, one of your friends from Liverpool, she's married to Martin and he's in the Slade too. See? You're all connected, you're easy to find. Sally said you'd probably know, being a friend of Sue's. Can you please find out for me? Anything?"

He was the second young man she had met lately who said he was sterile, it was perhaps a way to cheat a girl into having sex. Not every woman was on the pill and Stella had yet to meet any man who had a condom. If she had produced a packet of them, her name would have been spread round the pubs as an easy lay, quite beyond the pale. The rules were strict even though never said out loud. It was all a guessing game, and here, Sue had fallen at the first fence. Stella was gambling with her own fertility too, depending on using only the day before an expected period which should have been quite safe. But it was frightening like balancing on the crest of a waterfall.

Contraception was a dirty secret still and mostly devoted to women who were already mothers or married, or both – exactly as it had been when she was a teenager. Women with prams and extra toddlers would be seen waiting outside a clinic in Gambier Terrace back in Liverpool, and her mother would purse her lips as they walked past on the way to Windsor Street library. The women were breaking some sacred rule by not wanting extra kids to the ones they already had. It was women only; nothing to do with men, who never entered the building.

She did not like Rutger, there was something untamed about him, a coarseness, probably a really good trait for a sculptor, but he deserved any help she could give. It was not a good time to mention Gordon, who was now living with Sue and taking care of her.

"I can't say anything, no news, I haven't gone to the hospital yet." On Sunday afternoon, then, Stella dutifully went off to Harrow Road spending several minutes trying to find the right ward in the endless corridors.

At last, in one of the maternity wards, there was Gordon sitting beside a bed, holding Sue's hand, he looked as though he was almost pleading. There was a cot on the other side of the bed. Stella looked down at the baby and Sue caught her eye,

"Moses. I'm calling him Moses." The Old Testament princess finding a baby floating in a cradle woven from rushes – how had that name come about? Sue was not at all religious; in fact Stella herself would not have remembered the name. She looked at the baby boy seriously now. Its skin was dark, darker than any sunburnt child. She knew immediately it had to be Mahesh's, the creepy Indian who lived in the next room in that Belsize attic. He had quickly made a crude play for herself, after all, when she had moved into Gordon and Sue's old rooms on the top floor. When she had refused, he said she would be paid back by fate for being so repressed and she would find at the age of twenty-four she would end up going crazy and would be taking her clothes off at parties.

"You can only keep on repressing your feelings for so long, you know. Repressing sexual feelings will only lead to a massive breaking out later that will overwhelm you," Mahesh stated pompously.

"Well, that may be so, it sounds more like it's a strange idea you've probably just made up, but I don't see that happening. I'll risk it and see what happens when I get to twenty-four." Stella replied and adroitly got away from him in the narrow top corridor, getting back into her room and locking the door quickly. This was the problem with bedsitter houses, it was like living out in the street, you had no choice whoever might be living right next to you. But his putdown rankled, as it was meant to, and again she was left doubting herself and what was the right way of refusing these propositions and navigating the endless craftiness and resentments.

So Mahesh had managed to seduce Sue somehow. Surely she had better taste? But then he was in the very next room and would be difficult to avoid. They had to share the stairs to the bathroom and toilet and to the phone down in the hall. Just one instance of Sue needing a shoulder to cry on and he could have exploited her easily. Gordon had appeared like a knight in shining armour and taken her under his wing afterwards. Their needs coincided and a love of sorts soon worked for both of them, fate doing its best.

Right now the invisible Mahesh was back in India, a newly appointed professor in Bombay after his successful stint at the London School of Economics. From a postcard he had sent, Stella knew he had left on the SS Asia and it would take fifteen days, going via Genoa, to reach home. He had seriously given her the address as if he expected a letter in return. He had mentioned a wife and two sons waiting for him when he arrived onshore.

But also, in an unnecessary gesture of kindness, he had told Stella that she could help herself to anything he had left behind in his rooms. Stella stood there looking at the untidy debris of a life. The room was so desolate, even worse than the shabby one of Gordon and Sue's that she had inherited, and it was absolutely freezing.

However, the place was so damp that already an infection of minute white specks were moving all over the surface of the bedclothes. As it was too risky to take anything made of cloth, so she took some plates, cutlery and a tartan rug that would have to go to the launderette at once.

In a hopeful gamble she also took a collection of small wine glasses decorated with gold patterns. One day there would be a party to cater for. There was also a heap of important headed notepaper which might come in useful, *The Third All-African Peoples Conference – Cairo Troisieme Conference De Tous Les Peuples Africains – Le Caire.*

But of course, the main thing that Mahesh had left behind was a real live baby. A couple of wineglasses and bedclothes were nothing beside that. And there was Rutger, too, caught between all the possibilities.

"It's settled, just so you know, the baby's going to be put up for adoption," Gordon confided as they left the ward together. "It's only six weeks to go at the most, and then Sue is out of the woods here." She would perhaps go on to a mother and baby home to give up the baby legally and then go back to living with Gordon again. He did not want to discuss it further, Stela could see that, and they parted at the hospital steps. The baby would get a new name and it would all disperse like mist, except the actual live baby would grow into a man and perhaps start looking for answers one day. The answers were here and disappearing by the minute.

Stella walked home slowly, upset by it all, not knowing how to tell it tactfully, as Rutger would be calling round tomorrow evening and she would have to give him the bad news.

At last she could start painting in peace. Staying at Chester's had made it impossible, just a few covert sketches and being at Harry and Gloria's for nearly a month, there had been no space. The idea of doing 36 paintings had come to the surface again. It had been brewing for months now.

So, catching up with Hokusai and starting the set of 36 paintings meant dipping into her pitiful Post Office Savings account. The Post Office at the corner of Keats Grove also sold painting equipment and, fittingly, the silver-haired counter assistant had an arty fringe and wore a strangely patterned overall. The new account was reassuring. *Strict Secrecy Observed. This book is the property of the Postmaster General.* When any withdrawal of over £3 was made in a period of seven days, the book had to be sent off to Savings Bank Headquarters.

Stella took out a careful £2 and went off, ordering hardboard from the hardware shop along Fleet Road and then going back later in the week to buy some lengths of framing, a mitre block and a hacksaw which she found she could not use but the mitre block was useful to stack papers in. The wonky pieces of framing showed her various attempts at cutting sizes properly and ended up by the bins instead. The scratches and cuts on her hands mended later.

Paints cost far more at seven shillings a tube. She got Prussian blue (useful, though she hated it) ultramarine (beautiful enough to dive into) deep fast red (bloody), signal red (tarty), lemon yellow (looking as bitter as its name), mid-chrome (various butters) and black and flake white (poison, lead paint.) With glue size, linseed oil and turpentine, 3 small and 3 large bristle brushes bought over the next weeks, the show was on the road at last.

She often listened to jazz when painting, as it had the same wandering, exploring nature and was less distracting than pop songs or radio discussions.

Stella was introduced to Matt at the Tally Ho one Sunday afternoon with Gloria. The jazz session was a regular arrangement. He gave her his address, a new event from any man. Usually they hid wherever they were living, not wanting to be traced after any seductions. She visited three weeks later and apologised for the delay. He magnanimously said it did not matter. They became lovers in a haphazard way, tumbling into his gigantic bed, listening to music. An old wooden radio paced across the world of music as they lay in bed beside it. They listened as the broadcasters in every country closed down, each playing their national anthem.

"We could belong to all of them," Matt joked.

"This bed's about the size they'd need," Stella agreed as they fell asleep.

Gloria called round. She was excited - Fred was in town. One by one Liverpool was emptying itself and sending its residents off to London. There must be no one left in The Crack on a Saturday night by now, Stella thought. Fred used to call in on the way to the Saturday night shift at the tyre factory in those years. He had even bought her a drink once.

"And not only do I have to pay taxes that pay for your Art School stuff, but now I'm paying for a drink for you as well!" he complained. Stella looked at the begrudged glass of cider and tried to look grateful. And now he was here in London, transformed into a sculptor after years of night-shift welding in a factory in the small hours. It had to happen. Some worms turned and won.

Gloria said, "He's having an exhibition, and we're invited to the private view. So you've got to come to it too. Remember him?" This was the life Stella wanted, after all, one private view after another. Harry would meet them at the gallery straight from work, it was not far from St Martin's College of Art.

The Enigma Gallery was set in a basement in a court off St Martin's Lane but it was definitely in the best location and when they entered the place was already quite full. Rich people wandered round making muttered polite conversation and there, incongruously, was Fred right in the midst of them. He towered over everyone at six-plus feet, with a loud voice and his broad Liverpool accent booming around. The sculptures were set at intervals round the white room on waist-high white plinths and soft mood-music wafted around. It was as classy as you could get, a genuine West End exhibition.

Glasses of red and white wine were being offered as if from a fountain and Fred had indulged happily and was obviously already drunk. He was glad to see them and introduced them to his girlfriend, Anna. She was at least half his age, almost as tall and blonde. She assured Stella that she was going to be an art critic, that was her plan. Stella thought she was common, with that thick Liverpool accent and not very bright, but would get ahead because she had such an amazing self-belief it might carry her anywhere.

A beautiful Spanish man with soulful dark eyes and his equally good-looking boyfriend decided to buy one of the sculptures.

"We don't quite understand that piece, though. Why is it called 'Soldat'?" He pointed to a small brass coal scuttle standing under a spotlight.

"Soldat? It's German for Soldier. It's a German helmet! Thought that would be obvious!" Fred said brusquely, dismissing the questioner. However, the man moved away to a crucifixion piece and decided after a confab with his companion to buy that instead. It was a representation of Calvary made from three forks set into a block of wood. The forks' tines had been pressed apart to form the arms of the crosses and the figures of Christ and the two thieves were made from spilt solder, splashed silver ghostly figures that appeared if the onlooker used their imagination.

At this point two events happened at once. A distinguished figure descended the stairs, Alastair Burnet, the newscaster from ITV. It was surreal to see a television star actually appear in real life,

"Good God, I've never seen him as a person with real legs." Harry joked. "And that over there's a really expensive tweed jacket. Must be worth as much as one of any of these sculpture bits." Gloria could not stop staring at the TV announcer, trying to reconcile real life with image. Everyone, in fact, stared. But at the same instant Fred got into an argument with a collector about his method of taking everyday objects, adjusting them slightly - or not at all - and claiming they were his own creations. He took a wild swing at one of the guests, and missing, toppled over one of his sculptures.

Then as if set in motion, he dashed around the gallery yelling and throwing his pieces to the floor, followed by the plump gallery owner running after Fred, shouting at him and attempting to rescue them. The beautiful Spaniard grabbed the Crucifixion that he had been after and stuffed it up his wide duffel-coat sleeve to save it from the mass destruction.

Anna, the girlfriend, asked to cool Fred down by the gallery owner, was brushed aside as Fred continued his rampage. She staggered and backed against one of the plinths, and a *Head of a New Dictator* fell to the floor and shattered. It had been merely plaster, with an imitation bronze varnish finish giving it an authentic sheen. The TV presenter surveyed the damage and calmly climbed the stairs and escaped. By now Fred wanted to challenge everyone and anyone and people were cornered in various groups round the room, trying discreetly to make for the exit like the famous TV presenter.

One of the gallery staff wandered round trying to set the sculptures back on their plinths but several had broken apart and pieces were rolling round the floor. Fred tripped over and fell too, still thrashing around. As a piece of theatre it could not have been bettered.

"It's getting boring now," Harry said, "and if we don't get out right now, you know we're the ones who'll be landed with him for the rest of the night." Even Gloria, ever quick to follow the Liverpool label, agreed and Stella went off with them, as Fred staggered back onto his feet and continued whirling about, spectacularly destroying all his work. It was a disaster area. The few pieces that had looked like traditional sculptured heads turned out not to be bronze at all. They had shattered as they fell, showing that they were merely made out of plaster with a coating of bronze paint making them look authentic. Surreal bits of heads rolled round on the floor creating further hazards. Scared art-lovers tripped over the scattered remnants and fallen plinths.

The escaping guests regrouped on the pavement outside complaining and upset and the Spanish man with the soulful eyes produced the Crucifixion sculpture from his wide duffel coat and held it up. It shone under the street lights.

"It's all right, I've paid for it," he said, waving it about. "I made a cheque out to the gallery," as he went off towards Charing Cross Road with his friend.

"I bet that cheque bounces," Stella joked.

"But at least he's saved one of the pieces of sculpture after all," Harry pointed out. "And at the rate old Fred's going on down there, that lad's probably got the only surviving proof of Fred's work. It might be really valuable in no time at all." They watched the only extant piece of Fred's work left in private hands disappear into the distance. As he turned the corner, Stella realised what had been so familiar about him -he was the image of El Greco's portrait of Brother Hortensio Paravicino, dark and flamboyant.

And as for Alastair Burnet, it made all the difference when they watched the news again, looking out for the exact same speckled grey tweed jacket as Mr ITV gave the nation the News at Ten on its flagship programme.

14

There was worse for fate to dish up that autumn. There were power cuts, which meant that getting home was an achievement. No lights in the evening. After work you entered a black room, lit by candle or torchlight. The shops soon ran out of candles, torches and batteries.

It showed up how much of a release electric light had proved to be for the lower classes. Of course, there had been gaslight; Stella could remember the greenish glow of their living room light before Liverpool Corporation installed electricity in their houses in 1953, late enough to miss the Coronation.

Without evenings where anyone could go to evening classes, read books, study for any advancement, children or businesspeople to do work at home, society came to a halt. You became merely the person you were in your daytime occupation with no chance of improvement. The ploughman homeward wending his weary way could not have studied for any qualification by the light of a single candle back at his damp cottage. Scholars, academics, artists, were only able to exist if they were already of that class and functioned like that in the daylight hours. In the here-and-now, dressmakers could not do extra work, nor any designers or handicraft workers. Overtime in factories was cut, wages diminished.

There was a bit of excitement back at the house on a night soon after. Stella's room was near the bottom of the staircase and late one night she heard footsteps of someone passing by. It was easy to guess this time that it was the boyfriend of Emma, a glamorous girl who had recently moved into a room on the top floor next to Fiona. She heard him make a quick phone call in the hall and then close the front door quietly. A while later, there was a rattling at her door and a persistent shout,

"Are you all right in there?" with sounds of several footsteps and general bother. A young fireman, complete with thigh-high yellow wellington boots stood there, cheerful and enthusiastic. "Any fire in here?" She stood there in her nightdress as he demanded to inspect her room. He came in and looked around. Stella smiled at the bizarre encounter and could see as the door was wide open now, that several firemen were already coming downstairs.

"No, nothing going, All clear." They swished away. It was obvious it was Emma's new boyfriend, kicked out and bereft of a night of expected sex, who had made a 999 call as revenge. Stella did not mention she had heard the call and the good-natured firemen disappeared into the night, all excitement over.

On the 16th of October, a Tuesday evening, *'When the Kissing Had to Stop'* was on ITV. Tension was rising worldwide. And then on Oct 21, a Sunday , the Cuba blockade grew into a worldwide threat. John Kennedy and Nikita Khruschev or the other way around for those on the other side, were face to face in a nuclear crisis. It was NATO versus the Warsaw Pact. White versus black, or vice versa if you were Russian; you had to take sides.

On Monday the world was in torment. What was waiting behind all this, God or the devil, in millions of atoms? Stella turned up to work in the flatlet house to find that no one had gone to work at all. It was the end. They would not need to pay any rent or need food ever again, it might be merely a question of hours now. All organisation was finished. They talked to each other desperately, the charity of field mouse to field mouse as the tractor approaches. Now nothing was left to us, not even our own skin is our own now, the last boundary, she thought.

That morning there was an unusual number of women going into newsagents and coming out reading the papers right there and then in the streets, avid for information. Usually only men bought newspapers, whereas women bought magazines. Every news bulletin was listened to in silence. As Stella worked, everyone in the house was free to run into any room to listen to the radio, Fred's TV was on all day in the front room and they were free to go in and watch developments. She concentrated on cleaning each step of the stair carpet meticulously, like a soldier dying with his boots on. No running away. Poor Stephen, the American studying International Law, was at home and sat there fielding accusations as if he was personally responsible for his President's decisions. Jemma and Helen had not gone to work. For one day people could do without flowers or hair-do's.

Luke had stayed in bed, having given up completely. Whatever Stella had previously felt for him evaporated. They had spent an entire night talking in his room not long ago, intense, interspersed with helpings of coffee.

"We were really making love all that night, you know," he said a week later. It looked like a good beginning, sensible for once to be slower and careful. They then spent an agreeable night together in his bed as the next step. A grown-up and sensible approach, Stella thought, this is good, this has hopes. Then Luke announced that a friend would be staying with him, a girl from Australia.

"She's a penfriend. It's a sort of bed hospitality, somewhere for her to crash," he said in a worldly way. When Stella came to clean the room a few days later she gave up hope there and then. A serenely beautiful girl opened the door. She was tall with golden hair and totally golden skin. She oozed health and sunshine and sheer niceness. There was nothing to be said after that, even when this Emma had gone, continuing her travels. Luke's room was always immaculate, the only one that was fully carpeted in the house. Light grey, the colour of dust, she knew that from the contents of the vacuum cleaner.

If it really *was* the end of the world, lying in bed was the pits. You had to be with other people, perhaps even at a wild celebration, all-holds-barred party. Go out with a fizz. If everyone was going to be pulverised so easily, it showed up how false so much of their lives were right now. A spotlight was shining on them all. It looked as though they were not necessary at all as far as the politicians decided.

But after a couple of days the Apocalypse hype diminished and they all felt as if they had been made fools of. Headlines predicting the end of the world seemed abstract now. The world was still standing and the rent was due and work started again on the next Monday morning. The sliver of freedom that total annihilation promised had disappeared. Some people had made embarrassing decisions and now also had to back-track. Rows had to be mended, rapid affairs denied and money recouped all over town and worldwide.

Luckily Stella's painting "September Lawn" had been accepted by the Free Painters Group at the FBA Gallery later that October. Even better, one of the other entrants was John Keates, who had been one of their college lecturers. Not being too ambitious, the painting was priced at only ten pounds. In all the international panics it was completely forgotten and she did not collect it after the exhibition ended. Uncollected paintings accumulated a daily fine and after a week or two became too expensive to retrieve. No one ever mentioned where lost paintings went to, perhaps they lined the corridors of an endless Limbo.

15

1962 continued to surprise. It was early December after work and walking up Pond Street through the fog, only pedestrians were safe in the thick gloom. She could almost touch the 187 bus from the pavement as it tried to progress up the hill like the worn-out cart horse from a century ago that it had replaced. When she got indoors though, the smog was waiting for her. It had got in earlier and lay in wait like a silent burglar. The room was wreathed in grey-yellow stodge. But as it was also cold, she risked lighting the gas fire to give some warmth to the high-ceilinged room.

It got worse, with power cuts following the smog. People were getting flu and deaths were increasing.

While the entire city was cocooned in its fog, Gloria was in the Queen Mary Maternity Home, a transformed woman. She was sitting up in bed, a dressing gown given by a neighbour, glossy hair freshly shampooed. Gloria looked the best she had done for ages, she glowed with health. Like a parcel, a baby girl lay neatly in a cot beside the bed. Stella had brought a nightdress and a bar of scented soap.

"It's having a good night's sleep after all the fuss, and all meals provided. It'll be different once I get home," Gloria said candidly. Stella was lost at seeing this change, being the other side of life and death. The life of any single woman, constantly trying to avoid pregnancy, was so different from this. She helped out by babysitting for the boys so Harry could visit the hospital at seven o'clock or go out drinking afterwards in the evenings. His drinking had become more usual after work and this baby was like an interruption in the pattern. But he was overjoyed at this new birth.

"You only have to hold her hand and Gloria's pregnant!" he joked in the pub, boasting about his new baby girl. But once the ten days hospital rest ended, the pattern repeated of inviting friends back from the pub for Sunday roast, as if his family could be stretched as wide as possible.

"Look, do come round," was Gloria's plea to Stella, "I need someone sensible to talk to and help dish it up!" The baby was neatly bundled into its pram and seemed quite content with being the centre of attention.

"It is not a good sign," Jacques remarked to Stella, "when a couple need so many other people in their home at all times, especially with anew-born child. Not a good sign at all," he repeated like an Old Testament prophet. His own family was ultra-private and no one knew who they were, wife and two daughters, the other extreme.

Matters were getting too complicated to go on working at the Nassington Road House, it was time to leave them to their variations. She decided to go to an agency for cleaning work, that would be a useful stop-gap. Perhaps she would be a Daily Maid, there was a notice in Dove Brothers' newsagents window and it sounded encouraging. That settled it. The office was supposed to be next to a butcher's shop along Finchley Road but there was no trace of that address, no such number. She had to go into the butcher's and enquire where it could be. The man stopped cutting up some meats and pointed with his knife at a door at the back of his shop.

The way up the steep brown lino-covered stairs was no recommendation for the business. No soap and water had been near these stairs since the war. The landing was dark brown too, a mixture of old paint and general gloom. Inside the office a little old lady sat behind one of two mahogany desks, a large map of London spread-eagled behind her on the wall. There were dressmaker's pins of various colours inserted like a planned invasion around the local streets.

"I'd like to be a maid, if you have a vacancy." The lady looked at Stella in a distant and haphazard way. It was teatime and she was drinking tea and dunked a biscuit delicately.

"Have you any experience, my dear?" It was said kindly.

"Yes, I've been working already as a general housekeeper in a mixed house and I can give references. I left because the landlord changed." It was an edited version of the house becoming completely out of hand and each Monday morning when she appeared, there were more damage and problems. Stella had already arranged instead to get references from Paul's posh teacher wife to answer any enquiries as to her character, efficiency and state of fingernails. And, of course, her honesty.

"Six pounds ten a week and bus fares. Hours are from nine to one and then two to six, forty hours that is. If you work on Saturday mornings you can have Wednesday afternoons off. Some people prefer workers for the weekend, you see." Stella promised yes, that would be agreeable, which it wasn't. She needed the job as quickly as possible. Saying yes had become a habit - you could always change arrangements later.

"As soon as we have checked your references, we'll telephone and then you can call in here and receive your first week's list of addresses." Beside the large map of North London was a set of hooks with keys, their labels hanging down, keys to the best addresses in the area. "We send girls to some of the best houses, have been doing this even through the War," Miss Webster said proudly. No bombs had landed hereabouts, unlike Liverpool, where dusting would have been totally unnecessary in most areas. On her way out through the shop downstairs the butcher asked Stella if she was going to buy some sausages, he'd give her a special price.

"They take in all sorts upstairs. You don't look like all the rest of them. You'll see!" And he went back to slicing bacon rashers, this time with a broad smile.

Turning up on Tuesday morning, Stella saw what the butcher meant. A motley group of elderly women and a few younger West Indian women were waiting in front of the desk. Miss Webster and her associate, Miss Drew were giving out keys or addresses, plus some bus fares. These were doled out to the nearest penny.

Stella started off with a German family in Arkwright Road and a flat near John Barnes in the afternoon. The snag was obvious immediately; there was no lunchtime, it was spent going from one job to another, eating in the street on the way, in whatever weather. But now she was stuck. Only so much job-hopping was possible.

After a few weeks of ruined weekends, she asked to be changed to a solid five day week and work all day on Wednesdays instead of doing Saturday mornings.

16 By summer the Roebuck pub round the corner became Stella's community centre. Half an hour each evening soon built up enough of a presence for her to become accepted, safe.

Now and again there were gaps in the flow of the pub crowd and here she was sitting next to Felix. She stared telling him about the plan of doing 36 paintings.

"Oh that's a strange number you know. There's *Poltis' 36 Dramatic Situations."* He was about to tell her that when she interrupted him that she knew all about that. He recouped the lost ground easily. "Ah, but I bet you don't know about *The Love Romances of Parhenius of Nicea.* It's a collection of 36 stories of unhappy loves. I would have thought that would be more up your street. You could do a painting for each one."

She realised immediately that the only one already done - and definitely not a landscape – was the *Song for Nellie Bligh,* a riot of discordant reds. The poor Nellie Bligh, who probably did not know that Johnny had a wife or girlfriend called Frankie.

He got more serious, intimate,

"I've written about you, you know. Sometimes you say exciting, unusual things." The only thing she remembered talking to him about recently was pop music. Soon, she surmised, the Sunday Papers, quality ones, would have to start reviewing pop song releases. Felix was astounded at that. He was, in fact, most concerned, she remembered.

"What do you do that for? Are you going to put it into your scripts?" He was some kind of film researcher or a film journalist; it was, as usual, unclear what anyone's life really was outside of the pub life itself. The edges never joined. Felix gave her a strange look.

"It's possible, but I doubt it. All dialogue has to fit into a pre-arranged structure." He was warning her off entering his secret writers' world. "I can't really talk about my work, not to outsiders, just in case it affects the flow – and the confidentiality, of course." And accepting this warning about any invasion of this privacy, Stella was still allowed to be invited back to his flat as the eleven o'clock closing cleared the lounge and public bar.

After thinking about it for so long, his flat up Parliament Hill was a surprise. Opening the door at the top of the stairs, Felix showed her into a large white-painted room on the second floor, overlooking the street. There was absolutely no furniture whatsoever. A double mattress lay on the floor set between two windows, covered with a gigantic olive-green quilt.

"Oh, that's not a quilt!" he smiled, "It's a sleeping bag, pure parachute silk. Nearest to a continental duvet I could get." Felix did not admit that it had come from a government surplus depot past Finsbury Park. There was nothing else on the bare varnished floorboards except for a dark farmhouse chair in front of the gas fire, which was of course not needed on this summer night. At one side of the fireplace a low bookcase held very few books on it, mostly second-hand and definitely not the latest bestsellers. No sign of scripts, notebooks or a typewriter on a desk. A fitted cupboard on the opposite wall probably held his clothes, but there was nothing else to give any clues.

Of course Stella thought, he had an office to go to. That was where all his writing work was completed. Even so, there was so little sign of literature here, or anything else, that it was minimalist in the extreme. There was no television, just a record player. Felix did not let her into the kitchen, where the smell of freshly ground coffee beans was already spreading, but waved her towards the toilet. As this was a separate room with its own sink there was no reason to go into the bathroom and see anything private like toothbrushes or shampoo.

Felix came back with the two coffees and suggested they both sat on the bed, as there was only the one chair. With an Anglepoise lamp beside the bed, next to the large ashtray, he switched on the hi-fi and the discreet jazz of the M.J.Q. quartet filled up the shadowy corners of the room. Sitting down so near the floor level meant there was no view whatever now. The white walls, subtly shadowed or lit; the floor spreading to infinity; the crumpled bedcover. Only one sign of life: a framed photograph on the mantelpiece of a clapboard house surrounded by trees. He saw Stella glance at it.

"That's the house where I lived in Canada when we were married. You can just see our dog, Ruala, in the doorway. It's over five years since I was there."

Apparently Stella was not so much of an outsider by now, nothing to stop him from kissing her as soon as the black sugary coffee was finished. The mattress that was serving as their couch quickly unfurled to revert into a bed. Sheet and two pillows, she noted, in the same olive green waited beneath the imitation duvet. With his Russian-Canadian background Felix was as continental as any duvet; no one else had one except real foreigners with money. Everyone else she knew had blankets with a puffed up eiderdown on top, like punctured meringues.

At the lying-down-next-to-each-other-stage, still fully dressed Stella thought it was her last chance (and first opportunity) to mention she was plugged up with a tampon, it being the fifth day of a period. The blood could sometimes persist long after it should have finished. Felix said it did not matter and carried on as if she had not mentioned it. In bed with Felix, the intellectual, the scriptwriter, good-looking, foreign, in his thirties, interesting with a modern flat; what a time to tell him to stop. Everything would end if she objected. He pounded into her and she conquered the doubts and went on being brave.

Nothing awful happened and Felix gave her a hug, said she was a nice girl and then collapsed to sleep on her shoulder. He had no curtains at the street side windows, the moon poured pale blue light over the empty room. Stella lay looking at the blue-grey ceiling and wondered what would be the point of being the girlfriend of an intellectual who had no trace of any life.

"He was married in Canada, left her years ago," Brian had said in the pub, who traded bits of gossip as his method of paying his social way. "Works in some film producers place in Oxford Street apparently. Does some translation work now and again, he speaks Russian and Polish. Clever chap. He's writing a book." Stella wanted to reply,

"Aren't we all? But I think I'm living mine."

The room's white emptiness she could cope with, it was rather admirable like an art form. Sexually he was almost dull, though maybe she was tired and not at her best in the circumstances. When she said there was a tampon in her, Felix said that would be all right, he would be careful, but of course that was impossible without a periscope or a ruler or some scientific instrument. He achieved some kind of climax, with Stella not quite sure of what was going on, but it was too late now to stop the process. Within seconds they both fell into a deep and merciful sleep.

When they woke, Felix bounded out of bed, dressing hurriedly and he was already taking up the coffee cups and moving off to the kitchen. He came back with a cup for her, setting it down on the floor beside her pillow.

"I'm going to have a shower now. I've got some things to attend to. You'd best be going – and then I'll meet you in the pub at two o'clock." Washing her off and getting rid of her in one operation. No trace of her smell, no hanging around with toast and marmalade and long soul-searching talks, no heart-to-heart.

She looked at his bookcase again after dragging her clothes on and drinking the mug of medicinal coffee. Only a waist-high three-shelf fitment. Everyone's bookcase was the first thing you inspected in anyone's room; it was a quick diagram of their mind. Here there was a new copy of the A to Z of London, Trevelyan's English Social History, Palgrave's Golden Treasury, The Oxford English Dictionary, Nineteenth Century Poetry, Muirhead's Guide to England, The Home Lawyer, Cassell's Universal Cookery. Apart from the A to Z they all obviously came from a second-hand bookshop, most probably Oxfam, up the High Street. There were no notebooks or sheaves of papers, no manila folders and the only items on the bottom shelf were the usual four A to Z London phonebooks. There was no cracked or broken-handled mug full of biros and pencils either, nothing. No desk or even a table to work on. No typewriter.

It was the selection of a man who had no place. He obviously did not buy books or magazines. There were no newspapers either. It also hinted that he had no money. As the strident sound of the shower continued, it looked as though Felix was not coming back soon and Stella found herself out on the pavement by ten o'clock. After all, she had something important to attend to as well, far more than a mere shower.

At least it was a bright Saturday morning, the wide full moon had done its job, and the world had turned round. Already early shoppers were strolling down the hill; a woman was pushing a gurgling toddler in a light blue pram. An old man walked back, hauling a heavy shopping bag home for his weekend. There was a pain coming and going in her insides, giving her walking gait a slight stagger now and then. That was why she had not tried to stay.

Once back in the abandoned bedsit, Stella sat on the bed and took a deep breath. The operation would have to be done now. She could hear Bill from an upstairs room already using the bathroom upstairs. No chance of using the bath yet so she lay on the bed, removing yesterday's knickers and stockings and tried, squirming, to reach inside herself. Somewhere up there the escaped tampon was lurking. Even its string was missing. All those tunnels and tubes and secret places easily fended her off; she was a secret to herself. It hurt. Only Saturday and the doctor's would be closed until Monday morning. A morning off work then would cost money. Difficulty was already piling on top of difficulty.

And only a month ago, or so, in the Nassington Road house, she had been so superior when Irene had been telling her about exactly the same thing. Barging into one of the upstairs rooms to empty the rubbish and hoover the carpet, there was Irene lying in the bed in the middle of the afternoon, clutching a hot-water bottle to her stomach. She had lost her sophisticated elegance, the sharp tang of Blue Grass that usually surrounded her, and had obviously been crying, her eyes puffy.

"I can't go to work. Got a tampon lodged in and it had to be removed at the hospital, and apparently I've got VD as well. My innards are all churning round. Yes, you can clean the room if you like, it's nice to have someone to talk to and distract me a bit." Stella asked Irene if she needed any shopping but she said no, there was plenty of stuff on the shelf and she didn't feel like eating much any way, tea and toast was enough.

A few weeks; long enough for fate to dish out an extra helping to prove its random strength and even more random justice. No one was safe. It was never intended for safety to be worldwide.

Stella struggled with hips and buttocks, as fast as any part of the inner tubes was reached, the mattress bulked beneath and her fingers slipped. Climbing down and lying on the floor, to get a better grip, waves of panic, cold and lethal, swooped through her. Going to Casualty at the hospital round the corner would be the only way to get round this. Questions would be asked, files would be opened, records begun. Nurses and doctors would look at the problem and start seeing her as the problem instead. Felix would not be involved at all. By now he would be showered and shaved and renewed and had probably strolled out to get the Saturday Guardian (or perhaps he had it delivered) and would be reading it contentedly with another cup of coffee and some muesli. The Cona coffee set would have perfumed the flat again with its crisp purposeful aroma, the MJQ's *Take Five* floating across; the perfect Saturday morning sound.

Making contact with the magic little thread was like discovering radium or America; suddenly there was hope. The next worry was that by tugging at this little strand she might break it. It had never done, ever, before but there could always be a first time. In fact Stella had never thought of it. Writhing about, rolling over on this dirty carpet, she felt in sight of success. A lookout in the crow's nest. Land ahoy. With a sudden almost slurp the sodden tampon, almost bloodless, slid out. If it could have spoken it would have asked what had all the fuss been about. For a second, triumph at this achievement at this and resentment of Felix jostled for precedence. Clear. Now the weekend was safe, no great infections loomed, no time off ill, no deficit from the pay packet next Friday.

By now the bathroom was free. It sounded like that must be Bill now, pounding down the stairs. Gathering all her toiletries up, Stella galloped up to the still-warm steam filled bathroom. Perfumed soap and shampoo had never smelled so good. Calming down in the warm water Stella saw the funny side of it now. A small plug of cotton wool; total blockage of a woman's innards. A metaphor for sex.

The writhing about on the floor, going to and fro and the long bath time had used up a couple of hours without her noticing. Two o'clock was approaching. Combing out her hair from its tangles, then searching for unladdered tights, there was little choice of clothes. An apricot jumper with a navy skirt were the only items available and clean. A quick dash of Blue Grass perfume, bright blush lipstick, Sheer Genius foundation, chuck on another layer of spit-and-mascara and it was time to be off to the pub where Felix would be meeting her.

Saturday afternoon pub time was quite domestic and several people were eating meat pies and pickles here and there. Some had bags of shopping on the floor beside their seats. Stella had to make a way past shoulders to the bar, not recognising anyone but Brian. After being served, glass of bitter lemon in hand, she went across to the fireside where Brian was sitting on the deep sofa. She stayed standing so that Brian would not get any wrong ideas. He was mildly predatory, like all pub bores. He could also set off a rumour like a pack of hounds whether he intended it or not.

"Him! He's over there, already." She craned her neck and saw Felix in a small group, hidden in a corner. A blonde woman was chatting to him, they were laughing together. There were two men standing with them, obviously foreigners, tall and tanned. "That's the wife over there," Brian added, "She's just flown in from Canada." Brian sat back comfortably at ease on his Saturday afternoon off. His brother was neatly hidden behind that day's Telegraph, which was puzzlingly either a shield for the permanently shy or perhaps he could actually read it.

Half-consumed with shock, Stella stood up, putting the glass carefully on the low table.

"Oh look! I've just remembered, I've got someone coming round this afternoon. Sorry about the short visit, just checking who's here, see you this evening probably." She had to keep in with him as a guideline to save future evenings with his newsgathering like this. Brian was better than any newspaper. As there was a passageway from the lounge into the public bar she was able to leave the pub without Felix seeing her. But Stella had clearly seen the small blonde and the look of happiness of both Felix and the new-old wife. I helped towards that smile, she thought, I made him happy, a rehearsal for today. No clue except that photo on the mantelpiece. He should have said something, told me about her when he mentioned Canada. Nothing said. He had known this was going to happen, he must have.

He had planned the seduction, if that what it was. Sitting on the edge of her own bed again she remembered Felix walking across the pub towards her last night and stopping. Stopping to talk to her on purpose, not merely including her at the edge of a group. Staying with her until closing time and then suggesting she might like to go on up the hill to his flat, just to continue the evening with some coffee and music. Coffee and music she did not need, she had noticed him, intrigued, on and off for ages. It had all gone so smoothly. Now her innards were all over the place. His motives were strange, unfathomable. How vicious to set her such a trap as this. After all this trouble with her innards too.

That evening Stella followed the crowd to Saturday's usual after-pub party. There was nothing she could think of doing otherwise; to go home alone would have been worse. As they all trooped up Parliament Hill it became more and more obvious they were making for Felix's flat. Too late to draw back now. It would be obvious, someone would notice and draw their own accurate conclusions. Stella followed the others up the garden path and up to the wide empty flat again.

The non-furnishing made it possible to crowd in so many people, as most sat on the floor, clutching the bottles they had brought up with them. For those who wanted it, coffee was begun on the stove. The party had obviously been decided on the hop, with no planning, no drinks or eatables. The crowd hid the emptiness of last night. Felix glided about slowly, as if half asleep. His wife, suddenly matriarch of the strange flat, gave out plates and saucers to be used as ashtrays; there was nothing to eat. Someone started records playing, and first play was Modern Jazz Quartet. It was difficult to work out if it was meant naively or ironically. It was the same stuff as last night. He probably did not have a wide selection of records.

Stella walked across to the mantelpiece where Jean, the wife, was looking at the photo of Felix and the dog in front of the log cabin.

"That's Felix in front of our old house in Canada," she said serenely.

"Yes, I know, in Manitoba, wasn't it and that's Ruala in front with Felix." Jean looked startled for a second and as their eyes met, a pathway of possibilities spread wider and wider, the way suspicion always spreads out, realisation spreading its virus widening and widening.

Jean sat down heavily on the big farmhouse chair, gallantly waved towards it by one of the guests. She sat in it, wrapped in its wide brownness as if wrapped around by all of Canada itself. Months of silence from Felix hid from these smooth geeks as well as Jean that he was really unemployed and that the film business gossip he purveyed was, like Brian's similar pub currency, carefully gathered from pubs round Soho. Keeping connections with guys he had worked with in the past was crucial, any link was important. He had been dreading this for weeks. Jean was over here to expedite a business arrangement, to arrange some television tie-up with a new on-trend book. Episodes were being carved up; she was here to use any of Felix's know-how about the London end. Bits of gossip, addresses, phone numbers, links –anything which would further that cause.

Stella, exhausted, felt she had won the small obstacle race and now it was time to go home after all. There were times when sleep fell like the Iron Curtain and you had just enough time to be on the right side when it came.

During the week there were no tears as she realised that Jean, the returning wife, had taken a potentially deadly boring man off her hands

17 Harry and Gloria were thrown out of their semi-furnished flat suddenly one dull November afternoon. The landlord came round on an unannounced visit, inspecting all the rooms and had found Gloria using the electric light socket by plugging in the flex to do the ironing. As the basement flat rent included free electricity, he saw this as stealing and evicted her on the spot. Gloria frantically phoned the police from the payphone in the hall, but they said they did not come out for evictions, it was a private matter. It happened too often these days and was basically a landlord and tenant affair. The reporter from the Ham & High said more or less the same.

"We only report evictions if it's something exciting, unfortunately." It was not dramatic enough although all their belongings were being dumped on the pavement by some sort of bailiffs. It was just as dramatic as any of the old engravings of the evictions of the Irish Famine. It was exactly the same, but made more ordinary The baby in the pram did not count as important enough apparently and they were all, the two boys back from school by now, standing on the pavement waiting for

Harry to dash up from the advertising agency in the West End where he worked. Their clothes were piled up on a couple of chairs, and pots and pans were cluttering the ground.

Gloria turned up, desperate, at Stella's the second she got back from work. Could she put up Gloria and baby in its pram? Of course Gloria could stay. One of the many-layered mattresses put on the floor; a blanket and a coat each; the pram in the middle; they could just about manage to circle round each other and reach the sink or the gas rings. As she was out at work all day there was not too much of a crush, and the baby was good-natured. They cobbled together some sort of routine and Gloria provided some food. As long as Lawrence did not find out, or Mrs Grint or Miss Spedding inform on her, all went well for the fortnight it took for Harry to find a new flat, conveniently over an Indian restaurant.

Harry luckily did find a flat up Rosslyn Hill, almost luxury, with a food waste mincer in the sink, which the children broke within days, fascinated with how it worked and shoving a fork down the shaft. There was an all-pub moving-in party when Neil went off halfway through and bagged the bath to sleep in, as the Irish lads often did. They were a cross between apostles and anarchists, a private group, always good natured and never settling down.

They also took turns taking the kids to the fair on the Heath.

"There's a saying, 'You're in and out like a dog at a fair.'" Sam said. He was one of the pub drunks that was like one of the planets in orbit round the family. Everyone joined in looking after the kids. It worked both ways. Harry and Gloria's children gave a substitute family for the odd group of single people with no young relatives of their own

There was a casual network of care for the family. The door was always left on the latch and whoever wanted to would call in and see if the kids needed anything. Mostly they wanted, needed, jaffa cakes, which seemed to solve all difficulties. Calling in one afternoon after a visit to the dentists, Stella found the flat empty and started to clean it as a surprise. It was what she would have been doing anyway on any afternoon these days. It would be a surprise for Gloria and another thank-you for when they had taken her in and let her stay on their sofa.

18 Dot appeared next from Liverpool, with new American husband, Glen, and a baby in tow. She phoned without explaining why they had arrived and how her new family had happened so quickly. Glen had important official appointments in London.

"Look, we've got just a week here to see to Glen's tax and residency permits, all old legal things that Glen's never got round to tidying up. So I wonder if you could help us?" Of course Stella would help, memories of staying at Dot's years ago; favour for favour, the invisible bank account, its debts and payments.

"We're staying at a B&B down Haverstock Hill but we can't manage to get out after six in the evening because of the baby. So we thought, you could take the baby Roy for the night and we could collect him in the morning before you go to work. We've got our own cot. The B&B don't take babies. We smuggled him in, but it's taking a risk. Please say you will?" The cot was stashed in Glen's car. Stella said yes, as there was no real way of saying no.

Baby Roy and cot and Dot and Glen appeared promptly at 7 p.m. with a more or less sleepy Roy. Glen assembled the cot, Dot produced a bottle and a packet of baby milk powder and some rusks and nappies, and it was all done so rapidly that Stella and baby Roy were left looking at each other in shock as the couple's footsteps clattered off along the hall.

Luckily Roy was amenable and did not burst into tears. But crowded into the room with the cot meant Stella could not make any noise, no radio, nor have the light on too late. So she hung her coat across the side of the cot to shield some of the light away. It was a trap. She had to live baby-hours now and go to bed very early.

In the morning (he had only woken once in the night, luckily,) Roy woke loudly at the dawn and started to jig about, throwing the coat off the side. He held onto the rails full of joy with the new morning, dancing up and down merrily and cooed at her. His nappy must need changing, she thought, eyeing him from her pillow.

Up well before the real morning then, and making a bottle for him she realised yet again, from babysitting services, that most parents were on the run from their children. She managed to clean him up, laying him on the floor and putting the new nappy on inside his plastic knickers. They smiled at each other and she felt sorry for him. He was obviously not Glen's child, his skin was dark and he had olive black eyes. Dot had been frantic for a baby and it looked as though she had eventually got pregnant on purpose by someone unknown.

Glen had been a lucky addition, an American who wanted to stay away from the USA. Sitting reading an old copy of The Listener from Fred's wastepaper basket, Stella tried to read as the next hour went by. Roy crawled round the floor probably picking up germs by the million. He was fascinated by the shoes scattered under her bed. She lifted him back into his cot where he chewed randomly on a rusk, gurgled and played at throwing his teddy out of the cot repeatedly. She had forgotten this part. It was something about experiencing space or reciprocating favours. It was quite wearing and boring, but the child thought it was hilarious.

In their Modern History book, ages ago at school, there had been a reproduction of a nineteenth century cartoon where the lady of the house was passing a crying baby to a servant woman, with the words 'Take this screaming child away while I write my sonnet on motherhood.' Stella knew how she felt exactly. A baby ate up all your attention, it had to; otherwise it would not thrive.

Dot and Glen eventually showed up and took Roy away. He did not seem too bothered either way.

"See you about seven then," they both called cheerfully, going rapidly out of the front door before Stella could object about the cot which was still left in her room. It repeated the next night. It was not so bad - he only woke once, but again, Roy was merrily dancing about at 5 in the morning. Stella was exhausted and was not in the best of moods when Dot, on her own, came to collect him.

"I'm in a rush, Glen's got to go to the Foreign Office and the American embassy about his papers." She wafted off with a jiggling Roy. On the way to work, Stella met Gloria on Haverstock Hill and told her about having to look after Roy every night. Gloria exploded in a mixture of anger and amusement.

"Don't you know? They're out drinking all evening! They got kicked out of the B&B for leaving the kid crying all night while they were out. So that's why they picked on you!" Stella agreed she was totally fed up, plus the weekend was approaching. The minute she got back that evening, Stella dismantled the cot and stacked the pieces on the landing, plus the bottle, rusks, powdered milk and nappies. She then went back into her room, switched off the connecting bell to the front door and hung her coat over the door, covering the keyhole. It meant she had to sit in the dark, unmoving, waiting for their visit. Sitting transfixed like an Egyptian mummy, Stella listened as they got someone else to let them into the house and they knocked on her door. But obviously they had noticed the parts of the cot lying against the wall, left there with Roy's supplies. She heard their swearing and complaints to each other.

"What'll we do now?"

"We'll have to take him back. Come on, I think we could go and get Emma to have him for the night, she's got a kid already, it'll make no difference to her. We should have used her in the first place." And so Dot smoothly moved on to a new adventure, which was what she was good at. Glen obediently moved in her wake.

19
On November 22nd, 1963 a Friday, John F. Kennedy was assassinated.

For reasons unknown or perhaps caught from listening to the world on Matt's large wooden radio, Stella had started to listen to Radio Francaise. Luckily she knew enough French to follow the main news. It was a novelty to hear international names scattered amongst the different languages. And here it came.

"President Kennedy vien de etre tué dans Dallas hier." She knew enough to realise that 'vien de' meant 'has just' and 'tué' meant 'killed.' Switching rapidly back to the staid BBC Home Service, the news confirmed that the American President had indeed been assassinated on a visit to Dallas that day.

Edward, another late arrival from Liverpool and a friend of the poet crowd called in at this point and was shocked to the core. Whereas Stella saw it as a serious crime on an individual, Edward saw it from a political viewpoint,

"This is going to change the world," he said, shocked, just sitting down on the bed. "Let's get out of here, go round to the pub and see what others are saying." So, like new orphans they clustered with the nattering crowd just back from work. Tomorrow's newspapers would tell more; they had to fill in the gaps themselves meanwhile. Theories, comments, speculation, forecasts;

they made up a story that would fit for the time being. Various experts appeared on television or radio with explanations and analyses.

The world fell apart and then had to restructure itself like bad knitting. Drinkers in the pub worried at it like terriers.

Summer saw Stella back with Matt, although as usual there were gaps in the texture like moth-holes. One night, ensconced in the dark and settled in his wide bed, the door opened and the wide beam of a torch shone directly at them. Oh goodness, a police raid, Stella thought. There had been several raids on the house already; the police were not daft. Dope was the poets' pollen and honey. She was worried, however that they would think that she was some kind of informer – always turning up on a Sunday afternoon after the trouble but never being around while it was actually happening. Although it was likely that there would be a party on any given Saturday night, they also disappeared like a flock of birds to a poetry event up north or other secret places. The flag had to be furled.

So here it was. Fate. A police raid. The one time they were totally innocent and both of them being investigated. They both sat up in bed, shocked and naked but trying to be impressively dignified. Matt put his hand over his brow against the piercing beam shone right at him,

"It's OK, Olive, can you stop that light, please? Er... I'm a bit occupied right now. I might get in touch some time?" And the Olive person said something that was probably a swearword and shut the door. Stella was suspicious, amused and puzzled at once.

"She's an usherette at the Plaza and she calls round sometimes after her shift, that's all," Matt explained blithely. *Calls round* did not need to be translated. Free love is for everyone, you all bought a ticket, remember?
It was another nail in their relationship. But as she was passing by, a few weeks later, Stella called in one evening after work along Adelaide Road. It was well after six. Matt was standing beside the always-empty fireside and next to him was a woman of uncertain age. She must have been in her twenties but was wearing a dark green suit and could have walked right out of a book on rationing. No make-up and short black hair. There was nothing to connect them that Stella could see and Matt did not give any helpful information. The woman was introduced as Angela and they smiled at each other. Then the door opened and a matching young-old man entered.

It was like being on stage in a Terrence Rattigan play. He too wore a proper suit, though it looked rather threadbare. His hair, also black, was brilliantined. This was Angela's husband, Stan, apparently. They both had pale white skin and looked as though they had been dug out of a nineteen forties film noir. Matt stood there being affable, like the landlord of an invisible pub. Then the pair of them left, leaving Stella puzzled. She imagined a battered 1930s Austin car tootling off round the corner like a stuttering silent film. Matt decided to explain.

"D' you know, I'm really glad you called in right now, that was great timing. You turning up like that managed to change the circumstances, so that Stan had no idea that Angela and me had been together all afternoon." He was omnivorous. There had been no atmosphere of recent sexual activity – surely Stella would have picked that up? Her antenna must be off. And the poor wife looked so ordinary and worn out, not like an afternoon lover should look. Stella felt like a disappointed mother finding a son in trouble yet again. But there was still that link between them, old friends, old battle mates. The wide desk set in the middle of the room was covered in papers and books. Stella picked up a small book of poetry, *The Whip*, by Robert Creeley.

"But it's a Migrant Book from America, they're famous! This is important! 1957! How on earth did you get hold of this?" Matt said it had been left behind by someone, he'd forgotten who and she was welcome to keep it. It was as if she had been given a certificate, however late. It went into her bag, nestling along with the apron and indoor shoes. Something important to look over and learn from. It turned out to be almost a how-to-do it book which had obviously influenced all of them. Short vivid poems, like dried flowers that trapped a life. She had come late to the party, having had to invent it all by herself.

20

Strange choking sensations in the throat Almost unable to swallow. To the doctors after work; tonsillitis. But it grew stronger and soon she was weaker and unable to focus. Fiona called in her room that evening and saw what a bad state Stella was in. Laughing from the tusselled bed she said,

"Do what you like, if you want to get a doctor, I can't walk to the phone." So Fiona, worried, called in the doctor immediately to come round, her friend was in quite a state. A figure appeared and said it was now glandular fever. Her temperature was apparently at 103.

She realised things must be bad when she saw Laurence the next day standing beside her bed with a bottle of Lucozade, saying it didn't matter about the rent yet. The days and nights passed in a blur. It was quite exciting, whatever was going on in the bloodstream. The inside was far more powerful now than anything happening in the outside world. Nights passed in a brilliant fever as Stella drew diagrams on the wall above the pillow. When she recovered, they did not make sense though at the time they had held the secrets of the universe. After the heady days of the fever, which were really exciting, the come-down was drastic. The body was scoured, empty. She could hardly walk without staggering, even getting as far as the toilet down the hall.

On 20th April she walked gingerly down the hill to the doctors for a sick note that would authorise a support payment. In the cramped waiting room the patients sat with their lifetime's medical notes as given out by a rushed receptionist. Their records were kept in small cardboard pouches. The patients sat listlessly, their entire history in their hands.

"Let's look at our notes," Stella called out. "We can have a look now!" They all looked at her as if she had said something foolish. They were not going to interfere with their own official records. These details of their lifetimes illnesses belonged to the doctors, not themselves; they did not want to be caught reading them.

Stella found that good old Dr Bligh, in the 1950s had written in his careful fountain-pen handwriting 'She is depressed because of her father's fits of anger.' Later, after diptheria, measles, chickenpox and whooping cough he had categorised her as ' highly strung and extremely sensitive.' As she should be, if she was going to go on and become an artist. He also, in conversation had said to her mother that most diseases were the fault of either tinned food or the government. His other motto was that most illnesses disappeared after three weeks or were so serious that the patient was going to die.

The new doctor signed the medical certificate and she was sent to the Royal Free for a blood test, which luckily was on the way back home. As they put the needle in and took out the blood sample, every colour drained out too and the nurse and surroundings were all in sepia. She almost told them they were all in an old film, but they might have detained her for further tests.

Not going to work meant no wages on a Friday. As soon as she could manage to walk further outside the house, Stella slowly traipsed up to the National Assistance Office at the corner of Downshire Hill. The applicants sat on long benches in a dismal, institutional type of room, waiting to be interviewed. Dot had brightly said ages ago that the National Assistance Board, Hampstead branch, was more charitable than most of those offices because they knew that the unemployed residents they dealt with were likely to become real musicians, writers and artists in the long run and it was a form of investment to support them for a while. This did not work for Stella. She was treated like some sort of criminal. The official appeared shielded by a metal grille and demanded proof, her rent book, any wage slips, proof of identity.

The woman gave her a mere fifteen shillings through the grille, with great distaste, as though Stella was a modern leper and even though her rent book said the rent was three pounds a week. She trudged down to the Post Office later and withdrew as much money as possible from her account, two pounds, leaving 15/9d remaining in the account. The sick pay would take weeks yet before it came through.

It took a 'fortnight' to walk just as far as the toilet down the hall and walking round the streets was a slow process. It was enlightening - this was why old people sat around on benches and any low wall – they were not being picturesque; they could not manage to walk any further without a rest. Now she was one of them.

The fever-soaked sheets had to be washed now, so stuffing them into a pillowcase the next day she went down to the launderette in South End Green. Sitting there across from the tall trees at the edge of the Heath, the seeds of a new poem started to grow, about how the evidence of love and sex is cleansed away, all traces removed, of any affair.

Affair, that word right out of a Noel Coward, *'awfully flat, Norfolk,'* situation, nothing to do with the attempt at settling down with someone. She walked back slowly and managed to go out again round to the corner shop for some real food at last, hunger coming back.

The few days left were drastic, and on Saturday she went round the room raiding all pockets and delving into the lining of the old handbag, corners of drawers for any precious pennies. Enough for a pint of milk at last. Starting work again, she could ask for the money to be paid to her direct by a client and have it as a sub from the week's wages. That would be seen as a bit of sharp practice by the Daily Maids ladies, but these were disastrous days.

And coming up the steps, Stella stumbled and the precious bottle of milk shattered, the milk flooding down to the path. Its whiteness was magical, it was like watching her own life flood away. I don't exist now, she thought, I have absolutely no financial existence and here in London that is all that counts. Matt had told her that his grandmother had promised him £750 if only he would marry a proper Jewish girl. Money could manipulate anyone's life for good or bad.

"She says she is worried I won't be settled before she kicks the bucket and she wants to make sure I marry in." He said this as though he was outside any rules, but the family obviously thought differently and thought this emotional blackmail would work. Stella knew that, amazingly, was the exact price of the hire of St Pancras Town Hall for a concert. The price of fame was lethal. He could weaken after all and it was one more nail in the coffin of their relationship at the time.

Through the glass door she could hear the phone ringing and so went inside, leaving the broken glass and streams of milk. It was Harry.

"Good, glad it's you answering the phone. We need a quick favour. Look, we are in a bit of a state here. Gloria is really down in the dumps, so I wondered if you could come up right now this evening and babysit and do a grand clean-up of the flat, starting tonight? I'll pay you a fiver for that and for whatever food you cook for the kids, would that be all right?" God in heaven, moving lives and possibilities around. She agreed, laughing and going along the hall, collected the brush and a bucket and humming merrily, cleared the broken glass into the bins and swilled the steps clean with a few buckets of water. A fiver was a real treat. Plus, she liked the kids and they would have a good time together. They would feast on Jaffa cakes and macaroni cheese and watch TV. They were all saving each other's lives.

To celebrate being better she went to the next Poetry and Jazz concert at St Pancras Town Hall. It was crowded, with a real buzz of excitement though no one could have told exactly why. The poets and musicians, that was obvious – but the general public? It was as if there was a new outbreak of measles, caused by the Poetry & Jazz people. In all the excitement while the performers were on stage with Stevie Smith someone ran off with the box office takings. The story ended there, perhaps because they could work out who it was directly and so did not want to involve the police. Whoever it was, was a friend. But it was never talked about again as far as Stella knew.

It was their own circle after all. That world was small and intense, robbery notwithstanding.

On Thursday she was back at work again at Daily Maids. There was some sick pay due, they assured her, it would arrive in her pay in a few weeks' time. The government attended to that, it took time, sorry.

Fiona brought a visitor round, a friend from her hometown. Tony was tall and fair and gently mad, but well-off. He was staying in an hotel in West Hampstead. He was here for an interview for some prestigious job, something to do with fragrances that were in capsules that were plugged into electric sockets. Stella said it was just an electric form of lavender bags which he did not take as an insult but thought was an hilarious idea.

"We could present them *with* a free lavender bag, past and future combined! I'll put that to them in the interview! Marvellous!" He took them out for a meal in a proper restaurant and they got on really well. Stella was still grateful for all Fiona's help when the fever had taken hold.

"After all, you're the one that persuaded the doctor to come round. I was totally off my head, I couldn't have made sense, let alone even dialled the right number."

That early June weekend Fiona and Tony took her up to Nottingham in his car along the brand new M1 which was proof of the bright Britain of the future. Fiona's mother was going to put them up,

"You're going to be in my childhood room!" Fiona joked. Stella was not sure if she was better yet, still rather light-headed, which actually added to the excitement of the weekend. She couldn't remember the journey back with them both. Tony pronounced that a salad should have seven ingredients and she remembered that forever, always counting lettuce, tomato, beetroot, cucumber, spring onions, cress, celery to see if they were there. They went out for a curry on Saturday evening with his mother, golden and dying. Cancer prowled about even when the sun shone, people looked perfect and the roads were new.

The entire weekend was magical, a treat after the privations of the weeks before, Fiona being a fairy godmother.

21

Matt said he had written a song for a new pop group, it was in the hit parade already and so Stella took the Perdio radio to work and listened to it (via the shopping bag) as she walked from one cleaning job to another at lunchtime. She heard it halfway up Arkwright Road in the midday hits countdown. It was a perfect spring afternoon.

The third affair between them was starting again but the new distraction with the musicians killed it off quickly. Matt announced he was going off to Wales and would not be around for the weekends any more. Things were getting exciting for him right now. The £750 that his grandmother had tried to use as a carrot was irrelevant now, more was at stake.

"I won't be around weekends, Saturday night and all that. It's the busiest time if you're doing gigs and stuff, you see," he said cheerily. "So you could be a Wednesday night woman, that would be best."

Wednesday Night Woman. A song not yet written by the Rolling Stones. A definite sign that you were on the way out, a clear label. Fill in all the gaps on Friday, Saturday, Sunday. Do not write on the other side of the page.

22

The party was over; Ken, the host, was sitting on the draining board singing folk songs and Pete was playing a limp guitar accompaniment. It was after one in the morning and all the interesting people had left. Even Gloria wanted to leave now and Stella found that Scott had also palled up with Gloria and wanted to go and look for a taxi now. He was someone from the Roebuck, a writer with a Dutch wife and that was as much as anyone knew about him.

"That's the worst thing about ending up at parties outside of your own lot, you pile into someone's car and end up God knows where. Unless you stick right by them and get a proper lift back home, you're stuck," Scott said. "We can get a taxi together, that'll be easy." Once settled in the taxi's deep leather seat, Stella gasped how good it was to have escaped.

"The trouble with you is you're afraid of life," Gloria spat out as they smoothed through the empty streets.

"I'll get out with you both here by the hospital taxi rank," Scott said although he lived over in Highgate. "If I can come in, I need to use the toilet at your place, and then I can phone for another taxi off to Highgate the other side," As they got out, of course Gloria had no money on her and Scott only had a few shillings spare, which he needed to pay for his taxi to go over to Highgate later, so Stella, as expected, ended up paying the lot. And so as Gloria left them and walked home up the hill, back to husband and children, Scott and Stella walked off together down past the hospital alleyway and into the silent house.

"There's the phone and there's the toilet, Goodnight," Stella said breezily, waving good bye, going off to her own room and shutting the door. Within minutes, though, Scott was knocking on her door and saying

"What about a cup of coffee? Come on now!"

"Goodnight, and goodbye, Scott, it's time to go home," she said from the other side of the door. He rattled the handle, asking her to open up and then started to pound at the door with his fists. He demanded to be let in, what on earth did she think was going on? Then he began to make runs at the door, wildly kicking the bottom door panels and Stella began to be really frightened.

"Let me in! What are you playing at!" The door began to shake as if to give way. The lock was not the strongest but it was still managing to keep hold against the thundering attack.

"*Good Night*," she answered from the other side, "It's after one o'clock!" She still had not taken off her coat. Then, absolutely terrified, getting hold of one side of the wardrobe, she gradually shunted it across the floor and pushed it against the door. Then she placed the armchair against that again and sat down on it to add more weight. Scott took several running jumps, ending up with kicking the bottom of the door viciously, shouting all the time, then wildly thumping at the door with his fists. Then he continued kicking viciously, and the lower panels were beginning to splinter, she could hear them

"I thought we could talk! Open up!" As well as being scared, Stella was frightened of all this scandal which the other tenants would be listening to while he continued like a human battering ram. Eventually he gave up but she had heard the wood splintering and it kept her worried. She heard his steps down the hall and the slam of the front door. But she did not trust that Scott had actually gone. He might be out there sitting on the chair by the payphone, pretending to have gone and waiting for her to come out; she would not put it past him.

Thoroughly shaken by all this, Stella remained sitting in the chair for a while, still wearing her green coat for some time, as if soaking up the silence. She had switched the light off and was sitting in the dark. So much for being afraid of life.

Scott never reappeared in the Roebuck afterwards, an admittance of guilt. You could not trust even men you thought you knew. It was rumoured that he and his wife's marriage was in trouble; and now they had one less pub to go to. The pair of them often made a childish scene when it came to closing time, going on about how it was not like this on the continent and only in this benighted country were grown-ups treated like children Stella watched them each time as they demonstrated how scared they were of being left alone with each other. They needed the crowd and the alcohol and no timeline.

The next morning, removing the wardrobe and shifting it back against the wall, Stella stepped out into the silent corridor. Luckily she had a strong bladder and had not needed to go along to the toilet in the night. Inspecting the damage, Scott had splintered the bottom panel, certainly. It was quite obvious. The shame was left with her; he had escaped.

On Tuesday the same week, after work Stella came home to find her gas meter had been done in, her door bust open. Her other pair of shoes and slippers, left under the bed as usual, had been arranged in a little procession along the side of the bed as a joke. Amazingly, Stella's first reaction was relief and the second was amusement. Now she could tell Laurence that the room had been broken into and the two crimes could be told as one. She left a note through the office door right away. And Laurence, coming round the next evening and looking at the damaged door agreed that it was obvious what had happened and the door would be mended as soon as possible.

The shoes display was Lloyd, she knew that. He was the only one who would be playing jokes while burgling.

"Yes, you're right it's probably Lloyd." Fiona said it must be him. She had seen him coming down the stairs with a plastic bag full of pennies only a few weeks ago. "I didn't like to say anything, you know what I mean, we can't get someone we know into trouble." So, he had even raided the bathroom meter, where they paid four pence for hot water for each bath.

"I think he used to live here in one of the rooms, a while ago, could be years ago. So he's still got the keys. But the front door's usually open anyway, so it's not really a difficulty for someone like him," Fiona added. "He gave me a bright smile, you know, his usual sunny self. He knows he can call in whenever he wants."

Laurence, thank goodness, did not question too much about the event and the two damages were seamlessly blended into one. Scott's destruction of her door would get blamed on Stella herself, seen as some kind of flirt bringing men of dissolute character into the house – it would reflect on her more than him. Miss Spedding and Mrs Grint must have heard everything that happened. The small room next door was still empty now that Pete had moved out.

Scott was clever enough to not reappear in the Roebuck at all and must have had to make up some excuse to his wife for their decamping to another pub. It was well-known gossip that their marriage was becoming a public farce. Every closing time promptly at eleven o'clock, the pair of them protested at the English pub rules re closing time. Marika screeched about Continental pubs being open all times, that no one was treated like children in this ridiculous way. They wanted to go on drinking.

It was actually fear; they were afraid to go home and face each other. As long as they could keep socialising or just being with people they did not even like, Scott and Marika could survive. It was the same with several others, Stella herself and probably most of the pub. The house that was public was a refuge from their own myriad lonelinesses; the worst of all being the loneliness of married couples.

It rankled that Gloria saw her as not taking chances. Only the week before, there had been a chancy episode too, what kind of a coincidence was that? A sudden downfall just as a party at Rita's was closing and as the crowd dashed into the rain from the front steps and scattered homewards up and down the street, Brian turned to Stella and said,

"You can have a lift with Kevin~~Colin~~, I think that's his name, over there. He doesn't live far from your place." Kevin~~Colin~~ appeared at the side of the steps.

"My car's over there if you want a lift in all this." He was apparently a friend of Mal's, who was a friend of Barbara's, that is to say, from the hinterland between strangers and friends. She hopped in as Kevin~~Colin~~ politely opened the passenger door and then went round the front of the car and got in the driver's side. Chat was limited to where she worked, did she share a flat or did she live on her own; pointed questions that could give a lot of information. As they drew nearer to her road, Stella stopped him, not wanting him to know the real address. He had wanted to know too much all at once.

"It's all right, here I am, thanks," and she reached to open the car door. But there was no handle there at all. It had been removed or fallen off. Kevin~~Colin~~ or Paul or whatever his name was, gave a slight smile. As her panic grew, she kept up a silly patter, all the while winding down the window, and still chatting merrily, Stella managed to reach down to the outside handle of the door.

He shouted at her then and tried to reach across the seat and grab her back, but now she had scampered out on the pavement and pretended to walk back along the street, so that he would not see what house she actually belonged to. Removing the passenger's door-handle. How low could you get. Desperate and creepy, whichever came first. The car sped off into the distance. Never get into a car again unless you fancy the driver.

And to counteract Gloria's remark even more, what about the other time that she had ended up in a guy's flat recently, also trying to be sophisticated and worldly-wise?

That other Saturday evening there was the usual pub routine, the bumping around with a crowd of strangers until the 11 o'clock crescendo of friendships and settlings of parties. Keeping with Brian and Gloria she got into a taxi.

"There's another party too, you should have gone with Tony and all that lot." Gloria had great territorial knowledge at these times. Stella mumbled something about this one being nearer. "Trouble with you is, no sense of adventure. You are afraid of life" said Gloria sharply. They both went into opposite silences. Her own marriage as a comfortable mattress annoyed Gloria; while not having the courage to break free she enjoyed seeing others live it up by proxy. She was always chasing an excitement that could not be caught easily without sacrifice. Harry was always left at home, still drinking with pals he brought home, in a form of wild babysitting.

This party was in a basement flat. People last seen in Saturday afternoon shops or half-limp after afternoon drinking sessions blossomed again in the half light and loud music. Someone's front room, now ornamentless, was now an imitation club where the drinkers leaned against the walls hung with pictures, avoiding the halo of light from a standard lamp. Eventually one dancer's arm knocked it and the lampshade hung, lolloped to one side. Some people danced, others loitered in the kitchen waiting for it to really warm up.

Posses of partygoers would arrive later from other pubs or on the run from dull parties that had died the death. They would arrive like the cavalry rescuing stranded prisoners, bringing a drunken merriment with them but not usually any bottles. Already there was a little group waiting for the ladylike pink toilet. Two rooms to move in and a large wide hall. There was no sense of excitement, almost a safe 'duty' party, the night going past uneventfully and it would have been much better to have stayed at home. Stella wandered out into the hall. Might as well go home, there was no one here she wanted to talk to or prance about with for the next couple of hours or whenever.

The hall had a green carpet and a few people sat on the floor by the phone, drinking and talking. Suddenly it went past like a large poster: You are afraid of life. Gloria's remark still irked. As she stopped to collect her coat from the overflowing coat-stand the nearest man noticed her. He had a blank clean face and was the usual door-or-hall loiterer. Not brash or skilled enough to risk socialising in the fast-moving rooms, these men used the kitchens or hallways of parties as their territories, picking up passers-by with a gentle predatoriness that usually worked.

It was something more complex than that they simply could not dance or did not like music; music with a beat seemed to frighten them and they usually remained at a constant distance from any source of loud music. As with football the real men were in the thick of it; these were merely onlookers, critics. Sometimes however they blended into the doorjamb too successfully and disappeared from view completely, like a spider absent from a magnificent web.

Stella had fallen, ideals foremost, into this one. The flag marked 'Adventure' fell limply to the ground.

"Well, I'm going soon too," (he noticed the coat) I live near the corner, so we can walk up together. You could come round to my place for a coffee on the way, it's still early." As easy as that, all settled now. Over the bridge and off to coffee, the life of a sophisticated Londoner. Girls were doing this all the time after all. They all said so.

He walked up the hill with her, talking of his job as an industrial designer, designing shop fitting mostly, and how much money he made out of it. Down one of the roads sliced off the Heath and up to his flat. An old solid building of the nineteenth century with all the nervy stylisation of the mid twentieth century applied to its surface, rickety white smartness clung onto old-fashioned strength. The flat was deeply carpeted, in an oatmeal or light cream colour, like walking on pillows. Stripped pine walls, low leather couch, sheepskin rugs. Space, fashion and money equally applied.

"Do let me take your coat," he asked politely as if it was an arranged afternoon visit. Usually Stella kept her coat on in such situations (which had not in fact occurred before; going back to a complete stranger's place at night was a new move.)

"Oh yes, of course." He walked off with it before she could stop him. Well, it would look so childish to be bleating about a coat disappearing into another room. Children crying in the hallway of nurseries,

"NO, NO, I want to keep my boots ON, On, I Want To!"

"Now, now, we can't go into there with our boots on can we, dearie?"

He went into the kitchen to make the coffee as that was what it was all about. Long white hands. He must just direct the carpenters and painters from a large sketchbook and a swathe of samples. Wait. Those hands were some clue; they were the same length as those of the bridegroom in the Arnolfini wedding portrait. Long tapering fingers and long white rabbit face, a sinister whiteness throughout, She still did not know his name. Had it been mentioned and she had missed it? Probably John or something ordinary.

A large silver-white (it had to be) fridge hummed gently. There must be some food the other side of that slim white door. Better not ask for food, not get too involved. He was not too friendly, come to think of it, still sending up a barrage of information on his current work arrangements. Whereabouts? Some big refurbishment along Tottenham Court Road. West End, of course, it had to be, and occasionally the provinces. Really they were stalling until they could settle back in the lounge. It would probably be called a lounge in the plan. A view of where we are.

They went back into the lounge, coffee at the ready, for more polite conversation. After all, this was when one discussed life, when exchanges, soul for soul, took place. Do you believe in God. What do you think of the Conservatives. Do you think George dyes his hair. All this would be discussed with Fiona tomorrow afternoon in swaps for what she had been doing too; they ran an impromptu information course and forensic investigation of each weekend. This was the grist of life, the conversation.

"Actually the record player is fixed in the bedroom. Come along here. You must listen to this." He took her hand and led her into the next room. He became very technical, fussing with wires and knobs like a mechanic as though his life depended on it.

Stella was now parked on the corner of the floor, leaning against the side of the bed, listening to gooey music, Frank Sinatra, pour across the carpet and thinking how boring it all was. He got up from the flexes and sat beside her. His name she had forgotten and now it was too late to ask. She would be going soon anyway.

His conversation was getting into deep waters. The monologue on work had changed into autobiography.

"You remind me of my girlfriend. She's in America now. I don't know if she's coming back. Yes, she had the same green eyes. She's getting over a suicide, partly to do with me and partly another guy. She's cut up about this guy out there, so I said it would be an idea go out and see him. That way she'll really get over it. And I'll still be here. She's costing me over a hundred pounds for a Harley Street abortion too."

How cool. And tragic. Just right for long white fingers. How expensive these people's emotions are. The return fare to America and £100 to Harley Street. A lotta money. Wonder how they'd manage on six and a half quid a week. Probably far better.

"My eyes. You got the colour wrong. They're brown." That was fatal. He took hold of her face, looked at her brown eyes and started to kiss her. She joined in because it seemed impossible to dodge and place any formality back between them. Wandering fingers started trying to undo the buttons of her blouse and his body spread out alongside hers against the bed behind.

"Why don't we lie down on the bed? We'd be far more comfortable," he said. At this point Stella wondered if this was what happened all the time. All the other girls' stories of evenings out ended with "And we went back for coffee… Met and just went round to his place for coffee…This guy and we went to his flat for coffee"… Surely not every one? How neat the translation had been from lounge to bedroom. (She had noticed that, but again it would have appeared fraidy-pie and little-girlish to ask for the record player to be placed dead centre in the lounge, for fear of a bedroom seduction.)

Quickly she realised she must do something about the situation, this was only going to lead to more trouble.

Luckily, she still had her shoes on. Shifting her elbows, she sat up,

"I'm sorry, I didn't realise things would be like this, let's not get entangled any further."

"Didn't you?" His arm encircled her waist closely. Frank Sinatra went on crooning as if nothing was wrong.

"I think I'd better go. It's fairer to leave now than later. It's not going to work." Pulse beat, red stars of tension blaring round. She smoothed her blouse together.

"No it's not fair at all. I'm not letting you go." He put his other arm across her neck. Oh dear, what to do now, left for dead. She smiled and at the same time quickly twisted round, getting her feet and legs away from him and hoisting herself out of his looped arms in one quick swerve. The action made him fall back, rolling over onto the carpet suddenly. Luckily her handbag was on the floor, she almost tripped over it. He was shouting at her that she was a stupid bitch and there was something wrong with her, when Stella remembered her coat, her only one. Too much to risk leaving behind in the rush. It had a pound note, after all, hidden in the hem. Stopping at the bedroom door she said coldly,

"Where did you put my coat?" She had debated whether it was worth losing the coat in the dash for freedom, but could not afford to buy another one. Besides, he seemed to be more offended dignity now than brute anger.

It was an awkward instant, because it interrupted both of them – his accusation, her running away.

With supreme distaste he pointed a finger at the fitted wardrobe,

"It's in there somewhere," like a disgusted aristocrat. While the line of light from the lounge streamed in, opening the smooth teak doors with jittery fingers she saw her old green coat there, like an old friend inside. On a hanger, even. Grabbing it she quickly slammed the bedroom door and ran down the soft, superbly olive-carpeted staircase.

The record player went on playing Frank Sinatra's *Songs For Swinging Lovers* and she could still hear it as its bad taste followed her down the stairs to the outside door and freedom. Strangers in the Night, indeed.

Once outside the house it all became a mix of the ridiculous, so utterly embarrassing and yet so potentially dangerous. She looked back at herself still being there, so stupidly vulnerable. No more going back for coffee, life or no life. Sinatra indeed. Along the grey pre-dawn streets the sense of cool peace drew her round the edge of the Heath, space to think as she rounded South End Green again. By the time she got home enough of the event had dimmed for her to fall to sleep immediately. She put her problems into her sleep; it worked.

Morningtime Sunday brought the self which told her not to be so silly, and definitely not to tell Fiona. For in its way the incident held a great deal of valuable information. If it had been in a prayer-book, that page would be much thumb-printed and furred at the edge with much use. It ought not to have existed; life on the downside. Minus centigrade, perhaps, on the private thermometer.

23 Collecting the morning post, she opened the envelope while walking up Pond Street to work, and here was Lloyd walking down towards her. He started doing a fancy cake-walk, all across the pavement like a professional show dancer. In the envelope was a cheque for one of her paintings sold in the Hampstead Artists' Council Exhibition that month. Their Open Air show was held further up Heath Street over the past three summer weekends. It had been inspired by an item in the Ham & High about someone drowning themselves in the ponds earlier that summer. Titled *'Night, Grass, Ponds'* it had a glamour and mystery, a melancholy beauty.

Last year, the first year of exhibiting with them, a swirling *Summer Greens* had been bought for £10 by a Mr Green. So this year was an obvious improvement. This time the original price before commission was £15. This was what success looked like, or its beginning.

"Darlin'," Lloyd said, with his usual self-mockery. "I was just coming to see you!" He did a dance step or two right there, nifty footwork on the morning pavement.

"At this time? But I'm off to work."

"Well, it's a bit of a problem, that's why I got here so early, to find you, you see, we absolutely need the rent, it's already overdue. It's sort of an emergency. Well, actually it's a very major emergency."

"You are *so* lucky, I've just sold a painting! Got a cheque here for £12! What a surprise" and in the merriment of the moment and all the success it symbolised, Stella endorsed the cheque right there in the street, leaning against the wall of the Indian house. She gave it to Lloyd happily. This is what the bohemian life was like, success was getting closer. She also had a painting *'Black Rose'* accepted for show with the Free Painters Group later that year. He looked serious for a second.

"You do realise I won't be able to pay this back, don't you? But what we can do, what you can do, is to come round each Sunday for dinner with Netta and me until you think you've eaten about twelve quids' worth. That should sort it. I've just started work, it's a problem with the wages, got to work a fortnight in hand, that's why we've got no money." His girlfriend, Netta did not seem to work these days so was no help. Her family lived over in Dalston, rather a mystery.

"Work?" Fiona said, "He's a milkman! You can see him driving that milk float all around the roads waving at everyone and grinning like a film star!" And just as she said this, Stella did encounter him a day or two later, with his rattling cargo of milk, orange juice and heaps of potatoes and other groceries progressing along South End Green and turning towards Keats Grove. Suddenly he was everywhere, cropping up unexpectedly.

So, on Sunday lunchtime, Stella decided to explore what the possibilities would be. Lloyd and Netta had the entire top floor flat in a professor's house on Rosslyn Hill. The tasty warm smell of roast chicken was already spreading down from their landing door as Lloyd ushered her up to their flat.

And it was definitely a real slap-up meal. She was surprised. Lloyd and Netta had provided a genuine classic Sunday dinner. Roast Chicken, roast potatoes, stuffing, and veg, followed by tinned peaches and real double cream followed by tea or coffee.

"Oh, this costs us nothing," Lloyd said contentedly, "There's all these filthy rich people with monthly accounts or even longer accounts that they don't bother to pay for six months and then they go off abroad for ages, so you put something extra on their bill and they never question it, they haven't a clue what's going on. And even if they did query it, I've got extra receipt books to come up with something different." He smiled happily, a successful businessman.

The third course was cannabis, as Lloyd was also Hampstead's pet cannabis dealer. His life was perfect these days. Stella did not like to refuse; you had to pretend to be cool sometimes. The one fat roach was passed round slowly as they each took in its contents. And quite quickly it had results. The carpet moved upwards and substances became fluid, the furniture started to float. As usual to sober up, Stella made for the sink and started to do the washing up. It was what she did at parties to sober up, it was always both soothing and practical.

But the floor tilted from side to side and some tree branches from the garden came in through the panes of glass and spread across the carpet, making navigation difficult. Her feet went down further and further into compressed air. The dishes were like seashells underwater and although obviously they were solid in real life, now they shifted and slithered as if alive. The sink was an ocean and the dishes folded into each other. Looking at them she could hear colours too.

But now a ring on the bell caused Lloyd and Netta to startle. He opened the two windows wide on the garden side and started fanning the air wildly as if drowning in smoke. Of course, what they were doing was illegal and anyone could report them. The smell would give them away. But it was only a customer calling in to Lloyd; a dealer had no regular hours. He dashed downstairs to the door. Netta and Stella could hear the voice in the hall now, no more alarm, they could relax.

On the way home soon after, steering along the pavements, Stella ended up holding onto some iron railings along Hampstead Hill Gardens for a grasp of reality. This feeling was so near to what she experienced when a painting went well; you went through into another reality. It did not happen every time, in fact it was a hard-earned bonus. Lloyd himself had thought she was stoned when he had burst into her room one Sunday and found her painting. This was the illegality; this experience should not have become a commercial transaction. It was a bonus from nature, not supposed to be a frequent treat. You were cheating nature by purchasing something that should have been a reward for efforts made. And not every grappling with self could attain this reward; that was the ultimate magic of life. To be able to merely summon it up by naming a price was destructive. It was like taking the rainbow and turning it upside down.

The room waited, not impressed with all this goings-on. She had a couple of black coffees and tried to get back to normal.

Next Sunday was a repeat of the same menu as the milk-float could only ever come up with the same ingredients. This time a strange young couple called in for their supplies and sat on the sofa smoking with them. Lloyd said afterwards he did not know them at all, it was the freemasonry of drug-dealing. They hardly spoke. It was not possible to refuse the spit-wet roll-up as the five of them shared it. You shared the spit as much as the smoke. Again, a ring on the bell caused a frisson of fear. The merriment, the pseudo spiritual was all illegal. Lloyd dashed downstairs again, to deal, in both senses of the word, with the callers. But it could as easily have been the police too.

The third Sunday went according to plan until four French beatniks turned up, three lads and a girl. They had an air of vagabonds and Stella was glad they did not know where she lived. They looked dirty and desperate. Even their foreignness did not disguise that wild and threatening atmosphere. They were nothing like Lloyd or Netta. If the flat was raided right now, she would have to appear in court with them, there would be no difference, they would be seen as drug users together at the Old Bailey. So many humiliations navigated already; but this was the end. She had to get out.

"I've got to go off now, just remembered there's someone coming round. Thanks for the dinner, again, it was perfect," she blathered, "I'll let myself out " The grey carpeted staircase drifted like a seascape and she kept near the bannister, holding on to keep from floating down the stairs. She decided never to come back here again, no matter how many more Sunday meals would have equalled that one painting. It was a strange coincidence that the professor who owned the house was the writer of a definitive (if that could be possible) book on ambiguity, and here she was experiencing two or more different things at once in his very hallway. Even stranger that he had taken Lloyd on as a tenant, dealing in the very stuff that was lifeblood to confusion.

Outside, the sunny streets were reassuring, quiet and tree-lined and suddenly so valuable in their Sunday normality. Very few people were about to see her wavering stroll home.

Lloyd, of course, continued his merry tour of Hampstead daily but Stella tried to keep away from him after that. There was probably a wrap or two of dope secreted on the milk float now, well hidden beneath the piled-up potatoes or tins of peaches. The milk bottles rattled as he turned the corner of Keats Grove, waving happily to her as she went into the Post Office to buy more paints the next Saturday afternoon.

She had met Lloyd at a party, he was leaning in the curve of a grand piano, wearing glasses and surveying the room with a superior air. They started talking about pop music and how it was a public diary that they all shared. Their emotions followed the charts and the charts captured their emotions. They ended up in bed together without any real reason except a mutual easy-going. Plus, as Lloyd wore glasses he looked like an intellectual with his world weary sophistication.

A week later Lloyd took her round to meet his family. They walked up East Heath Road to an unmarked lane. Right there in the Vale of Health was a wooden bungalow that was right out of the West Indies, complete with veranda and an old man sitting in a rocking chair. This was his father, reading The Daily Worker, retired but still interested in politics and the rights of workers.

"My Dad's an old shop steward, used to drive buses, he's always going on about rules and regulations," Lloyd said in a teasing way. The father looked her over like someone assessing livestock, but smiled at Stella kindly. Lloyd's sister came out hearing their voices and gave Stella a suspicious look, not friendly at all and then ignored her, chatting to Lloyd and taking him into the house for a talk with Mum. Stella was left with the Dad, who, looking worldly wise, started talking to her quietly so Lloyd could not hear.

"Are you getting involved with him? It won't last, you know. In fact I thought he had a proper girlfriend, over in Leytonstone or somewhere like that. I'm only telling you because you look like a nice girl. He may be my son, but he's not really a good catch. My other two sons are far better boys, but both settled down now." He took out a pipe from his pocket and started to fill it with tobacco. The sun was shining on the surroundings, making him even more authentic. She thought they could easily be in an exotic travel advert, only a few roads away from a London tube station.

Lloyd's Mum came out of the cool dark house to meet her. It was obvious that the sister, Olive, had told their mother to come and have a look at Stella. Again, it was a rather guarded but polite greeting and suddenly Lloyd stepped out from the dark interior carrying a bag of clothes and kissed his Mum goodbye. So that was what the visit was about. Lloyd, everyone's free spirit, brought his washing home to Mum. Stella had already got round to realising that just because a black guy wore glasses did not mean he was an intellectual.

They walked back along the edge of the Heath and into the organised chaos of the rush hour.

He was easy to be with, until he admitted about having a girlfriend already.

"Darlin' I've got to tell you now that I've got a girlfriend called Netta, she's seen you in the pub and she said she didn't mind me being with you, she said, because you're nice, so she's not too mad at me. I mean, we're going to move in together. I thought it was not going to happen, but we've got a chance of a place up Rosslyn Hill together now," he gabbled on. Stella, the insurance policy for lonely guys.

"I wasn't thinking of moving in with you, if that's what you mean," she said in defiance, thanking his father for that instant of prewarning.

"Oh, good," Lloyd smiled, "That's a weight off my mind, all clear now, then." Netta turned up in the Mag that very weekend, a tumble of red curls cascading over her shoulders. Apart from her ravishing Pre-Raphaelite appearance, she had little to say and merely sat there looking pleasant. She was the image of red-haired The Lady of Shallot. Stella could see that Lloyd would get bored but would keep the relationship going because it was not difficult. He would be guaranteed centre stage forevermore while Netta smiled vaguely.

But she did have Lloyd to thank for telling her about Radio Caroline. Its rebel pirate-boat programmes gave out every necessary ration of music that any young person would need. Unfortunately the station, being illegal, shut down at 8p.m. each evening with its haunting closedown of Jimmy McGriff playing '*Round Midnight'* It was the perfect ending to every summer evening.

Then she would switch to the Third Programme and whatever jazz could be found. The meandering of jazz was the perfect accompaniment to painting, with its sudden sweeps and valleys and its musing with time as if it was endless. You could think to jazz whereas pop music got you by the throat and did not let go, pressing every emotional button. One evening it was the Colin Purbrook quartet which was the background support as she painted. Going off to the pub up the hill, talking to a plump man sitting near the door, Stella mentioned this and he said

"But I am Colin Purbrook" which punctured the mystery completely. But it showed how many of the nearby people were creating, making, exploring, if you could hear someone from the Rosslyn on the Third programme.

Summer Sundays at the Magdala were often ruined by tourists turning up to inspect and even photograph the marks outside the doorway made where Ruth Ellis had shot her lover, David Blakely, to death, in 1955. The last woman to be hung and the last official hangman, Albert Pierrepoint, twinned in death. Stella could remember as a teenager the tense silence as it was announced on the BBC Home Service that she was dead.

Beside the windowsill where outside drinkers left their glasses there were definite chips in the stonework where the bullets had hit the wall that Easter Sunday. It was ironic that several of the women drinking there had almost the same grounds for resentment, but luckily had no access to a gun. Married lovers and secret abortions ran underground through society. Stella had seen women at New Year's parties loitering, on edge, round the host's phone in the hallway, waiting for that important phone-call from their married lover, ringing secretly from his family home. The girl would have given him the probable phone number of a few watering holes or party venues beforehand.

"I might be at Fred's or we could all be at Barbara's, so here's the numbers. Keep them in your diary." And he would tell his wife, when midnight struck and all the bells rang and fireworks exploded,

"Darling, I'm just going to phone up that old uncle of mine up in Glasgow, can't leave him out at a time like this," and then the valuable whispered endearments that kept their secret relationship going. And then the semi-tearful girlfriend would turn back to the party, make for the whisky decanter and whirl around dancing with whoever was nearest, a fabricated merriment.

24

After the glandular fever episode the Labour Exchange noticed she had some educational qualifications again. A different woman behind the counter produced a wonderful job at London University's Senate House. It was a specially constructed job for graduates to fill in time while they decided what to do next.

"You will be working in the school exams department. It's a general clerical position, you'll soon fit in."

To celebrate the new proper job, Stella thought it was well past time that her place needed a good clean after the previous accident with a splinter of broken glass she had not bothered. Kneeling down she washed the high dull grey skirting boards and swept away the detritus collected under the edge of the matted grey wall-to-wall carpet; peeling the edge of it away exposed hair clips, drawing pins, buttons, crumbs, edges of envelopes, the scraps of years of residents buried in dust. There was no way to improve the greyness of the indistinct pattern, faded and worn, but Stella thought she was improving things. The result was indistinct, however.

The new job at the Senate House was interesting in more ways than one. Examining people's examination scripts was a chance to save some scholars from doom by finding even one mark that the enumerators had missed. It was a job made up for ex-students to find some time to look for a proper post somewhere. For Stella, it was the dream job. And one day, checking over the physics papers, the writing was familiar, the same italic script, the same fountain pen. In spite of the tight scientific answers, it was Dave again, the love-letters she still had somewhere in the old hatbox. He was living up north now, they had changed places too. It was not worth keeping a note of his address, but it was a magic link. He might have been a million miles away, not just Bradford.

Stella had felt itchy all the time now, and was losing sleep because of it. Scratching was beginning to cause a rash. Brian, who was checking maths scripts with her today, advised her to go to the doctor's.

"You don't have to take a day off, you're technically a student after all, working in this department. The student doctors' place is over Gordon Square, you can go in your lunch hour, easy." Egged on by this Stella went off and was accepted after a bit of a suspicious start. She soon found herself lying naked on a high inspection couch as a medic surveyed her with disapproval.

"Do you keep yourself clean, or perhaps you borrow other people's clothes? Or do you live in a dirty house?" He took off his rubber gloves. "You have got scabies and they only come from dirt." The penny dropped.

"I've been cleaning my bedsit as it needed a going-over and I was ashamed of it. So that's where this has come from? The carpet?" As the proper reason came out, the medic could relax. She was not a slut after all. Time she could get her clothes on and here was a prescription for a cream. But meanwhile he could give her this powder to apply right now as it would be contagious for anyone near her. Jumping down from the couch, Stella put her clothes back on, after sprinkling powder all over, saved. You try to improve your surroundings and you become a pariah by default. The young doctor's disturbing disapproval remained with her for several days.

The walk from the bus stop meant a stroll past RADA and Malet Street, the students union HQ. But the 24 bus was often crowded in the mornings and it was less chancy to go by tube from Belsize Park. It became a chant most days – Warren Street, Goodge Street, Tottenham

Court Road. But the tube was also packed, standing room only. Stella stood squashed, hardly able to see past someone's shoulders, always touched by men in the crowded carriage, pushing themselves against her, fingers searching, pressing. One morning, fed up with the humiliation and hidden threat, she called out loud, for once she was not going into work with the feel of strange men's handprints upon her,

"Will the person who is handling my behind and the other man who is rubbing against me just stop it!" The invisible men drew back and even the ones in front managed to withdraw a few inches away. They obviously expected women to exist in silent acquiescence. She had to invent her own respect.

If she had invented a motto, it was that if she had to be a slave, then she could have a change of masters. A new job was easy to get in any lunchtime. Thursday, dash into an agency, arrange it, leave quietly at 5.30 Friday and reappear somewhere else on Monday morning, National Insurance cards 'to follow.' But being harassed by other slaves was not in the social contract. It was bad enough as it was, working every day and arriving back home with only the husk of one's real self remaining. It usually took until after 7 p.m. before the system regrew after cups of tea or coffee and met pie and pickle, followed by a hazelnut yoghurt.

The Senate House job, however, was interesting and set in a beautiful Art Deco building, even though they worked in the basement area. There were other benefits, being able to work here at the university. In the lunchtime she discovered the Courtauld Museum, set in an ordinary house in Woburn Square. It was like being someone in a Virginia Woolf story, merely calling in for a quick visit in the smallest of the Bloomsbury squares.

And there it was, in the empty gallery. There was no one else in the building apart from the receptionist downstairs at the front desk in the hall. Edouard Manet's *Bar at the Folies Bérgère.* She could have reached out for one of the bottles, talked to the barmaid. It was two realities at once; no, three. One version was a girl standing in front of a mirror; another version was of another girl behind her, with the reflection of the waiting man. And for a magical second, both versions combined and you could hold two truths at once blended into a third. Just like Borgia coffee in the recipe book for all occasions, with its cocoa and coffee mixed – again, a second where the two flavours amazingly combined in a new caramel? butterscotch? A new flavour, definitely. It was the sort of place you reached after several glasses of gin and not a safe place to be.

And Toby was in that place right now. Matt said he was in a mental home, Springfield, he thought, not sure. In the lunch hour she went to the British Museum library to look up the address but there was no Springfield near London, they would not have sent him further away, surely? There was a Springbank University Hospital in Tooting so she took a chance and sent Toby two postcards. One was *The Family of Sir William Young* by Johann Zoffany and another one, by Laurence Alma Tadema, of a harem, saying "We all miss you and the old crowd send their love." It probably never reached him and Toby never mentioned it.

One morning two girls appeared at the long tables that were used to stack the exam scripts and as usual it was a chance to talk while they worked checking the margins for extra marks that could save some scholar's future. Stella was sent to help them start the process.

One girl realised who she was.

"You're Matt's girlfriend, or you used to be! I live in the same house, the basement – you must have walked past my door a couple of times! This is amazing!" Trudy was bright, arty and had the slim figure that nervy people always had. "Now, there's another party this Saturday, well, that's more or less the usual now, you know that." She glowed with enthusiasm as the bright future spread out. They would all be friends. The quieter girl, Jean, was far better looking and it was obvious that they split any social encounter between them. Trudy would win men over by her force of personality, but it was Jean's Madonna-like good looks that lured men towards the twosome in the first place.

Trudy was here to fill in time before something exciting in design or fashion turned up. She had contacts all over the place and enough confidence and verve to take up any lead. Meanwhile she was giving a life class at Kentish Town Evening Institute. In no time at all ("I even had to ask Matt and he's fed up being a model, besides the class didn't like him,") Stella was rounded up as a model for the class. Anything for money, and a bit more exciting than babysitting.

So after work, Stella, on the promise of receiving some expenses, got into a taxi straight after work, remembering to perch on the edge of the seat so that the suspender pips did not leave a red impression at the top of her legs. To make extra certain she also had a tin of talcum powder to disguise any marks. Her dressing gown was stuffed into a shopping bag for the intervals.

It was strange to be on the other side, as an artist's model. It was obvious that any girl who had been to any art school would see it as more or less normal to take off all her clothes and sit still in front of a roomful of strangers. That was the easiest part. Trudy arranged her arms and legs, an ordinary sitting position to start with. The difficult part was remaining still and using all strands of self-control to keep static while remaining human. It was a form of vertigo where the mind went off for aeons but only ten minutes had passed in real life.

The rules were that the model had five minutes rest in the hour, when Stella retired into the corner cubicle and put on her dressing gown brought from home. She could go round and look at the various translations of her appearance, and see what Trudy had been commenting on. Many of the drawings were unrecognisable, only two looked anything like her this first evening. At five to nine, the class ended and there was a pass-the-hat collection to pay the model's expenses as it was called. Stella was amazed at the result, a week's rent already. It was worth the pins and needles that she kicked away.

Trudy suggested they all go off for a drink after the evening class, but Stella pretended tiredness and escaped. This strange arrangement continued for several weeks until the end of term. Jean, with her Madonna looks would have been a far better choice but of course not every girl would do it. In fact, Jean disappeared about this time.

There was a limit to how many people could belong to any group; perhaps this one was already full.

So Stella duly appeared at the house for their usual Saturday night party again but found it boring. Trudy had said about Matt and her,

"You two are made for each other," but Matt did not seem to think so and when Trudy sent her to the other room where Matt was sitting, it did not work, it was more a duty. "He's depressed, he won't join in, just go in and cheer him up, will you?" Trudy suggested. He sat alone on a chair, brooding and looking dramatic while people thronged around dancing merrily.

"You can't make any difference," Matt said miserably. Something must have gone wrong in the fame they were all after. The Inland Revenue had been after him already, looking for missing income tax payments. He had told her a while ago his answer. "I told them, no income, no tax." That might have been the source of his downbeat mood. The outside world was telling him that his poetry was nothing.

She went into the cold bathroom and sat on the edge of the bath for some peace away from the others. Hugh, one of Matt's musician friends, dashed in and gave her a large spliff,

Here, you can have this, I've got something else," and he disappeared as quickly as he had appeared. She sat there looking at it as Toby walked in and snatched it off her.

"I thought you didn't go in for this stuff," and pushed it into his mouth frantically, drawing on the wet draggy end and all as manic as usual.

At work, Mr Drury drew her aside for a chat.

"Now, you've been here for the complete year, and it doesn't look as though you are planning to move, are you?" He pointed out that the exam room job was really meant for graduates as a stop-gap while they fixed up their proper careers. "What you are doing is not meant to last much longer. There is another way out, though. Now, what I think should happen is that you should join the permanent staff and have a proper contract."

Stella could think of nothing worse. The permanent staff worked on analyses and rolls of computer printouts. They had separate desks along the side wall and did not mix with the clerks on the many tables, who were ferreting in the scripts and able to sit with whoever they liked and talk all day. History and English papers were the best, often a good read, whereas no one wanted to go through the physics or maths ones. A move like this would be imposing an early middle-age on Stella, which was absolutely worse than death itself. Miss Pickford was only last week talking about life insurance plans although she still lived at home.

Toby reappeared in her life as though nothing had happened. They carried on as if there had been no break, as usual service resumed.

When she got back from work, shattered, she looked round the room for any message, any trace of Toby. It happened every time, that change in the atmosphere, that hunger for any sign of belonging. There it was. All across the fireplace mirror, a bright red piece of witty graffiti, "Go to work on an egg," taken from the latest ad on the side of buses. The sketched outline of a scarlet bus stood above an egg. It was done in her favourite lipstick, Summer Cherry, and he had been so liberal with it that she would have to buy another one soon. Later she started to wipe it off, then stopped, needing to save it. He might turn up next weekend after all. She realised yet again that she was now the only one of the group that went out to work properly each morning at half-past eight.

In the lunch hour it was a luxurious treat to make a shortcut through the British Museum. She felt it was almost illegal to use the Museum as a shortcut when it was not even raining. People travelled from all over the world just to visit here. Right up the steps, along past the Elgin Marbles and then through the Reading Room. Sometimes a quick flick of the thick green velvet curtains that sheltered mediaeval manuscripts from the danger of light. And then past a crystal figure of a woman, probably a Japanese goddess, set on her plinth. A benevolent half-life-size figure, she stood at the centre of the corridors as if to signal the way to the side door off to Montague Street and round to Senate House.

Out of the sunshine and back to the basement, to continue rescuing students from their fate, by discovering a few extra marks in a margin, if possible. All late summer after the official GCE Ordinary and Advanced results came out, they worked overtime rescuing failed scholars. August was crunch time; they worked overtime, even coming in on Sundays. Richer parents and annoyed teachers sent in their complaints and requests, their chickabiddies could not possibly have done so badly, surely the universe was wrong? And sometimes they were right, the examiners had left out a page or had added up the marks in the margins wrongly and suddenly a failed thirty-nine would be changed into a successful forty-five.

The scripts could have coal dust in the margins (marked by a fireside, Would you put some more coal on the fire, darling) or traces of marmalade (Have you finished with the newspaper yet, darling?) or biscuit crumbs (I'll have another cup of tea, thank you darling.) It showed up that the exam scripts were marked in domestic surroundings, at the mercy of doorbells, phone-calls, visitors, and any family interruptions. Stella was shocked at this as she had always imagined that exam papers were marked in the same stringent circumstances as the original exams. Silence, in a large hall, concentrating on the work at hand.

The fee for being rescued was two and sixpence a time. There were very few scripts where they did not find a crucial extra mark or two hiding in the margins, and so someone got the necessary GCE Ordinary or Advanced levels in history or physics or Latin and their life was sorted immediately. The work gradually decreased in the autumn but then there were the November retakes, and after that the system repeated yet again.

In the winter, the Australians went crazy, never having seen snow like this before. They spent their entire lunch hours over the week, until it turned to sleet, dashing out and taking photographs of the local squares and any tourist spots that were near enough. The Londoners looked at them as if they were crazy, and found it hilarious.

But Stella remembered her own first few days in London. On the top of a bus going down Grosvenor Place, it was possible to see over the wall of Buckingham Palace and into their gardens. But as they turned the corner the real shock was the grey ordinariness of the palace building itself, not as glamorous as on any postcard or Pathé Pictorial newsreel. It looked like some county council offices, grey and unspectacular, As the bus went past the front of the Palace, her first impression was how dirty the net curtains looked. Any housewife, even a Queen, was judged on how white her net curtains were kept and here they were a dun white as if drenched in smoke and coal dust. Perhaps they were special, some gift, handwoven; perhaps they were some safety weave against any attack of gunfire shattering the glass, but they still gave the wrong impression.

So the enthusiasm of the Australians was understandable. It was merely that the rest of them had become jaundiced over the years about the joys of snowfall in city streets and knew all about sleet and the sleazy pavements after the first day of brilliant born-again whiteness.

25
Christmas loomed like an iceberg yet again. Roy came across to her in the pub after managing to avoid her for some weeks now. Some relationships disappeared like a wisp of smoke; here was the proof.

"What are you doing for Christmas?" he asked sociably as if they had never met.

"I've not really thought about anything, just staying here."

"No family to go to?" he tactlessly said. "Well, never mind, I've decided we must all gang together for Christmas, it's the only way to cope. All that festivity going to waste. So I thought of making an arrangement for all the lame ducks, what about we contribute a couple of pounds each, say two pounds, and we can make a feast lasting as long as the food can stretch out. What do you think?" He smiled his sunburnt accountant's smile. Having no other plan except perhaps an invitation to Harry and Gloria's, Stella said it sounded a good idea, what was the start, she had a ten shilling note spare right now and gave it to him. People were already giving Christmas tips to the cleaners before they left for holidays abroad, guilt disguised as generosity.

"I've got it all arranged now, don't worry. What I'll do is I'll come round and collect you on Christmas Day then," Roy said the next week. "We're going to be cooking at different people's flats, the shopping's been sorted, there's already six others, so it'll be good." Stella felt efficient and realised a gap had been filled.

On Christmas Eve she went into the Roebuck and found it packed with strangers, visitors who had drifted in for the holiday. Fiona and other friends had already gone off to stay with their families, leaving Christmas cards behind for her. Her mantelpiece was full of the display. The house was empty except for the couple in the top floor and the invisible Mrs Grint. Even Miss Spedding had a mother to go to. So, spying Louis and his gang in the public bar, she sidled through the screen from the lounge to join them. As she had let him stay in her room when he was homeless, they were considered friends enough to let her mix with his much younger group. Boys and girls from posh Hampstead families, ministers' sons and the double-barrelled, they were out mixing with the commoners in the public bar, as a joke, where, as it had no carpet, drinks were a penny or more cheaper. In the daytime it was the hangout of old men and a place for decorators and workmen to call in for a break at lunchtime.

Among the merriment, Louis, Max and Ben had a sudden scathing row with the others – something about politics, important even now on Christmas Eve. It led to three of them running out of the pub to settle for a real fight, but in no time Louis came back, worried that Ben, totally drunk, his glasses knocked off, had run off into the night. Deirdre and Vanessa began to cry.

"He's almost blind without his glasses! And he's got asthma, he can't be left to wander around. It's far too cold." In an instant, they all became concerned.

"We've got to search the streets now. Did he go home? What on earth did you go and say? Which way did he run?" They all pitched in together accusing each other while the two sisters got hysterical.

"I know, what about we all go back to my place, have some black coffee and sober up. Then you can think of what to do next," Stella suggested, being the peacemaker. They all trooped back to her room round the corner. Jim ran in saying that Ben had not gone home. Paul suggested Ben's grandparents' home,

"He sometimes stays there when his lot have had a row," but no one could think of where else he could go. A tall gangling lad, drunk, myopic and upset, not a night to be lost. The girls tried every address they could think of while Stella whirled around, a haphazard hostess.

And then as the mugs of black Nescafé, ladled with sugar were finished, Max dashed in,

"Found! On a bench round by the hospital! All clear!" And in an instant, like a flock of sparrows, they all vanished and Stella was left in a silent room scattered with mugs, cups and bowls, amazed that she had managed to cater for all of them. Surprisingly exhausted, she began the washing up but a sudden bout of nausea stopped her. She leant over the sink and began to vomit. The room started to reel around, da-dum da-dum. Where had this dizziness come from?

But someone was here - Greg was walking into the room; the front door must have been still left on the latch and her own room door was slightly open. There was no reason why he should come back. He was really a hanger-on to Louis and the gang and she had hardly even spoken to him all evening. He was always at the edge of their group, watching, buying his own drink, never a round. Smallish but burly, the only thing she knew about him was he apparently wanted to be an actor, but seemed not to realise that his black eyebrows that met across his brow and his fierce glowering expression would not be much use in the world of stage or film except as a trainee gangster.

"They've all gone," she spluttered. He saw what was happening as she bent over the sink.

"Put your fingers down your throat, that'll make it all come up easier," he advised. Bits of food gulped up. The dizziness grew worse. She grasped the edge of the sink for balance. As everything went red and the room began to swing around, Greg guided her across to the bed and slipped off her shoes as she crashed onto the eiderdown. "You should have lined your stomach with a glass of milk beforehand," he said sternly. "Here you are, let's take this dress off, you'll be more comfortable then."

She had no control of her body now, it was heavy, falling down a dark tunnel. He got her comfortably settled into the sheets, shuffling her around.

"You can rest now." Stella slumped her head on the pillow. But now he was getting in beside her. Calmly and deliberately he stripped down her tights and knickers and lunged into her. There was nothing she could do, she was not in her body, it was a lumpen object that he was more in charge of now. But her mind, ever rebellious, remembered a joke of her mother's *'Oh, no, Sir Jasper*!' and now it was happening to her, like a modern serving-maid. Greg's face loomed over her as he took possession of exactly what he had planned to happen. Her arms and legs did not work and her mind was trundling off somewhere else. She did not think of screaming. There was no one to come and help, Mrs Grint was probably out and even if she was in she would have been selectively deaf.

Luckily Stella then passed out completely or fell into a deep sleep and woke on Christmas morning feeling calm and ordinary, except that Greg was in bed beside her. She had no hangover but many questions. He was more ugly than ever in the Christmas morning daylight. She surveyed him as though he was a cardboard box.

Not fazed by his own behaviour he announced that if she was ever his girl-friend he would see to it that she was on a diet and he would hit her if she didn't follow it properly.

At last, someone who cares, she thought sarcastically, looking at his eyebrows.

"Anyway, you should definitely think of going on a diet," he said, getting dressed and slinging his black leather jacket on. He looked as indestructible as a cockroach again. He must have taken off all his clothes last night; she had been in no state to notice. "I've got to be going off now, my Mum'll be starting the Christmas dinner. She gets up early and has everything laid out neatly in advance, but I always help her."

The loving devoted son. He lives at home with his widowed mother in a basement, Louis told me. He had the prison pallor of someone who did not see daylight often.

Time to go over the events. Last night she had had two glasses of Merrydown cider, her usual drink. Or no, perhaps she had finished only one glass before they all ran out of the pub after Ben? That did not explain why she had been so drunk, it would have been impossible. Home from work early after a mince pie and coffee at the Pack's house in Arkwright Road, her last job on Christmas Eve. Dinner at six o'clock had been a meat pie, pickle and a yoghurt, the same as so many other evenings, followed by coffee. There was no reason why she had been so drunk. Surely if it had been only food poisoning, there would have been more vomiting and less of the passing–out. Something was wrong.

Greg had not spoken to her in the pub, that was certain. There was something iffy about the chain of events. In fact she could not remember him being with the others in her room earlier. He was always the one hovering at the edge – how could she have not noticed him? And she should go to the police right now. But what would that do apart from dragging her own name through the mud? You could not accuse someone of rape, it was too serious and the trouble would go on forever, she would have to move to get away from the scandal. It was rape, but all of Louis's friends would get involved, there would be a report in the local paper and all the people in the pub would have their own opinion on it. She could never go out again to the same places. It was a blank wall. A solid hit. She would have to keep this story under wraps until some time in the dim future, whenever that might be.

So, it was Christmas morning and time to go upstairs for a bath, trying to start a new life. Pregnancy was a possibility after all, another worry, but she could only deal with one problem at a time. You had to pace your disasters properly. That would be a month ahead. You could manage meanwhile by cramming in enough distractions to dislodge the current problem from the surface and deal with it later at a deeper level. Roy had arranged that he would be calling for her at two o'clock and there was the Christmas eating-party to look forward to. He'd said it was starting at someone else's flat, so he would call round and take her there.

By two o'clock Stella had managed to resurrect a passable self. The radio was kept low, to make sure of hearing anyone fumbling at the front door if Roy had not remembered the right bell. By three o'clock the Queen's Speech had happened and she was beginning to worry. She pinned a note on the front door with 'Gone off to your house, 3 p.m.' and started out in the untreaded snow. Not one taxi at the rank on the hill, no cars on any of the roads. Absolute silence. Everyone was indoors, busy eating. Roy would have to be walking towards her as it was the only way up from his place down Haverstock Hill; they'd have to pass each other in the silent empty roads. In any other circumstances it would be quite a romantic encounter in the snow.

Reaching his gate, she rang one of the two bells. Perhaps something had gone wrong – the chicken or turkey not properly defrosted, causing a delay; something like that. No answer. It was a 1900s imitation Tudor semi, just two floors, two flats. She rang the bottom flat's bell too in case he had gone downstairs. Silence. Ring again and again. Nothing. Remembering romantic scenes from films, she threw a few small stones from the tiny front garden up at Roy's window, risking breaking the panes. Tiring of digging up pebbles from the snow with bare hands and missing the glass several times, she admitted the entire house was empty.

Turning back up the hill was surreal. A white streetscape stretched as far as the eye could see. Only one person in the distance, a man carrying a heap of brightly-wrapped presents, a late arrival. They smiled at each other like conspirators in the grand emptiness. Still no taxis, but now and then the odd car going past in the melting snow. The reward though, was a brilliant early sunset, dashing orange light along the skyline and no one else to see it. Letting herself into the silent house, she put the gas fire on and surveyed the possibilities. There was no food because of the Christmas dinner plan. It had taken most of last week's money, an investment on future food. Some cornflakes, a plain yoghurt and the standard Nescafé and sugar. Getting on for four o'clock; the pubs would be open at half-past seven, she could easily last out that long. So, Radio Caroline and painting, it was being an artist after all that was important. There was no one to phone.

At half-past seven Stella was the first person in the pub, trying to look casual, just dropping in early. Food at last. The meat-pie display unit on the bar, however, was empty and when she asked Myrtle about it, the answer was, who'd be needing extra food like that after stuffing themselves? It made sense, of course. Brian and his brother then came in and leant on the bar in their usual places. He told her that the landlord had invited the local lame ducks upstairs for the Christmas dinner. They had a wonderful time, he added.

Stella was annoyed with a type of jealousy at there being a rival list – were there bands of lame ducks all over the place? – without wanting to be labelled as one. But the thought of being upstairs in her favourite pub, in a sort of fake family, was a temptation. Who on earth were in this branch of the lame ducks? If it was Brian and his brother, she really was better off alone with a plain yoghurt and the radio.

"Speak into my watch," Brian's nameless brother said yet again, giving a Christmas smile. He never said anything else except "Talk to the hand." Both phrases were so abstract that they fooled most people. If he was so backward, how had he chosen such extreme sayings?

Too much philosophy on an empty stomach, Stella bought two packets of salted peanuts. But it was impossible to eat more than two packets of salted peanuts at once. The salt was as strong as barbed wire round the peanuts and she could not get anything else to eat. Salt and vinegar crisps would only make it worse. Tomato juice was as near to a food as any drink so she just sat there making conversation and waiting for the shops to open the next day. Many did not function on Boxing Day, but at least the pub might start its usual meat pie display again.

One by one the regulars filed in, full of cheerfulness and jokes, with Boxing Day to look forward to. After going round to a deserted Roy's flat again, she went round to Harry and Gloria's with some extra presents for the children and joined in a consolation meal of yesterday's remains, with an extra serving of Christmas pudding.

"We don't want to waste it and it's useful, rather like roast beef," Harry said, heaping the plate. "In fact you could probably fry it if you wanted to."

The next day, no Roy either. Stella phoned up, then walked round at midday, to find the house empty yet again. Same the next day. But by now the shops were open for a couple of hours and she had some basic foods. It was Thursday before she caught up with the roving party at last. He opened the door as though nothing was wrong and implied it was all her own fault, he had called round and there had been no answer.

"Never mind, we're all here now. We're all a little tired about eating chicken and turkey, so we are making a gigantic curry." They had got real saffron, quite expensive, to colour the rice. Stella was past caring as long as the stuff was eatable and she sat down to the most expensive curry ever, price two pounds' worth. It was interesting looking at the people, a quiet couple - he much older than his girlish wife; a cheerful middle-aged man; a rather curt woman; and Roy's new girlfriend, Moira. She looked like an adolescent boy, dressed in a lumpy grey jumper and non-descript jeans, no make-up. Roy was proud of her and mentioned to Stella that she was pregnant.

"Yes, it's a nice surprise isn't it. The baby'll be living in her flat, it's too small here." Then he dropped to a whisper. "I'm keeping on the other place along Finchley Road for my other activities." The way he said it implied that the naïve girlfriend had no inkling that he was bi-sexual and this was only half of his life here. Three flats to house them, no wonder there was a growing housing shortage. A child dropped into their cats' cradle was an experiment, Stella felt sorry for all of them.

Several months later she saw Roy coming into the Mag with a group of three or four men, all wearing navy overcoats. They were shorter and darker than him, his golden hair stood out among them. He looked across at Stella and a message crossed, a mixture of regret and a plea for help. She semaphored back that nothing could be done, it was too late. Perhaps the men were other accountants, they had come from some official meeting; or perhaps not. She wondered about the baby that must exist somewhere by now.

26
Alarm clock cutting off dreams. The world claimed her loudly, sharply. Mediaeval strip field workers, surely *they* did not just go out to the master's fields to work out of sheer community duty. No, there must have been bailiffs pushing them but that was not discussed in history books. The peasants, being peasants, just rolled up to do the extra toil out of the goodness of their hearts, in all weathers, of course they did. Here in the twentieth century the best 24 bus to aim for left at twenty past eight for town. Later ones would be full up immediately from the morning queue at the South End Road terminus.

She could go upstairs and have a cigarette on the way, to ease into public morning life along with all the men in the top deck. Downstairs was for non-smokers and women who had such high stilettoes that they could not navigate the stairs easily.

Back to work, its neutral wasting of time blanking out any other preoccupations. On Wednesday morning, as usual, Stella went round to Miss Kirkham's. It was one of the eleven addresses on the Daily Maids cleaning round and one of the easiest they had given her. The large Victorian house on Winchester Road was shabby but carefully looked after. It was like a private museum. Even the rowan tree in the front garden was apparently under some type of protection order.

"It had a special number given to it by the council. They said it can't be cut down, not ever and it's only to be pruned by a properly qualified gardener," Miss Kirkham said proudly. Stella glanced at the unspectacular tree that blocked light from the bay window. "They are magic trees, rowans. that's why it's got to be preserved even in the middle of London. They're fairy trees," she said again. Down in the basement Stella changed her shoes in the corridor and said hello to Mrs Grove, a widow who acted as housekeeper and cook. With her daughter Elsa, she lived in the basement. A serious accident at the garage where he worked had led to Mr Grove being crushed to death, she had brusquely told Stella some weeks ago. Although there had been some compensation money, Mrs Grove did not have the means, she said, to keep up the mortgage and so they had lost their house. These days she and her daughter hardly saw daylight, stranded in the electric-bulb gloom of Miss Kirkham's basement.

It was not complicated to look after upstairs, Miss Kirkham kept the place trim. In every room there were vases, each one containing a clean yellow duster. She showed Stella where they were hidden.

"I go from one room to another, a bit every day, dusting here and there. It's the best way to keep on top of it." The work today entailed taking down the lighter summer curtains and putting up blanket-thick winter ones for the front room. the big stepladder had been left in the hall by the odd-job-man. Up the high steps, Stella leant down as Miss Kirkham handed up the folded lumps of cloth. Their weight was astounding although they had no real colour – grey, the colour of winter fog. Once up and drawn-to, they were so thick that the noise of the traffic outside became muffled with the power of heavy cloth.

"That's all ready for the real winter now," said Miss Kirkham and sent Stella off downstairs for midmorning coffee and two digestive biscuits in the gloom of Mrs Grove's kitchen-living room.

"She's going to put me in her will," Stella said brightly, "If I come here and work on Wednesday afternoons too."

"Oh, she's putting you in her will too, is she," grim-faced Mrs Grove poured out hot milk for the coffee. "There's almost everyone in that will by now. Of course we've none of us a hope or a clue. What are you in it for?"

Stella shook her head. "Well, it's not going to happen. Miss Kirkham wanted me to work here all day Wednesdays and she's put me in her will. But I need the time off to paint, I work Saturday mornings instead." The idea had been to go to galleries and see what possibilities there were, midweek when everything was open for business.

"You're best not counting on her, I can tell you. There might be nothing in it at all. Nothing for any of us," Mrs Gove added mournfully.

Stella finished the afternoon by polishing the brass stair rods which were unusual and probably extremely expensive because they were triangularly shaped like bars of Toblerone. The flat-faced brass shone now as far as the top flight. Beamish, the sleek black cat, sauntered past, disdainful of all this interference in the calm household.

Miss Kirkham's life centred round the cat. Beamish was all that was left of the original family, where she had been engaged as companion to the two Misses Langham long ago. They had left the house and an income plus Beamish's mother-cat, to their dear Miss Kirkham. Nature had taken its course; hence the arrival of Beamish.

Beamish was not let out often.

"The local cats are disappointingly vicious, he's not able to cope well with them, you know," Miss Kirkham remarked as she let him downstairs via the dumb waiter. As he descended by the rope and pulley, it was Mrs Grove's job downstairs to let him out and then, after his 'airing' in the back garden, to deposit him back in the hatch, shout up to Miss Kirkham and send him slowly whizzing up to the front room again. Beamish would step out as if all this toing and froing was beneath his dignity.

It all went wrong though, one Wednesday. Stella arrived to be let in by a distracted Miss Kirkham.

"I've had no sleep at all. I've been up all night. Hour after hour of cups of tea and I even took a glass of whisky at one point.

"Oh? What's happened then?"

"It's Beamish. He's been out all night. I've even rung up the police this morning but they said they could do nothing about it. He's done this sort of thing before, but never all night." Stella murmured some consoling snippets and started on the hall carpet using the ancient carpet sweeper. There were no modern appliances in this time-warp establishment but it did not matter.

Poor Miss Kirkham, in love with the only male in the house, Beamish the gad-about. To distract herself she showed Stella into the upstairs so-called needlework room. The house was so large that there were still many rooms that had remained locked and unused, falling back into history. Miss Kirkham had one room downstairs merely for having breakfast in, a proper breakfast room. The rich had to have at least one room for each bodily function. This room was a trip back to the nineteen twenties. A wide worktable stood under the front window – they were somewhere above the bedrooms on the second storey and could see the rowan tree beneath them. Ceiling-to-floor cupboards on either side hid secrets, while on the central table and on racks beneath it, bolt after bolt of cloth lay untouched.

"We used to go to Liberty's sale every New Year and the Misses Langham would choose dress material and upholstery stuff. Then they would engage a dressmaker to design and make a season's outfits." No one had entered here for years and they both diligently inspected the bolts of cloth in the cupboards and those laid out on the tables for any evidence of moths. Miss Kirkham and the two Misses Langham who died, going to one New Year's sale after another, picking up fashionable prints, stocking up for a future that never happened.

The Groves, mother and daughter, lived in the basement in permanent gloom, the peeled potatoes always waiting. A dumb waiter trundled up and down from the front room to the basement kitchen, ferrying up meals, packages and the cat. On the top floor there were empty bedrooms and the storerooms with unused sheets embroidered '1911.'

"We used to go off to Pontings and Derry & Toms as well, regularly, every sale time," Miss Kirkham told her as she moved some of the shelved unused materials – art nouveau prints gently fading, the bolts of cloth like an imitation shop. Each multicoloured heap of cloth holding so much promise of parties, celebrations, picnics, dances, events that never came about, locked in a promise

Then Stella had to begin scrubbing the patterned lino floor from edge to edge. It was like working in a museum; each bolt of cloth must be valuable by now. Some might be original William Morris prints; she recognised the sumptuous Strawberry Thief pattern on one shelf.

The next week all was peace and light. Beamish had returned home.

"I waited the next night too, stayed up all night, kept the hall light on so that he could see it. And he turned up at six o'clock in the morning. He'd obviously been involved with other cats and got into a bit of a fight."

Stella could just see it all. Beamish, monocle and cane, top hat and tails, looking raffish, collar askew and with the over-bright eyes of the all-night stop-out, leaning casually against the doorpost. And Miss Kirkham, so glad to see him, gathering him into her arms, petting him, giving him something tasty to eat, putting him to bed, wiping the scratches gently, not knowing what had happened, full of questions and devotion. And all the while her own life whirled quietly away, the bought-in companion, frozen in time.

Stella knew about dealing with the same problems with a real live man, how like a cat he was, that same inscrutable triumph as the dawn chorus sang in the city trees with the same secrets kept behind his over-bright morning eyes. Miss Kirkham's life was the other extreme; you could stay safe if you did not engage emotionally with anyone. But eventually the repressed feelings would erupt and a clever cat would run away with your heart. It was a pity about those vintage Liberty's prints kept away from the world, though. They had come round in a circle and were the height of fashion now, William Morris's prints of birds in hedgerows, *The Strawberry Thief* being the best known.

The Daily Maids clients were mostly within walking distance; any house further away, their bus fare was given too. The two ladies were meticulous. Everyone worked in a position of trust. One day Stella was given the keys to a judge's house, set in a Hampstead by-way.

"You might find a list in the hall of what to do, but otherwise it's the usual, don't forget to empty the vacuum cleaner bag afterwards and all the wastepaper baskets, you know the routine." Sometimes the people had not paid by cheque and the session's money was left in the hall.

There was another place in St John's Wood she went to on Saturday mornings that was a posh version of a high-rise. So often those places had become notorious slums that this was a surprise. It showed that architecture was not necessarily the deciding factor; money was. It certainly helped that everyone was rich, and that there was an attendant, or caretaker, on duty at a desk in the hall. All the corridors were thickly carpeted; otherwise the design was exactly the same as any slum high-rises, door after door down characterless corridors after ascending in a featureless (but immaculate) stainless steel lift.

The Levines, a retired couple had a farm somewhere in Hampshire, where they went away for most weekends and left their keys at the desk. They left instructions too, like,

"Clear out the fridge, you can eat it all." This meant free chicken and chocolate dessert to take home. One weekend Stella risked having a shower in the entirely windowless bathroom. Its pink comfort, its carpeted floor was utter luxury. This was tempered with a frisson of fear in case Mr and Mrs Levine reappeared, their car breaking down, something forgotten, a sudden illness, coming in and finding her there, naked in their bathroom. She thought of various excuses to give as she used the fluffy pink towels before putting them in the washing machine and getting fresh ones out of the laundry cupboard. No excuse sounded authentic enough when faced by an angry rich Jewish business couple just arriving home.

"I felt ill. I spilled toilet cleaner on my skirt. My own bathroom is out of use. The shower started to spray over my clothes, so I thought, why not have a proper shower?"

As she went to take rubbish out to the communal chute beside the back stairs, a blue china coffee pot was there, left standing on the concrete floor. Someone had had second thoughts about sending it down the hatch, too precious to be left to crash into pieces at the bottom of the chute. It was waiting for someone like her. She took it back to the flat, putting it into her straw shopping bag and carried it triumphantly home. It became a coffee pot in its own right again, plus a random vase and sometimes a jar for long paintbrushes. There was nothing wrong with it, just a crack at the end of the spout, hardly noticcable.

Mrs Levine had to go to hospital, which left Stella and Ed the chauffeur doing all the housekeeping. Ed was better at cooking omelettes than Stella and was clearly an all-round efficient cook. He stood by the stove, and told her ruefully,

"At home I have a wife and kids. And I used to run an antique shop. It's not right, you know." Ed was put up in a B&B somewhere near, ready to drive Mr Levine to the farm in Hampshire. Other relatives kept up the visiting rota in the hospital over the weekend.

Another on the usual rota was a Mrs Emer who shared a flat with her widowed brother-in-law. A large photo of the dead sister-in-law was displayed on the mantelpiece as a memento.

Mrs Emer wanted the gigantic chandelier that dominated the dining room to be cleaned. A tall wooden stepladder was already leaning against the wall and soon Stella found herself up on the next-to-top step, cleaning a chandelier right in the middle of the Vietnam war. News had come out that the USA had started to use Agent Orange, a defoliant that came in metal orange containers to expose roads and trails used by Vietcong forces. Stella had a photo of a Vietnamese prisoner taped to her wall beside the mirror.

"We came across to England as refugees, we had nothing, nothing at all," Mrs Emer wailed to Stella, marooned up the high ladder, cleaning the chandelier with a bucket of soapy water balanced on the top step.

Stella looked across at the gigantic carved wooden cupboard, large enough to sublet as a separate flat. Mrs Emer followed her gaze and tried to recoup the story.

"Oh, we managed to get some of the furniture shipped out, just in time before the war really started." Later, going out to the bins with the rubbish and seeing the boys from University College playing cricket on spreading green, a vision of an England she was not part of, Stella came back into the flat to more misery.

Mrs Emer moaned that a sapphire had fallen out of one of her rings, inherited from her mother.

"I have looked all over the floor, it's nowhere at all, but do see if you can search too, don't hoover it up, but I think it's lost now. It was the central stone too, it's irreplaceable"

"I think it would make a slight noise, it might rattle, if it went up the vacuum cleaner," Stella said reasonably. "I'll take special care, though." Mrs Emer then went off to John Barnes department store where ladies like herself all congregated in the café for a gossip while their houses were being cleaned. Within seconds of her leaving, Stella found the sapphire on the multi-patterned fireside rug. It gave out shafts of blue light across her palm.

It must be worth quite a lot and it's here in my hand. Hatton Garden deals in gems like this. But she had no idea where Hatton Garden was and perhaps they did not buy separate stones from individuals like her. Best not to risk it? There must be forms to fill in, how it was acquired and so on and she would perhaps be identified as a type of thief. It was a definite temptation but she did not know how to carry the plan out. When Mrs Emer returned and she gave her the surprise sapphire, the lady gave her half a crown. It emphasised that Stella should have gone to Hatton Garden and risked it anyway.

Like a few of the other ladies, Mrs Emer had done the usual sixpence-under-the-armchair trick. They hid the coin dead centre under an armchair. If the sixpence disappeared, the cleaner was a thief; if it was still there, she was a cheat, not moving furniture about to clean the carpet thoroughly. They must all have learnt such tricks from their mothers surely, no one ever, ever, had mentioned this ploy at the agency as a warning. Stella would have loved to have just walked into a new place, moved the armchair, retrieved the sixpence and to have said,

"I've found the sixpence, I've found you out, I'm going to go home and you can pay me right now."

There were creative moments though – almost an entire afternoon spent under a table in Golders Green polishing a neglected parquet floor, bringing it back to life, feeding it with polish. In all places there was that moment of real pride, looking back at a room, thinking, I made that, I did that, it's all new and shining.

There were a couple where the wife reclined on the bed quite happily eating chocolates and reading Mills and Boon romances. She was like a 1930s film star in a silk nightdress; her husband was worried, though.

"Do you think you could persuade her to get out of bed? We could all have something to eat together, that would be a real step forward," he pleaded. His wife was flattered with the attention and they had lunch together of tinned soup followed by various cheeses, grapes and crackers. Stella wanted to tell the husband that his wife was suffering with absolutely terminal boredom, probably with him, but that would have been too brusque. It was a problem, then an idea occurred,

"What about a trip to the theatre? I'm sure your wife would like that, an excuse to dress up, that's what she really needs." He was delighted at this and brightened up, hurrying back to the bedroom where his wife was already hovering by the bed preparing for her afternoon nap, as she called it.

"Help yourself to a box of chocolates, as an extra thank-you," he whispered, "There's several in the kitchen cupboard, the one by the window. We get them every week with the groceries."

It was impossible to draw or sketch at work even when a house or flat was empty. But she always kept a small notebook in a pocket for any rapid lines of poetry that might occur, worried that if not written immediately, they would disappear forever. Otherwise entire days were wasted with nothing to show for her efforts. The houses re-dirtied themselves, there was no result much longer than an hour. So much of the work ordinary people did was like this; untraceable and repetitive.

Working until six in the afternoons meant that going home in the winter was a walk through dark streets or waiting for crowded buses. Snow, sleet, fog, it made no difference; flat shoes were for stomping through rough weather. Stella came out of Arkwright Mansions one afternoon after cleaning a large flat and realised that blood was starting to flood out of her, although period time had finished a few days ago.

She knew there was a public toilet across in the Finchley Road and Frognal Rail Station and she fled into the Ladies. Grabbing her cleaning apron, she managed to staunch and wipe away the signs of the flow, as the blood was already streaking down her legs to her knees. Thank goodness it was so dark, so people might not have noticed, a real hazard. Perhaps nature had intended her to have twins last period, and this was the second one making its surprise appearance. In future she must always carry a supply of tampons at all times.

Grateful for this last-minute escape, Stella washed her hands, applied fresh lipstick and went out to the platform. It was bitter cold, with flurries of snow adding to the discomfort and her hair and coat were already covered. The station porter noticed her and, as she was the only person around, he invited her into his snug office.

"I can't leave you standing there like that, the train's a few minutes yet, eight minutes easy. You can wait in my office out of the cold, here you are." He ushered her into the small room. It was like a wild animal's nest, cluttered with newspapers, lanterns, broken signs, overcoats, and two cane chairs set beside a small woodstove. The shabby chairs had lumpy cushions of an unidentifiable colour, a faded grey or the actual colour of decades of dirt. His enamel teapot and a large black kettle stood on the stove and he offered her a mug of tea. It was all quite domestic and warm. He was right out of *The Wind in the Willows*, a modern Mr Badger, the same kindliness, with his comfortable home from home. He looked as if he had been here since before the war, totally forgotten by all officials. It was quite an interruption when the train actually appeared and broke the domestic cheerfulness. It was, of course, an extra expense but it went right to South End Green and it was an instant when a bit of luxury was necessary.

Just beside the Finchley Road station there was a minute office which was an employment bureau and Stella had once gone into it out of curiosity. There was nothing better on offer than what she was already doing, except lower-grade clerical work. However, the owner, a large olive-skinned woman, perhaps Greek, leant towards Stella and said, reaching for a tray of file cards,

"We also run a marriage agency, and you would be very well advised to join my system. You are just the type of girl that the gentlemen here are looking for." She waved her bejewelled hand over the stacked cards. Then drawing a photo out, she told Stella, "This is a wonderful gentleman here, he is sincerely looking for a wife, a successful businessman, wanting to settle down, you would be very lucky to be introduced to him." A plump middle aged Indian man wearing what looked like an expensive suit smiled at any possible ladies.

Stella said she had no plans of marriage right now, thank you. It was a possible risky set-up; girls needing employment being fed into a marriage bureau system; strange coincidence.

The radio continued being a close companion. It issued various parallels to what was going on, pop philosophy at its best. The Moody Blues' *Go Now* melancholy beauty was not enough. It did not cure – it curdled her innards and hit between each thought. It held safely all the hysteria of the break-ups and loss and the black territory you were left in to navigate alone. Bus stops, lipstick, work. Their smooth yearning was unnecessary now. She was here in the very place all these songs were about. Invincible, the inside of the golden castle that everyone needed to live inside, and so many could not; a few days, weeks, and most people were cast out. Heartbreak was for others now, the outsiders; and then suddenly, banishment.

27

On the 19th October, a Tuesday, she took the day off work to commit suicide. It was her twenty-fifth birthday and she could see no way out of the repeating pattern of work, rent, love, let-down, see-sawing constantly between desire and despair. Refusing to get up to go to work responsibly, this day, she had a weekday lie-in for a change and tidied up the room in a desultory way. It did not matter much but people walking into an untidy room afterwards and talking about her was unthinkable. All papers shuffled into a drawer, rubbish taken out, mug and plate washed, bed made; perfect.

Stella walked round and round the table, round and round the room. Once, on holiday with her parents in Llandudno, they had passed a convent with a low wall. From a pathway on higher ground they could all look down on the convent grounds and see in the gardens that the nuns were walking to and fro, saying their daily office. Each had been allotted a length of ground, about ten paces each, at the end of which they turned and wheeled back on their tracks. Pace, pace, turnabout, the click of wooden rosary beads. Although it should have reminded the holidaymakers of caged animals, it did not – by a crossover of ironies it seemed the nuns were freer in their chosen limits. The holiday crowds had the duties of pleasure, tourist trails, ice creams, souvenirs, healthy climbs and fairy glens to navigate.

This was no gentle, rueful sadness, it was more like a wild beast which had her by the throat and was shaking her body, a mad dancer determined to make the marathon. Each gale of tears felt so strong that it must be the last one. Yet no sooner had she stopped, rinsed her face over at the sink and skewed up the handkerchief and gone across to make tea or open a library book or try some little stumble back to normality – each time, another wave would come to land, and tears fell through her like water through a sieve.

She thought of whatever ways there were to kill herself. Pills. It would mean going down to the Welshman's and buying several hundreds of aspirins – a couple of bottles of a hundred each should do. There had been someone in Canning Street, a sacked musician who had attempted suicide by taking aspirins, but who eventually came round, as there had not been enough pills in the bottle to manage it. How could she manage to get enough bottles without arousing suspicion? She would have to go down to the Co-op on South End Road and then try the small shop round the corner, pretending to have a headache. There were no chemist's shops nearby and anyway, here came the onslaught of tears again. What if she vomited half way through? Or it did not work and she remained rolling round the floor in agony, unable to cry for help? What to say at the hospital when 'they' brought her round? How could she ever apologise to Fiona, who would be the one most likely to find out something was wrong?

There had been enough suspicion at the hospital across the road when she had gone to outpatients with a sliver of glass stuck inside her fingernail. The nurse looked at the problem.

"How did this come about?"

"I was cleaning the floor."

"Didn't you clear away the broken glass first?"

"I didn't know it was there."

"What?"

"It was from a previous tenant, I'd moved the carpet up, you see." The nurse had gazed in unbelief at it all. An unsuccessful suicide attempt would be even worse.

Jump out of a window, then. Her own window was not high enough to do it and was set over the basement flat's patio. It could prove embarrassing to land in front of the couple downstairs' living room. A couple of broken bones, or a hip in plaster and disjointed for life. The staircase window would not open and the bathroom one only opened at the top for ventilation. Stella could not really go up to Fiona in her top room with a window over the garden and a lovely view towards the heath,

"Excuse me just a moment, Fiona, can I come into your room for a sec? It's not really a social visit because, well, really, I want to jump out of the window."

"What for?"

"I want to kill myself."

"Sit down and we'll have a cup of coffee..." And so on. No way out there, no escape; as usual, hours later they would still be sitting there, discussing, theorising dissecting, analysing, laughing, planning.

Razors. There must be some left in the little cupboard over the sink. But how was it done? Having cut the left wrist with the right hand, how did you cut the right wrist with the left hand half-severed and already gushing blood? So much mess, slippery too, and then having to sit and watch it happen, unless of course she took the aspirins first. But maybe that would not work as a combination - the aspirins perhaps making everything shaky to start with. Stella was not afraid of blood, as such, but left with half-skewered wrists and neither one thing nor the other, again, if 'they' saved her, it might mean ending up with weak wrists for life and how could she work or paint like that?

Gas would have been convenient, just roll a blanket along the bottom of the door to stop any draught of air, but again she did not have enough shillings for the meter to do it properly right now. All she would achieve would be a bad smell and perhaps an explosion. Again, a lot of apologising and explaining to do afterwards, with everyone in the house gasping for breath and exiled onto the pavement for their own safety. They would never forgive her. She could see Miss Spedding and Mrs Grint being extremely angry and even Fiona and Max and the nice couple from the top floor being puzzled.

Run under a bus. The 24s were regular but there was such a snarl-up at South End Green, with so much traffic, as well as being a bus terminus, that all that could be achieved there would be a trapped ride on the bumpers, lost shoes and a hefty fine. And the 187 going in the opposite direction took so much effort going up Pond

Street that it would be cruelty on her part to make it more difficult for the driver too. Coming down the hill would probably be quicker and easier. But he might skid, and hit someone else, plus the mess, the scene, the poor driver in court after, the blood on the road, the shock for passers-by.

Have to wait until the rush hour tomorrow and try it in central London. Or under an underground train. Or there was Waterloo Bridge, that was quite famous. But all these plans entailed getting ready, make-up and coat on – and that was impossible because she was still crying. And she might be in a different mood by then if only there was a *then* out there that could be reached. It was the present that needed to be broken more than herself, but how?

Drowning! That was it, it was easy, cost nothing and made not too much mess, perhaps you would sink and never be found. There were several ponds on the Heath, all in easy walking distance and that was settled then, decision made. The crying stopped at this, she almost cheered up with the decision made now.

This took up to the afternoon, already a dull ending to the day, the summertime hour already changed. So she went along to Mr Melbourne's bakery on South End Green and bought a large home-made apple pie, family size. It was the sort of cake she lusted after and could never afford, but today was different. Waiting for the dark, she wandered round that part of the Heath, eating bits of it, random scraps falling for observant sparrows.

If she was going to drown herself over in the ponds, it would have to be in the pitch black so that no one would notice and be dashing into the cold waters to save her. Terrible headlines in the Ham & High told of this sort of thing each summer, plus occasionally rescuers themselves even drowned too and that would be a real tragedy. Why make it difficult for everybody else; it was bad enough as it was.

She had sold a painting last year about this very situation *Night, Grass, Ponds* – about a suicide mentioned in the Ham & High. Now she was going to walk into her own painting.

The grey afternoon dragged on, eventually turning to a rain which in turn changed into sleet. It was still too early – she had gone and timed it wrongly, now people were beginning to come home from work, the sound of the buses was clear from here. To pass the next hour until the real evening set in, she called into the nearby Magdala to sit it out and wait patiently with a half of lager and lime.

The landlord, who did not like her, served her listlessly. He could not ignore her as he usually did because this time there was no one else around in the space.

The pub was deserted, just opened at five thirty, so no one she knew would be here yet and she looked around it coolly, a deserted stage set. A couple of commuters called in, quite a different type from all the people she knew from so many evenings and parties that started from here. Feeling calm and decisive, all problems solved, she enjoyed the actual drink unlike most times when it was social necessity. The theatricality of the bar showed up in this emptiness. It was the crowds in the evenings or summer Sunday afternoons that gave it life. The couple of stuffed fish in glass cases looked as bad as ever against the dark panelled walls.

And Toby walked in. He had no connection with anyone here and would not have thought she would be here; they had never been in this pub together and she hardly ever mentioned it. Torn between trying to get rid of him in order to go off and neatly drown herself as planned, she drifted into chatting with him and spending the night with him as usual back in her room. Life claimed her back.

He boasted he had a novel something to do for sex.

"Women love it," he asserted. He clambered over her and proceeded to stroke his penis in between her breasts. Nothing happened, in fact it was boring and she lay there being patient and wondering how many women told lies in order to keep hold of a man by praising his every move.

"Can't we just do it in the usual way? "she complained as they got back to normal and could relax again in enjoyable sex.

Next day she had to apologise at work for the sudden day off, trying to be truthful, resenting the day's loss of wages and the now-deferred plan. But at least there had been a rehearsal even if it had ben scuppered by Toby. His mercurial energy was everywhere, untraceable. She never thought of him as saving her life, more that he had muddled it up even further than ever.

The day off was docked from the week's wages as it was obviously not a real illness so the blocked suicide attempt meant that the apple pie was definitely a once in a lifetime luxury.

28

Calling into the Roebuck as usual one Thursday evening in early February, Stella could see Gloria was already there, sitting chatting on one of the sofas with a man who looked vaguely like a younger Prince Philip, the same fair hair and grey eyes,

"This is Andy, he's from Manchester" she introduced him, "And Stella's from Liverpool, she's an artist," and then Gloria abruptly got up and moved off to the bar, leaving them together.

They shifted together in the space. They looked at each other, eyes locked. Love at first sight. Two magnets connecting together. He said yes, he came from Manchester.

"Manchester! You know we Liverpudlians look down on you inlanders! Without us and our shipping and the canal you wouldn't even have had any cotton to sell."

"And without our canny business sense you wouldn't have had the cotton trade at all or the exports" Andy smiled. The two cities rivalled each other through the centuries.

Their lives almost tallied. They were both artists. He said he went to Manchester College of Art and then got a scholarship to the Slade. While he was a student there he started working part-time in restaurants. But working part time in restaurants had taken over.

"I turned into a chef at Père Nicholas in Chelsea and got so involved in it that I got promoted and then I used to have a restaurant in Englands Lane. We called it a bistro, really, but it didn't catch on." Stella knew it immediately. It was the one she was always too shy to go into. Walking past it last winter after work she always looked through the window, fascinated. Through the steamed-up windows there were clusters of interesting people, but it had looked a bit too expensive to risk going in. She walked past with her apron and indoors shoes in a straw basket, not exciting enough to make an entrance or able to afford a proper restaurant meal.

They almost matched in life stories, artists who got by in other occupations. Gloria did not come back; no one else counted. They left the bar long before closing time and crashed into a new life together back in her room and bed. Desire met desire, their bodies crashed together, then joined seamlessly.

It was almost dawn as he left on the Friday morning as the birds sang out all along the back gardens and the sun blazed through the long thin curtains, already bleached by decades of summer mornings. In fact it could easily have been mistaken for a summer morning right then, and not an ordinary February day.

"I've got to dash now, work's all over the place.You know, you could fit an extra floor up here, it's high enough" he said, from the comfort of the bed.

"If I had that sort of money I wouldn't be living here would I? She eyed the massive unused space above them, like unuseable life. He reached down for his clothes said no, he wouldn't be staying for coffee, must rush, and kissed her goodbye as she still lay in bed. As soon as he had gone she felt sad, as though she had done something wrong, should have dashed out, got dressed with him and sauntered along home with him in the golden morning.

The next time they met in the pub he said he was in the doghouse back at the shared flat.

"My flatmate, Ralph, went and lost his key and I wasn't there to let him in, so he had to climb up the drainpipe and climb in the back window. I've got to get back early anyway, for a lift to work. Sometimes I'm a film extra and that has an early start. It's miles outside London now, past Elstree. Other times I do market surveying, door to door with a clipboard. We have to go round suburban houses door to door to do surveys. Market Surveying is all the rage now, planning for the future advertising campaigns. And it's not just groceries, we do political surveying too. Government parties want to find out what people are thinking."

"And then they can go about changing it, or doing the opposite. At least you get to see something of the truth."

"Yes, they use the social survey information to create a new narrative, better suited to what they want to do. I don't like being part of the scheme, you know that. We are all cornered, just trying to earn a wage."

On Saturday afternoon Andy turned up at her place and asked would she like to go somewhere to look at furniture. Fittingly, it was St Valentine's Day.

"The landlord says we can have an extra wardrobe or cupboard thing for storage. We've got nowhere to hang coats or leave our shoes. So he said there's a furniture warehouse Islington way that's cheap, he's used it before. I thought you'd like to come along too." It was hardly a glamorous outing but could be interesting, their first time out together in the daytime.

The place was an eye-opener. The property was a rambling collection of sheds and outbuildings. In parts the roofing was corrugated iron, except that sometimes the sections had shifted and rainwater dripped down. The furniture itself looked as though it was dying and this was its cemetery. Ranks and ranks of wardrobes, dressing tables, chests of drawers and three-piece suites advanced across the dirty floors. In places the puddles were disguised by sacking laid out underfoot. The lighting was poor and dangerously looped electric wires hung above their heads.

"Luckily," Stella whispered to Andy, "the whole place is too damp to actually go on fire." He strode around, looking even more handsome in this incongruous background. They could be any young couple setting up house on a small budget and looking for bargains.

The furniture, however, was so miserable that it would have broken anyone's heart to take it home and have to look at it day after day. Only sandpapering, bleaching, painting it white or any colour in fact, would manage to drag this wreckage into the 1960s. It had long lost its nineteenth century smugness or respectability. It had invisible scars from First World War, the Depression, the Second World War and every disaster known to local history. None of it was antique or ever could be. And here was Andy, swashbuckling around in the midst of it all and growing better looking by the minute. His navy car length coat gave him a fashionable silhouette.

They were separated by a fleet of occasional tables and other obstacles. Stella saw visions of herself, ghostlike in several wardrobe mirrors where the silvering had decayed and an indoors grey lichen grew instead. The hidden previous owners kept their secrets in the fog.

Andy settled for a tall cupboard, not really a wardrobe and went up to the office above the main storeroom to settle the deal.

"They say they can deliver it one afternoon, that'll be OK. And I managed to get them to reduce the price a bit too." That meant they could go for scones and tea out of the money saved. There was nowhere trendy nearby, the district was as neglected as the furniture and as ripe for exploitation. A small café had several empty tables as a slight rain began. But they were both cheerful in their snatched intimacy, safe here where no one would know either of them.

A couple of months later, one evening, Andy told her he had something to tell her. As they came out of the Roebuck at closing time he said,

"Oh yes, that. I'm married, I had to tell you some time." He was married! He turned aside, talking to an unknown man after he said this, and as they all left the Roebuck, coming down the steps, Andy turned away and walked down the hill with a group of people, moving away on purpose to get lost in the after-pub companions. Stella could not go screaming after him in the crowd. She gasped and blundered off, tears blurring the way.

Stella almost bumped into Tom who was coming down Pond Street. He put his hand on her arm.

"What's wrong? Why are you crying?" Tom was large, warm and sympathetic, which made it all worse. She sobbed that the new boyfriend had turned out to be a married man.

"He's got a wife, I've only just found out."

"Look, we can't go on standing in the middle of the street here, you can't just be on your own, why don't you come back to my place? You can come back with me, give yourself a chance to cool down a bit." Tom hugged her, the big best-friend-brother. They walked off to his basement room off the High Street. By the time they got there she had mostly stopped crying and had reached the sniffing stage, followed by complete exhaustion. Tom's room was darker and shabbier than her own, but this was no time to be critical. He made some cocoa,

"I hope this milk's not gone off," and then they fell into bed, such as it was. It was a good job, she thought, that the light bulb was the lowest wattage possible, as the sheets were probably grey, judging from the smell. But at least Tom was a human being who seemed to care. He did half-heartedly try putting his arms around her, but she shrugged him off and he soon fell asleep.

They had tried a night together some time ago with disastrous consequences. His penis was too large for her and she had ended up begging him to stop. Tom said it happened all the time, he was used to it, unfortunately, and he was not going to force her about it.

Some time later Fiona told her that Tom was living with a lady doctor, someone who would have known what to do. Perhaps there was something medicinal that could be found or perhaps the woman was differently constructed and they were luckily matched. It showed that couples should have a chance to experiment together to see if they actually fitted sexually in an easy way; goodness knew what horrors some virgin brides had encountered on their wedding night through the centuries.

Andy had disappeared like the Cheshire Cat. But he appeared at her room door during the next week. Not shamefaced, not different, not able to stay away, as he admitted.

"I knew it was dangerous from the start, but I obviously couldn't tell you right then. I'd never met anyone like you."

It was impossible to break away from each other and Andy and Stella continued to meet at the pub and go back to her place and fall into each other's arms. Iron filings can't avoid the magnet. He stayed, as usual, until early in the morning but the gold was wearing off, a wife always in the background. They could not go further, nor draw away from each other. Complete stasis. She theorised – why have to change where she went, just to avoid him? It is impossible to stop loving or fancying someone when they are standing right beside you and being as charming as ever.

Was Andy a cheery deceiver or was he trapped in an awkward and hermetically sealed marriage, desperately looking for escape? Stella could see it that way, but being the fire escape was no fun. There was no way out, except outplacement itself. You watched a film or a theatrical play all too conscious of the doors either side of the screen or stage marked *Exit*.

She had strayed into uncharted territories and now she was lost. The heart could skip all the back alleys and sideroads but sometimes fell into swamps and meres. The

Monday morning world, however, had to do with fact, and here there was a big wedding ring somewhere. Romance and fact, emotion and reality, constantly at war and that was exactly where she was trapped.

"I can't break away though. If I was free you wouldn't be." He said this as he unzipped the back of her dress. It was a fractured proposal of marriage. It was easy, their bodies knew each other completely and their hunger for each other was more than greediness.

"Wake me up again if you want some more," Andy said as he crashed to sleep after their fireburst. Stella always felt bereft the instant after, yes it was like a sudden death, but there was always the promise of renewal.

There was nothing sexier in the mornings as she struggled putting on her bra and Andy leant up from the pillow and casually slipped the hooks together. She would feel his hands on her through the day, along with every other part of her body. They could not break away from each other.

Later, Fiona said she saw him with a baby in a pram on the Heath. She had words of wisdom to impart as usual.

"First they break themselves, then they break you, or they break you because they are broken themselves, whichever you prefer."

Andy said he had no money the last Christmas and he did not have enough to buy Marjorie a decent present. Stella knew that if there was enough love, an ordinary bottle of shampoo or a bar of scented soap would be enough. But obviously if he had something to hide, he was trying to make up for something – like the loss of the café – things had to be different.

"So I went to a gambling club and I won enough to get her a proper Christmas present," he said smoothly. Playing cards were also known as the devil's playthings and gambling casinos were dangerous places, but Andy was always ultra-confident. And, he won. Obviously Marjorie expected something special. He said a while ago that when the café had ended – he never explained why – she blamed him.

"Marjorie held it against me. She'd got used to us raking in eighty quid a week and it's all been a bit of a comedown since the way we lived then." The disappointed wife, permanently aggrieved, a daily reminder of his defects. "I got a job in market research in a hurry, to plug the gap. Don't know where it's going to lead, it was a dash, to pay the rent, just to give us a basic regular income to work on. And of course, we had to get somewhere to live, after having to give up the flat over the café." He never mentioned where Ralph had come into their lives and Stella really did not want to know.

Stella remembered night-times in winter walking past that interesting café in England's Lane, steam running down the windows, groups huddled at tables, all interesting looking and young. She was far too shy and poor to chance going in. To think that she would ever be girlfriend of the owner was strange.

Andy had been kind enough to employ Matt as a washer-upper when he needed the money. So they were all linked, without realising it, but that was the only time he mentioned any of the poets. It was ironic that the apparently aimless poets were on the way up just as Andy was on the fall. Their worlds did not join at all now.

The baby, Cristopher, was not enough ballast to keep things improving. That was why Andy was here with her. It was a pattern duplicated from pub to pub, party to party.

She tried to work it out. He wants his wife at home and he wants a girl from the outside world. Then he doesn't really want his wife and neither does he want the girl either. He uses the girlfriend to give excitement and escape and the wife for the rest, behind closed doors, Christmas, New Year, Easter, birthdays and Bank Holidays. A girlfriend adds spice, excitement, danger, the beginning again, running the Grand National from the start each time, all the wide possibilities, being reborn. And the wife becomes reassurance, safety, home, somewhere to go to when he feels ordinary again. Because eventually he becomes unavailable – even to himself - and that's when everybody wants him.

And in the middle of it all is his little son, growing like a sunflower whether he likes it or not, a hostage to fortune or failure.

Mornings started with the half-seven alarm and leaning out of bed reaching the Perdio radio on the floor beside the bed, to find what Bob Dylan had to say that day. Beatles, Rolling Stones, Smoky Robinson.

In a gesture to what was really going on in the world, a picture of Vietnam prisoner was stuck up over the mantelpiece. A protestor was in the High street most

Saturdays outside Woolworth's with a petition against the Vietnam war. A polite list of people's names versus complicated international disagreements and a profitable arms industry needed more wars and more people to be killed. She signed his petition and wrote a poem on the subject; every poet was doing the same, plus song writers and artists, all the voices of the concerned, who could see the dreadful results without having any motive. They also, though, it had to be admitted, advanced their careers by inventing new protest material. No one could disagree except arms manufacturers who did not buy poetry.

Tom Jones singing '*It's Not Unusual*' whirled around, attaching itself to the situation. Andy was at the centre and yet also totally far out of orbit. It was difficult to work out if the pop songs helped or merely prolonged any agony.

One evening a tall man came and joined them both in the pub. Andy and herself were sitting on the same sofa where they had originally met some months ago. Andy introduced him as his flat-mate. Ralph came and sat beside her. His eyes ate her up. He was the most sex-hungry man Stella had ever encountered. He also, unfortunately for him, looked like any woman's idea of a rapist. Extremely tall, his long dark hair and beard disguised his face; in fact he was the image of Rasputin. A brown mac, tightly belted, gave the unfortunate impression he wore nothing underneath, though blue jeans poked out beneath. He wore sandals with no socks even in the cold April weather and his pale toes were as long as fingers. There was nowhere about him that was pleasant to look at. As he sat down beside her his extra-long legs had to adjust and refold like a seaside deckchair. She looked at Andy, who was oblivious to all this, or pretended to be. Ralph's tongue was almost hanging out.

Andy was changing tack these days. He had started to go on more and more about not being free, that in fact Ralph had more right to her than himself – Ralph was free and had more right to her.

"No wonder," Stella remarked, irritating him. There was no clue how Andy and Ralph had met. The Slade or a café? He did not mention art and was too ungainly to be a waiter or a chef. It came to a head when Andy suggested right then that she would be better off as Ralph's girlfriend. Ralph was 'free' Andy said yet again as Ralph came back from the bar with more drinks.

"What? No wonder he's free! He's totally repulsive! You want to play pass-the-parcel? I'm the only one who decides who I get involved with and nobody else!" The love that existed between them was abruptly hitting the buffers without explanation.

It was difficult to have a proper row sitting down and in public like this. Plus Stella did not want to cause a scene in her favourite and most useful pub. The Roebuck was far too valuable to be barred from; that was unthinkable. It was a community centre, well disguised. People would stare. And Ralph was right there listening to all this.

Andy shifted on the sofa and brightened up,

"I've got an idea, I know, what about we go back to the flat and I cook you all something?" Stella realised that this was going to be their funeral service but was intrigued at how it would all end. "You'll have to pretend to be Ralph's girlfriend and we all met by accident," he encouraged. At last she would see what was behind the scenes and find out the real address. Truth sometimes came out too late to be of use.

By now Stella was sleepwalking into the situation but did not want to go back to her room alone yet. Any distraction, however brutal, was welcome. The tears would come later, about Tuesday or Wednesday. Nature had always given her this delay, an animal instinct giving enough time to get away from the danger area before being able to let the real grief out of its Pandora's box. The one word that had not been said was the main one – Marjorie. The two women would be meeting at last, barrier to barrier, with Andy in the middle and Ralph hovering like an unnecessary midwife. They walked down the hill together and crossed the road by the Classic Hampstead Playhouse on the corner.

And here they were at last. It was that near. It had been, all along. Their entire world was held in these couple of streets as if it was any northern town. And their lives circled round an amazingly few pubs. It was a shock to see the truth of their lives exposed like this. Only two pubs, the Roebuck and the Magdala. Stella had one random other, the Rosslyn up the hill. Only three in all of London. The Railway they hardly ever used, or the George or the White Lion at the corner of Fleet Road. It became immediately obvious why Andy would not be using the White Lion as it was much too near.

The secret flat turned out to be over the newsagents at the end of South End Green. No wonder

Andy had never wanted her to walk down the street with him – the bay window above the shop had a wide-span view of all approaches. Marjorie, perhaps up early with the baby, would have easily been able to see them. The side door was discreetly hidden round a corner and up the stairs they went. The brown wardrobe they had chosen together on St Valentine's Day stood on the landing, an orphan with a new home, like a reproach or a souvenir. The entire flat was a vision of dark brown paint, something left over from the nineteen-forties when post-war colours were limited. Dark landlord's type of forlorn furniture, the exact kind Stella had seen in that warehouse with Andy, made the living room depressed.

And sitting at the dining table, surrounded by piles of paper, was Marjorie. She was listening to the radio, some music station on low, because of the baby. Red hair that could have been flaming and luscious hung lank and greasy round her shoulders. No lipstick, mascara, earrings, no jewellery except a wedding ring. No engagement ring glinting. No stockings, white bare legs, flowered cotton dress and navy cardigan. There were traces of who she must have been once, but Stella remembered Andy's only bitter comment, that Marjorie had never recovered from the loss of the café and their eighty pounds a week. Andy never said what had caused the café to cease trading. She had resented their come-down in life. Anyone who had to live with Ralph in their spare room had massive grounds for grievance, Stella thought, giving as genuine a smile as she could while being introduced as Ralph's new girlfriend.

They sat at the table, Stella feeling overdressed with black silk gloves and clutch handbag, new grey coat and navy suede shoes, perfume, earrings and full make-up. She felt tarty in these circumstances and even more so when Marjorie asked would she like to see the baby. She could hardly say no. Going into the small bedroom, she was extremely aware of the double bed cramped beside the cot. It was all so downtrodden and featureless. The bed was neatly made and the bedclothes tucked in at the sides like a hospital bed, a blue-grey coverlet, the colour of depression. It was the most unsexy bedroom Stella had ever seen.

Marjorie hovered above the baby and pulled down the edge of the blanket. Fair-haired and plump, the sleeping baby was perfection, the child that anyone would like to have. He slept on, building and replicating cell after cell, busy growing as he lay there. Stella made some remark about babies being completely perfect (again) and backed out of the room before anything was mentioned about babysitting and they all fell into a trap. As it was, Stella felt as near to a tart as she had ever done, confronted with plain motherhood and a sleeping child versus her own Saturday night dressed-up persona. She had stuffed the new black silk gloves into her handbag but kept her coat on.

In the meantime Andy had enthusiastically begun to fry rice, for reasons of his own, a party trick perhaps. Or perhaps he had promised it because there was nothing else to offer in the flat. He stood at the ancient gas stove that stood in the corner of the kitchen-living room like a magician ready to produce a rabbit out of a hat. Swish and swirl and now there were four plates of fried golden rice. He set them down with a flourish and Marjorie came across to join them.

I am not drunk, I am not seeing things, Stella thought, but this is surreal. She also had to talk to Ralph as though they knew each other well, which was difficult, as this was their first real conversation ever. Chatting was out of the question. He could not do it naturally. Ralph sat even nearer now, moving his chair, as Stella tried to think of something to say that did not sound too false. He, in turn looked as though he wanted to eat her, but had to make do with a plate of fried rice instead. She spoke about a party at Rita Rave's and the other one where the grand piano took up most of the space. He looked deeply into her eyes in his best Rasputin imitation and managed a word or two. He still looked like a rapist even here indoors at home eating a plate of fried rice at midnight with his flat-mates.

How on earth did Marjorie cope with this set-up on a daily basis? The thought of using the same bath as him (in spite of all the shared bathrooms Stella had ever used as she progressed throughout London) would be disgusting. Andy continued to pirouette at the stove, producing more fried rice. There was nothing else in the room except basic furniture, table, chairs, sofa and the other table piled with papers that Marjorie was listlessly working on.

"It's market research on mayonnaise" she explained. "We have to fill in the results for the team at headquarters to investigate the public's choices. The researchers visit various districts and go from house to house asking people what they think about various products. This pile of forms makes up the latest results." Andy hardly talked and soon there was nothing else to continue with. The space between them grew. As soon as she could, Stella said she would be going now, nice to meet you, thanks for the surprise meal, and started to walk to the door. Ralph accompanied her, downstairs to the front door, playing the part of the boyfriend. Andy and Marjorie faded away. Stella managed to get in front going down the stairs and open the Yale lock before Ralph could make a lunge at her.

"Goodnight, then," she said loudly for the benefit of Marjorie upstairs, and turned quickly up the road. On the walk home she thought how Andy had never talked about anything to do with art, no favourite artist, no mention of paintings he had done, no friends who had entered exhibitions, no pictures on his own walls and definitely no trained response to her own paintings, as from an experienced artist. He had never remarked on any of the latest ones stacked on the mantelpiece.

Perhaps, now it looked that all the cards had fallen down, he had never been to any art college at all and had always been in catering. It might have all been a false image. What had they talked about all those times? It was all gone, like a mist evaporating. So they were not twin spirits at all. And who in their right mind would have Ralph as a best friend? Andy had never talked about anyone else he knew, whereas her own conversation dripped with names, places, brand new gossip, what happened last week. No use asking those questions now, it was all too late. He had been so good at deceiving and dancing on the spot. The secret gambler, too, that was another facet.

"Knockout," he was always saying that. Did he say once that a painting was knockout? Or was it just a passing joke? Now that it was over, Stella could not remember one conversation they had ever had, it had all been such a whirlwind all the time.

And as she slowly walked home up the hill, Stella remembered another part, that Andy had said he was also a film extra. The bits did not fit, except he was good-looking and an obvious choice. Perhaps he did some market research while sitting round a film set.

Painful goodbyes like this were never said properly, out loud, and no real explanation was given, and here was another one of them. However, Andy turned up at her door a few evenings later.

"I couldn't keep away. It's all a mess, really." He told her later in the pub that Marjorie suspected something after the grand evening visit to the flat for the fried rice.

"You gave it away, mentioning that party at Rita Rave's. She said you were good looking too." It was irrelevant now, but she was as sorry for Marjorie's pain as well as her own. She already had a large red painting and here it was later, *'Song for Nellie Bligh'* the innocent woman involved in the Frankie and Johnny drama, failing marriages that needed a third person to support them along. He had to keep lying for the past few months and was sadly relieved it was all out in the open now, all the mess. At least Marjorie's silences now had real material to lean on.

It was impossible to stop loving someone merely because they said it was time to finish. Emotions were messy and did not work according to a timetable. She remembered Andy saying

"If I was free, you wouldn't be," and took it as a roundabout proposal. The whirlwind of their feelings was going to take a long time to subside. It was all found in the latest pop songs; Tom Jones and '*It's Not Unusual*' remained both balm and irritant. Slowly they unravelled, there was only sex left, with no future in it at all. And then Andy did not call round and did not appear in the Roebuck. Perfect. Stella could go round all the likely local four pubs, patrolling a round like a security guard. Or she could go and ring their bell and call for Andy direct, risking meeting either Marjorie or Ralph each time. He was utterly out of reach, not even where he worked had ever been named. Market research covered so many possibilities, all untraceable. It was as if all of that whirlwind had never existed.

29 Jacques appeared later that summer.. He was some kind of decorator and turned up in the Roebuck now and again. How they met was a mystery; probably, as usual, an introduction by Gloria.

"She ought to run an agency, she'd make a real profit at ten per cent introduction fees," Fiona said.

For reasons unknown, although Jacques was a builder and decorator, he was always running out of money and Stella, also untraceably, always had spare pound or ten shillings. This was in fact her random savings, a note stuffed under the carpet that saved fussing about at the Post Office savings counter. She also, as a safety measure, had a folded one pound note secured into the hem of her coat. Stranded somewhere and needing a taxi had to be catered for. Once she had put a folded pound note into her shoe, only to find at the end of an evening that it had got worn to a frazzle at the edges and had become almost no longer legal tender. But stuffed along a hem, it was quite safe and ready for extreme moments. The glandular fever aftermath was still whirling round: rent and food, rent and food, always have some backup. And always plan for the taxi home, if necessary.

Jacques was always quick to repay, which was what kept their alfresco system going. Once she had dashed back from the pub to get extra money one night when Toby suggested an extra drink, but had run out of money. He had then insisted on buying her a glass of gin, which she did not need and refused to drink and so he had merrily thrown the entire glass of gin over her, spilling all down her coat. A few days later, having forgotten the incident, she could not work out where the money had gone to, thinking someone had managed to work out her haphazard banking system.

But Jacques was different. She guessed that he was probably going off to a betting shop – that would explain the quick need and the equally quick repayment.

In return Jacques came round one evening to ask her about doing some work for him, proper paid work.

"I've just finished decorating a small church out in a village past Elstree and I wondered if you would come and clean it up for me before the place is opened again. There's bits of paint splattered and sawdust, wood shavings, plaster, things I couldn't help doing, that sort of thing. The place needs the benches cleaned and the floor scrubbing. Could you do that, say, Saturday?"

Stella was intrigued at this and said certainly, Saturday afternoon would be fine. He said he would throw in a snack at a country pub on the way back, plus a couple of pounds. They bumbled along country lanes in his van. He produced a handful of large keys and pushed the heavy doors open.

It was strange to enter a church that was not being used. Even in its empty state it still exuded a sanctified air. This contrasted with the actual smell of new paint. The entire place startled with its whiteness. Summer light filtered through the stained glass windows, splashing wild colours across the floor and pews. In the vestry she found there was a mop and bucket and some rough floor cloths and Jacques produced a brand-new scrubbing brush. But there was nothing romantic about being on all fours scrubbing paint blobs off acres of tiled floor and then the beautiful marble of the sanctuary. The faint blue veins showed up through the white grey of the true smooth marble. This part was creative and interesting to do.

"It's like painting in reverse, taking signs and blotches away all the time. That's why I like cleaning. It's the opposite of what I'd be doing otherwise." He knew exactly what she meant.

"I've heard the same thing from other women artists, I've found they make the best cleaners. Do you find that if you tell men in Hampstead that you're a painter, that they tend to jump up and down for half an hour in protest?" Jacques smiled mischievously.

"Yes. They do, they get really upset, even hostile about it, they say a woman can't possibly do anything creative. We are not supposed to have any artistic drive at all. It's like something out of D.H Lawrence, only the male's got the impetus and women can only create babies. And that's supposed to keep us totally satisfied. So I don't mention it any more if they ask what I do, just say shop assistant or cleaner. It's safer."

"That's a good idea. Keeping your powder dry, sort of."

Jacques was married and had two children, but had never mentioned his wife. This time he started to talk about her,

"She's a very intelligent woman, she's doing a further degree in sociology while she teaches history at a private school. It is not easy between us, we married young and we have developed in different directions. But our two daughters are a wonder, yes, we have produced two lovely young women, we are proud of them. You might get invited to dinner after this." Stella was confused, but an invitation was an invitation, something to be accepted. He went on, saying further how they were often at the brink of leaving each other or at least he was always on the brink of going. "You have to have respect for each other, whatever is going on. You still lay the table for breakfast even if you are planning to leave them that day." It sounded as if this was a reoccurring pattern. Stella was intrigued.

The day's work ended after six o'clock and they had a pie and chips on the way back. The invitation for Sunday lunch duly followed during the week and Stella got ready to meet the mystery wife. And mystery she certainly was. Pauline was blonde, tall, quiet and posh. Standing beside Jacques no one would have thought there was any connection between them at all. Jacques was wild, uncouth, just this side of dirty and unkempt. His clothes were shabby, whereas Pauline was wearing a trim navy blue dress with a pink cardigan and long pendant earrings, lipstick, face-powder and a hint of perfume. Her blonde hair was coiled in a neat chignon with no tendrils hanging down, perfect. The daughters were quietly friendly and also reasonably well dressed, as though they belonged to a different family completely from Jacques. In fact they all veered towards the neat and subdued.

The flat was on the first floor of an Edwardian mansion and all their rooms led off a square hall. Pauline produced a surprising Coq au Vin with silky mashed potatoes in a separate covered dish . But the dessert was genuine Angel Delight, butterscotch flavour, which brought back memories of Brixton days when Stella more or less lived on it, making it first thing at getting back home after work.

After the meal, Jacques said,

"I've got something for you here somewhere, about poetry stuff."

Jacques went into a bedroom across the hall, leaving the door open. She knew already they slept in separate rooms and through the open doorway Stella could see there were newspapers on the bed, it was covered with them as if they were actual bedsheets. It looked as though the room had nothing else in it, as he brought out the magazine he had promised her.

"Here, I found this, ICA Bulletin, it's got all the latest stuff that you're interested in." It held most of the poets' names, all neatly collected together in one of their performances.

When Jacques called in again to borrow some money, Stella said it was surely strange that he kept calling round like this, what would his wife think it implied?

"Oh, don't worry, if I was going to run off with you, we'd already be in Dublin or somewhere like that where it's a different jurisprudence. I think you need a guru even though you don't know the word *guru*. Your headmistress, teacher, neighbour, colleague, aged relative or the old age pensioner up the road who grows wonderful night-scented stocks. That sort of person. The sort who knows the woolly parts, who's been through all that. Not information knowledge, not even that, they're cleverer than you. Sometimes they're even stupid. But they've got this store of *something* and you need it. That's who you're looking for. I'm just part of it." Here was another version of Chester, even if far more benevolent. All these men wanted to remake her in another image, all so dissatisfied with the original.

30 The poets were staging a grand reading at the Royal Albert Hall. St Pancras Town Hall had obviously been a stepping-stone, this was the real thing.

Everyone knew it was going to happen, arranged quickly and news spread like a forest fire. Newspapers were irrelevant, they all knew each other and it scattered across London and further without trace. American poets were going to appear. Poetry was suddenly worth investing in.

Stella decided against it, having too many gripes against all of the poets. Without even knowing the line-up, she knew there would be no women reading, perhaps not even Stevie Smith. Ginsberg was in town; the lads clustered round, wanting a sprinkling of the stardust.

Plus, as usual she would be expected to pay full ticket price and be ignored as they began the transition into being famous. Trying to get into behind the scenes would just be an embarrassment. Even current girlfriends would be in the background, not needed in the photos or the interviews. Like any pop-star, a man needed to be seen as single in order to keep his attraction. And there was always the male loyalty, almost homosexual, they closed ranks against women without realising that was what they were doing. There would be a full report in the International Times later to see what had really happened.

When she had eventually accepted that the third affair between Matt and herself was over, Stella had sent him a batch of her poems as a sign she was fed up and when they met accidentally at the Tally Ho jazz session one Sunday afternoon, Matt said,

"I got your poems" (*miracle of the post*). "They were quite good, very good, in fact. But for God's sake, don't try and get into the scene, because there's not much money to go round and we already need anything we can get. It's bad enough as it is without more competition."

It was like being the girlfriend of a jazz-player and telling him she played saxophone.

So hearing about the coming Royal Albert Hall event, she decided it was easier to stay at home and listen to Radio Caroline until it shut down at 8p.m, followed by a short visit to the Friday night pub, a quiet aftermath of the week and then home to bed nice and early.

Sometime after midnight Toby crashed into the room (she must have opened her room door half asleep; the front door was often left open) wild with excitement.

"It was marvellous! You weren't there! You missed it! Everyone was there! Ginsberg! Ferlinghetti! Corso! And Adrian Mitchell and us!" Each word was a wild exclamation. He looked round the silent room. "I need something to eat. Have you got any bacon and eggs, something like that? I'm ravenous." He danced around, raw electricity as Stella stood there in her nightdress being calm and plain. She looked round at the cupboard.

"I've got some Weetabix and milk, if you'd like." It was half past twelve.

"No, no," he protested, still as high as a kite. "I need proper food. Put your clothes on, I know somewhere that's still open and we can get something." Caught in the slipstream of his galloping enthusiasm, she was soon in her green coat and stuffing a purse and the keys into the pockets. It was still a warm night, but it might be colder later.

He took her up to the main road, past the taxi rank.

"Where are we going? Camden Town?" She knew of Pano's café where coffee was still only fourpence, but it was still quite a walk from here and it would definitely be closed right now.

"No, we're going to hitch somewhere," And he stepped out into the road, telling her to put her arm out. Sure enough, a car drew up and Toby said to the driver, an ordinary middle-aged man, that they wanted to get northwards. They were told to hop in the back and in no time Toby was telling the intrigued driver that they were coming back from a wedding party and had missed the train to Watford. Stella was amazed at the story and all its embellishments, how Toby had gone to school with the groom and how they had not had much to drink.

When the driver dropped them near Pinner, Stella questioned him about the wedding story, where had all that come from?

"Oh, you have to give them a story. That's what they need, they wouldn't have stopped otherwise. They stop because they need something only the hitcher can give them. It's a contract of sorts, story for travel. We've cheered him up no end now, he'll go home happy he's met a nice young couple hitching back from a wedding."

"Where are we going?" She looked round the silent street. Not even a prowling cat.

"Watford." That silenced her. They managed two more lifts, the wedding story growing details that even Stella herself started to add, and they were deposited by a lorry driver at a café set beside the main road. He said it was his regular drop-off, they were lucky to have met him, what a coincidence.

Inside the café it was as normal as an ordinary afternoon, except for the exotically-dressed group of teenagers loitering near the juke box and the wan-skinned look of people who looked as though they never saw sunlight. It was more like a happy mental home serving a choice of breakfasts right now. Stella was not hungry, but decided on a coffee and a bacon sandwich, while Toby ordered a full English breakfast, enough to last two days for an ordinary person. He would never put on weight; his mercurial character burnt up any fat before it had a chance to settle. As she suspected, he had only a few coins to show and she ended up paying for most of it, still fascinated with the night people scattered amongst the regular haulage workers. He burbled on about the influence of William Blake and experimental works.

It would take a heap of money to catch up with books by all the poets he mentioned, if one took it seriously, but tonight had really been a massive party. At least seventeen poets had taken part, all men, Stella guessed. Heaven only knew where they all were right now, or what state they would be in. Of all of them, Stevie Smith would be the only one safely tucked up in bed at home probably because she had not been invited either.

She suddenly felt tired and as he had cleared his plate happily, they began the run back to Hampstead. Obviously they only had to ask around the tables of the normally-dressed transport workers for a lift back into London. This time the story changed that they were going back into Hampstead after a wedding in Abbots Langley, where they had missed their lift. He went through this so effortlessly that Stella suspected he had done this trip before. She asked,

"So, where have we actually been? What was the name of that place?" The lorry driver laughed at this innocence.

"You don't know? It's bloody famous, it's the Busy Bee, everybody knows it." As he was bound for the markets in Covent Garden he was able to drop them quite near Hampstead Heath so it was just a short walk back as the summer dawn broke. Of course, Toby did not have to wake up and she left him sleeping as she dressed for an extra shift of work in the sunny Saturday morning, astonished at what they had done in the night. She had just enough money to last the week after their exploit.

He turned up on Friday evening again. He was critical of her paintings while managing not to look at them at all.

"Of course the trouble with you is that you've never left art school," Toby said, dismissing the past and the present and probably her future. It was as if he did not want to admit that the pictures existed or that she wanted to do something other than being a shop assistant, waitress, office clerk or cleaner.

He told her that when he was in the mental home, he said that once they discovered he was a poet, they had given him a typewriter. For over a fortnight he had just sat there producing enough for a book. Food and drink regularly supplied, it was like winning the prize of a writer's residency.

"So how did you get that?" she asked, amazed.

"Oh, I wasn't crazy, just exhausted, I turned up at the doctors after not sleeping for a couple of nights and he sent me off to this sort of stately home for them to observe me. It was like a kind of Butlins, but with crazy people scattered round. I knew it was a good chance to do some uninterrupted writing and come out with a complete manuscript and a bottle of pills. The Social looked after the rent too, so it was all a good move, you could say." Stella was jealous as all this time she had been going off to work and any idea of getting a typewriter was out of the question so far. Her poems were a mere clutch of papers stuffed into a drawer haphazardly with various notebooks.

But right now even he was working in a plumbers' warehouse. The employment people had got hold of him. His madness was not serious enough to be an excuse for not working, apparently. Toby said he was surprised at the almost exotic names for the various fitments and pipes. Of course these new words could be blended into his poetry and make it exciting. Plus he could take notes as he worked, or even take some labels or information leaflets home and scour them for something out of the ordinary.

"Look at this!" Toby drew out a list from his pocket.

Push-fit elbow	Threaded Coach bolts
Flow-fit fittings	Coach bolts bright zinc
Straight Couplers	Blue-Tip Concrete Screwbolt
Stop–ends	Penny washers
Eye bolt steel	Easyfix Hex nuts bright
Large flat washers	Packers and shims

"All I've got to do is just to mix that lot up, and the poem will just write itself! It's surreal, the guys who thought up these names didn't know what geniuses they were. At the very least, I can write it all down as a found poem, but it's better if it's shoved round a bit, make it more original." He was delighted. "And d'you know what? That's what Coleridge did too, he said he went to Davy's lectures on human physiology to increase his stock of metaphors. That's what he said when they asked why he attended so many of the lectures." Stella wondered if a selection of poems on plumbing would hit the right note in this century.

"The problem is that there's a line that won't go away, I've got to use it somewhere –'the roses are quiet they have nothing to say.' But I can't stand all that nature poetry stuff."

There was nowhere where these poets learnt their craft; it was an accidental inclination, which was why they clustered together like some mediaeval brotherhood. And brotherhood it certainly was; apart from Stevie Smith there was no female involved except as something to screw or give inspiration, often confused by the women concerned as being the same thing.

There were so many ways of seeing things and so many of them running about too.

After he had gone, among the clutter on the desk she found a scrap of paper from her notes at college, with some scribbled lines.

Painters' Notes (from a lecture probably, not a book)

...are affected by perspective. The mind readjusts the retinal image of sizes. The judgement of real size and shape is always of more importance than the apparent size

of the retinal image. The apparent contraction of space does not worry the beholder. The rivalry between mind and eye image is a problem to painters, however. Few have used literal linear perspective. 1) The convergence of lines to a vanishing point makes a hole in the picture. They are dynamic and draw all other lines with them. 2) The kind of space, however, that a designer sees when he looks through his canvas, the volume of space, is different from the space that a painter depicts.

31 Mice. It had to be. She woke up, about the middle of the night, hearing a slight rustling in the pillow. Moving across to the edge of the bed, the sound was muffled – had she imagined it? And that was the first night she had what she later called 'mice in the pillow.' It went on for several months, on and off, startling and bizarre each time. Each time she thumped the stuffing and replaced the pillow, only to hear the same infinitesimal sound yet again. It went on all night. In the mornings she would open the pillowcase (washed more or less weekly at the launderette) and look inside. An innocent plain, lumpy pillow remained as ordinary as any pillow could be in the plain daylight. Nothing whatever was moving about inside it.

She was going mad. But months later it happened to Fiona too, who went to the doctor's about it, being far more pragmatic and brisk.

"The doctor said it happens to a lot of women who are 25, it's almost normal, he said it's probably worry, that's all. It's stress related. It's all to do with the life we lead and it's how we react." It was reassuring that even Fiona was being affected, and by coincidence the episode disappeared then, as if the imaginary mice had galloped upstairs and taken up residence in Fiona's place instead.

But there were more mad women about who were picking up on stress and being written off as truly, well, *mad.* In the Ham and High that week, there was a report that a madwoman had gone all along Frognal, attacking parked cars with a hammer. Police had been called and she was taken away to stop her outbreak and promptly sedated. There were many mad people around Hampstead; the Heath probably drew them to its centre, looking for solace in its spread of consoling green. But Stella thought the woman attacking cars was absolutely right, it was anyone sane's response, to react to the metal monsters cluttering up the roadway and blocking pavements. The woman had been screaming when they dragged her away. The stuff of suffragettes, probably a century ago.

But on this topic she was too early. It would be years before they would admit the toxic fumes poisoned babies' blood. But by then the woman herself would be on pills and her own system ruined completely too. Sometimes the totally mad pointed the way long before the rest of society picked up a whiff of the truth. They got to the pain first, before it had a feasible name or a cure.

It got worse. Stella woke suddenly one night as a black dog was coming through the window. Evil itself oozed across the room like a tide of mud. It was also engulfing like something hungry, avid to encroach, devour. Stella was just about able to say the name 'Jesus' to stave it off, a reverse blasphemy. It took all her strength to say the name once. The black dog grew larger and embodied a hunger that nothing would cure, wanting to bring her into its maw, until she could manage to say Jesus's name in a stronger and louder way.

At what point does forgiveness turn into supine acceptance of evil, she had read that only last week and here was a profound example. She was sinking into a mud that was gradually sucking her down. Sleaze grew infinitesimally until you could not get out of its danger area. Avoid getting into more of the same stuff, days, weeks, months of it.

32

She had to have a better plan. Too much had gone wrong and it was time to get to grips with whatever would give her some advantages and a modicum of safety in this sexual jungle

Only a week ago a thick green gloop had started to drip out of her innards. Trying to find out more before approaching the doctors with anything so embarrassingly personal, she thought of going to the library. It turned out it was probably gonorrhoea. It said symptoms developed within two weeks of being infected, though sometimes it did not appear until many months later. No help there, then. Half of women and one in ten men did not get any symptoms; other men got a discharge from the penis. The main news was that it was more common in people under 25, and men who had sex with men and people who live in large cities. Anybody in the last three months might be at risk of infection. All rather chancy then. Another medical volume said 'Symptoms begin in men within first two to five days of infection and for women within ten days.'

Women could get a fever, pain on passing urine or during sex or bleeding between periods or heavy periods or pain in abdomen or pelvis. Or, or, it all went on, piling on various possibilities. No wonder men like Rutger became sterile if the disease could lay so secret and do its damage at leisure.

On the weekend, Fiona from upstairs would call in and they discussed their current goings-on and plan the next week, inquests and forecasts combined. "What do other women do?" Stella asked in one of their usual natters.

Fiona said,

"You should go to the Marie Stopes clinic, it's in the middle of town, I did." In fact Fiona had covered much further territory in a neat path and could look back at her with pitying eyes. A fiancé, a ring, contraceptive appointments and the open road. There was a Marie Stopes clinic in Whitfield Street and so it was easy to call in for an interview right after work and get some contraceptive help. Time to get business-like about all these problems. Too much emotion whirling around, causing the mice in the pillow and the black dog entering through the glass window panes. Here was dry ground, logic at last.

That Monday lunchtime Stella almost ran into the Marie Stopes Clinic to make an appointment. The building had that mixture of medicine and homeliness which societies manage when they are trying to make friends with the public for something eventually subversive. There was no methylated spirits smell but Country Life appeared, in its magic way, amongst the magazines like any doctor's waiting room.

Stella felt dishonest about being here. It was so against her own code. But Fiona's pity (and triumphant handbag.) combined with the hiatus of the past week and former times was too much; enough to drive her into this foreign place. To be so scientific about future unplanned moments seemed a crime to her; surely the very value was in the accidental, the test of feelings. The number of men she had said no to – did that not count? A life of going out armed with pills, caps, creams and pessaries looked like opening a shop about it, separating life from blood by inserting objects in between.

"We could see you after work this afternoon, we're not too busy." The receptionist gleamed through her little window. The waiting room had some quite young girls in it, sitting around lackadaisically. Someone loves someone some time. Toby had said he had been with seven girlfriends already, all disappeared now. These girls sat, waiting. Who was right, them or her? Who had given in, who was winning or losing? Did it matter?

Getting the 24 bus back to Tottenham Court Road, to call in casually clean involved dashing home and having a rushed bath and then getting a return bus after six o'clock.

The lady doctor was, as usual, white-uniformed and nice. But the crisp whiteness sent out messages of 'don't trust me. I may be on the other side.'

She was.

"Well, you don't look twenty-five," was the doctor's first reaction.

"That's not really why I'm here. I need some contraceptive because none of the men I encounter use any condoms and I'm constantly afraid of getting pregnant. Men are so complicated and there are so many deceptions and I'm tired of being misled and let down." The doctor looked puzzled.

"So how would contraception help?"

"It would give me some leeway. I want to be able to make decisions properly, not just on the hop all the time. When I can see that the relationship is fading out and they are going to get rid of me, I don't fight it because I'm too frightened of getting pregnant this time and being left pregnant if the affair goes on any longer without any contraception. Then, after a gap, I meet someone new and it starts all over again."

It seemed perfectly obvious to Stella – why else would any woman be here? "I want something that gives me some power in the situation, some safety and not just risking it all the time. None of them ever have a condom and they always make jokes about them, about wearing Wellington boots and so on. Men don't like them at all. I wait until the day before a period, to have any sex, to be safe." But there had been a few scares. A three day delay of her periods had been scary and a ten day delay had left her going through all variations possible. From frozen fear that reduced her to a zombie going off to work to a future as an unmarried mother, the scope was wide.

She had gone as far as thinking how the baby would fit into the bedsit – it wouldn't. The baby would need a darkened corner to sleep in, its cries would disturb the other tenants, it would stop her going out to work, it would mean she could not go out, ever, again. But it at the same time it would be a wonderful, beautiful being to love forevermore, to flood with love. So when the delayed blood started to stream out, she had an experience of loss for the never-to-be born baby. It had been a violent see-saw of hope and dread. This is where the mice in the pillow and the black dog had come from. Seething fear, never talked about.

The doctor looked at her as if at a specimen in the zoo. There was a wedding ring on the correct finger and what Stella called a housing estate engagement ring – those with a large diamond solitaire flanked by smaller ones either side, somehow an obvious and vulgar design. Hard to judge if it was worth thousands or just ten quid. The husband would be another doctor, The Times, Telegraph or Guardian on the side plate at breakfast, chunky marmalade on toast, the daily woman just arriving. Once a year they would take the wrong briefcase from the hall stand, with embarrassing results. A joint bank account. Occasionally a visit to the theatre or a symphony concert. Not really together, not really apart, and seemingly eternal to the neighbours.

"So yes, I want to be fitted up with something or some pills." The doctor gave her a cold, assessing look. It was frightening.

"Well, we certainly could not give you anything in the present circumstances according to what you have just said. It would be impossible. It sounds too chaotic as a lifestyle to be encouraged. We could not help you at the present at all. However, when you establish a proper relationship with a boyfriend, a fiancé, we would be able to give you a Dutch cap and a cream, which will give you a form of protection." The doctor leant forwards.

"We could help you here, we could get you to take part in a study, investigate your case. Now, what was your full name again, and your address?" She was reaching for a manila folder, the kind all offices used. Stella knew how much information a manila folder needed to justify its existence. "If you could attend here on a Thursday evening, we have a special session at 7p.m. You say you work nearby?"

So now they wanted to turn her into a case and turn her life over into data for someone's research. How on earth did these people live? What categories did they dream up to shove everyone into? Stella rose up. The doctor looked surprised. No one had ever defied her here. They were all victims, supplicants.

"I'm not going to be turned into a case. I came here for information and proper help and you only want to pick over my entire life and turn it into data for someone's PhD."

There was a calendar on the desk and Stella could see that the moon would be in its last quarter on Tuesday and Toby would be round on Friday. It was all pointless, but she was not going to betray her own life for the entertainment of the medics here and their quaint opinions especially as they were not going to play fair.

Walking out through the waiting room, it was crowded with a legion of girls who looked about sixteen. Ostensibly engaged, they sat reading fashion magazines. She wondered what was going to happen to them, were they already enmeshed in the medical research web, or gaily already somehow on pills and potions? It was supposed to be right in the middle of swinging London but for their real lives it was something like 1865.

Off into the remains of the rush hour, with the inevitable future of an unplanned baby whether she wanted one or not. Temporary people could give permanent lessons, unfortunately.

"Disgusting!" Stella said to herself, feeling that some sacrifice to morals had been made (or someone else's strange code; it was hazy) as she walked out into the beginnings of the sunset.

She could imagine Toby's seven past girlfriends that he had told her about sitting round the waiting room. Perhaps they, too, would have been thrown out. Perhaps some things were inevitable and the life force demanded some workers on its side. Someone had to have the babies after all, or all society would grind to a halt.

It was a warm early evening and as Stella walked up Pond Street past The Roebuck, a man who had been walking up from the bus stop drew alongside her and said,

"I like a woman with a bit of meat on her myself, good legs, you need to have something to get hold of." He smiled at her in a proprietorial way as though they were friends. Just walking home was an unwanted game of snakes and ladders, you were there to be commented on and judged, trudging home after the disappointing interview at the clinic. The ploughman plodding his weary way was not hassled by any milkmaids.

She told Fiona what had happened. Fiona stared at her. Stella really was so stupid.

"Oh, You didn't!," said Fiona, "You should never tell them the truth, you were a real fool! I said I was engaged to a boy in the RAF and that he was stationed abroad and so when he was on leave, it was so important for us." Stella would never have thought of that, or even that the story was only a cover and the doctor knew it, but needed it as some sort of chit. How strange. Love and bureaucracy, of course they could not mix.

That there were two levels of reality going on at the same time – what was actually going on, and what society would say was happening. As usual, Stella had fallen through the gap. Fiona dashed upstairs to her own room and reappeared with a book.

"Look, you should have a read of this, it tells you everything you need to know." Fiona had managed to remain a virgin, regularly throwing men out of her room in the early hours of the morning. Stella could hear them clumping down the stairs as her bed was alongside the staircase wall. Why anyone would go to such extremes, Stella could not understand.

"I tell them I know it hurts, and they've got to stop, it can't go any further," Fiona stated. So far no man had caused any trouble, but it was a dangerous path to tread, taking men back after an evening out and then telling them to leave later on. She gave the book, Nina Farwell's *The Unfair Sex* to a bemused Stella. "You'll really find this useful, I've got to go now, another fitting for a new dress for the next cabaret show, it's up in Leeds! See you about Wednesday, then."

Fiona had a new boyfriend who motored her about and took her to the train or coach. He would meet her on return. He was nice because he did not have the oomph to be anything else. He could hardly believe his luck that Fiona was interested in him, not realising he was actually perfect doormat material and mostly sexually undemanding. As she was away so much, it was a perfect match for both of them at the time.

Glancing through the pages, with their many witty cartoons, Stella realised she had broken every one of the rules and had already done everything the examples warned against. But it only worked as a strategy if a woman did not actually like sex - or men, in fact, and was holding out, as it described, for proper marriage. In between was all the music scene around them.

All the pop songs plaited into each other in a vast evidence of human striving after something which might not have existed. Or perhaps it was all after that unimaginable height scaled when sex blasted all self to pieces and did not care where the bits landed. Walking up Pond Street with Fiona, on a Sunday evening at seven, new trendy purple shoes pinching.

"We're both 24 and we're dashing home to listen to Top of the Pops!"

July brought a hectic summer. Suicidal people ended up in her place, making her unhappy later in the week. It was as if there was a neon sign over the door '

Disheartened, desperate? Or actually suicidal? Apply here! No questions asked!' It was no coincidence that the Beatles newest song was "*Help*" as that summed up the sharp flavour of the time. One Saturday afternoon Sally arrived, another acquaintance from their Liverpool days, on the run from a collapsing marriage with a college sweetheart:

"Who are you seeing these days?"

"Well, it's Matt for the third time round. There's a party at his place, come along. It'll cheer you up." They walked along to the poets' Chalk Farm house, where Stella introduced Sally to Matt.

And with exceptional skill Sally immediately disappeared with Matt into the dark garden at the back of the house. Going round the sniggering couples in the dark garden like pervert, Stella tried to make out in the shadows if he was there but of course it was useless and by now perhaps she did not want to find him. Back in the dark room she sat on a striped mattress and talked to a young man who was yet another poet. There were too many of them, it was getting like a measles epidemic.

So it was definitely time to admit that the third affair between Matt and herself was truly over. His constant acquisition of new women was too much to cope with. But Stella remembered how kind he could be in the middle of all the chaos. Once, having left her at a Sunday evening gallery reading and going off with a young girl, Matt appeared at Stella's much later that evening.

After coping with someone else's depression and suicidal state, Stella had caught the same emotion herself. Pete (who she had fancied some time ago) had arrived in a desperate state and she had managed to haul him out of it, but had got too involved herself. A week later when his real girlfriend had collected him back via a telegram from Italy,

"I've got to go now, she says she's madly in love with me after all, it's all forgiven," Pete gloated and went off to Heathrow to meet his reinstated beloved at Pisa airport. Stella was dropped like an unwanted marionette.

Matt came back unexpectedly ("I just saw her into a taxi at the top") to find Stella standing on the desk, trying to open the window and crying constantly, trying to escape out of the window. He persuaded her to get down, and said she would come home with him, he could not leave her like this. She cried all the way down to Chalk Farm station. The new lodger in the basement was astounded to see what a bad state she was in. She crashed to sleep in Matt's large never-ending bed and woke in just enough time to dash back home for her overall and shopping bag and clean underclothes for a Monday morning start.

33

Toby and Stella drifted together again as there were no other possibilities, it seemed. Anything to blank out the gaping space left by Andy. Their relationship limped along in its random way. None of it was important, which is why it worked.

One night in autumn they came out of the pub laughing, whirling into the traffic, hurling each other into the road, careless of death. Night motorists stopping, swerving up Pond Street. Drivers swore at them as one or both of them dancing in the road or pushing each other further. Cars jamming brakes. Stella did not care if she ended up in hospital. The endless round of work food rent was just as meaningless as this bravado. Neither Toby nor Stella had any fear or concern about the consequences as they played at jaywalking. They skirmished with the manoeuvring cars and angry drivers, laughing at fate.

It was annoying to find she was awake yet again on a Monday morning, ready to go out to work. There was no escape. Each week's National Insurance and Income Tax had to be paid. No old age pension otherwise. Stamps on your card were paramount; it said so; otherwise you did not exist. National Insurance knew where you lived and could trail you from job to job, employer to employer.

Toby turned up on various weekends. He was apparently her boyfriend, if asked, though it was surprising to both of them. These days he shared a flat with two other teachers-of-English-to-foreigners. They were all writers, going off in different directions, a mystery to each other and deadly rivals. They wrote plays and poems which they presented to their befuddled students as examples of English culture. Their rich Chinese and Japanese students attended out of politeness, not able to make sense of any of it because even in English it did not make sense. Much of the writing was the outcome of a semi-lethal mixture of drugs and hunger. However, the productions gave the pseudo teachers extra dues and credits. Toby was a star performer and did not expect any payment either.

They acted out the playlets written in haste during the week. This performance had Toby being a do-gooder who was adopting an alien from another planet. He had painted a piano yellow in welcome and the puzzled foreigner did not appreciate why the cat was painted yellow too.

"But I have washed the radio in your honour!" It rollicked along merrily. The audience applauded. Then Mark did a modern version of Thomas Grey's Elegy Written in a Country Churchyard. The pastiche worked wonderfully if you knew the original, otherwise for its mostly Chinese and Japanese audience it was nonsense

One Saturday they both woke about eleven to a bright morning. Stella was glad that gin did not smell as she put last night's clothes on again and went across to the coffee pot to start the day. Toby had run out of money last night and she had dashed back home and retrieved a ten-shilling note hidden under the carpet. But she did not want the glass of gin that he insisted on buying for her after that; a tomato juice would have been enough and far cheaper and she had refused to drink it. Laughing at her, Toby had then thrown the entire glass of gin all over her, though she was laughing too eventually. They could pretend to be rich, for an instant.

Toby still lounged in bed, now hogging both pillows. Stella passed him a mug of sugar-laden coffee and he started to get dressed, stuffing into his jeans and sweater. She got the pack of bacon indoors from the windowsill and began frying a few rashers for bacon sandwiches. It was part of the usual service, after all.

"Oh, I can't wait for all that," Toby said, slinging his boots on. "I've got to push off right now; I'm getting married at half-past two. Veronica's father said it was about time, he's some sort of vicar after all, bit of pressure there. It's at St Pancras Registry office, everyone will be there, you're welcome, do turn up." He strode across to her, gave her a quick peck on the cheek and dashed out. "Bye!" She heard the clatter of the front door as it slammed behind him. The bacon curled obediently against the silver sides of the frying pan Mrs Harris had given her. The throw-outs of the rich, loved and cared for by the desperate. Pink, delicate rose madder, curling fat at the edges – what colour would that be – zinc white with yellow ochre, touch of grey? She would have to eat it all now, his helping as well as her own. But no, it was impossible to eat now. The half-eaten sandwich was cast aside.

A wild hysteria kicked in, beginning with this forensic freeze. Then, slowly, a drumbeat started, panic, panic. She had to get out of this room quickly, anywhere, just get out of here. Slipping on shoes and coat Stella went out into the street not knowing of anywhere to go, but anywhere would do that would fill in a couple of hours until this wild heartbeat could subside. The real tears, she knew, would not appear until about Wednesday, she had that much control, but the tide could not be stopped; any tide had to come in eventually.

It was as if the shoes knew where to go, she ended up at Queens Crescent market wandering past stalls of vegetables, fruit and cheap clothing. A voice in her head took over and told her what to do at each moment like a stage director.

Have to buy something. Get some oranges. Go into a shop. Here's Woolworths, that will do. The floorboards stretched to infinity like something out of a Toulouse Lautrec, or that spooky Night Café by Van Gogh. What to do here? Walk round properly. Look at things like a real shopper. Must buy something, you're in a shop after all. A lipstick, it will come in useful, Toby ruined your other one last time with that message all over the mirror.

I can't possibly go to the wedding. She will know. Women pick up on that sort of thing, bound to. In fact they'll all know, they'll suspect. But no one will know how I'm feeling. Not supposed to feel. But I'll go to the evening do, that will look right and it'll be the only way to get round this. There had been one time when Toby mentioned going back to the house and digging a sandpit for the toddlers, but it had sounded like a visitor doing something out of duty. He had never mentioned any link between himself and Veronica still existing otherwise. And by the time Stella walked back home, having bought yet another meat pie and a jar of Branston Pickle for tea the evening was settled. On stage again, in best make-up.

The wedding party was held in Matt's basement, with all the rooms open, including the ground floor flat. People drifted from one room to another and stumbled up or down the stairs already drunk or stoned or a mix of both.

Various bits of jazz oozed out from different record players. Toby and Veronica stood in Trish's room where the main drinks were, bottles lined up along the window sill and along the sideboard that was Trish's painting surface.

Veronica was a surprise. She was as tall as Toby, obviously effortlessly slim. Auburn and subtly red hair artlessly arranged in a loose chignon. Perfect cheekbones and violet-blue eyes, skin and bones of porcelain. It was as if a light shone through her and as if she was breakable. There was no sign of the two toddlers, left with the relieved grandparents at a vicarage somewhere in the Home Counties. She hardly spoke and Stella managed to congratulate her while Toby had gone to collect more drink. They were going off tomorrow to France on honeymoon, after being together, more off than on, for over four years.

Later news was that they had soon run out of money and ended up sleeping under a French hedge or two, only too glad to get back again to the council house in Hendon. and the waiting toddlers.

34

Every weekend was another escapade. This time the group from the Roebuck had ended up at a place in Wood Green over a shop in the main street. Sometimes it was not easy to navigate, they merely piled into someone's car and hoped for the best. It was the almost-end of one party. A small plump man walked across from the fireplace where he had been talking to another middle-aged man. Now he stood before her, a forty-ish man in black leather jacket and jeans. He was obviously angry.

"Why have you been ignoring me all this evening?" He jabbed his finger at Stella. His face was growing red with anger. As usual in embarrassing or hostile incidents like this, no one intervened, in fact there was a sudden gap all around her. She faced her accuser.

"I did not even notice you!" she said truthfully if not tactfully

"You've not bothered to speak to me at all!" he rasped. Stella assured him that there were several others she had not talked to.

"I don't talk to everyone, and anyway I'm here with some friends." He was not mollified by this at all and continued to point at her face. It was both embarrassing and frightening. No decent person would have treated him like that, he objected. As she spluttered more soothing words , floundering dangerously, his friend eventually came across after him, realising it was getting heated, and patting his arm, drew him away and stopped the altercation.

"Come on now, Gordon, you can see she can't say any more. You're wasting your time here. Let's go home." Gordon, still snarling, let himself be guided back to the fireplace to nurse his grudge. Their two empty glasses stood on the mantelpiece. As if by magic, the remaining party people filled up the spaces again, their cowardice changed now, the atmosphere different. Stella went into another room to find Fiona and Ben, the new boyfriend.

"For goodness sake! Can we go home now? I've had enough." It was like encountering a rabid dog disguised as a pudgy balding middle-aged man, a resentful bulldog. It had been deeply upsetting and she was shaking now and near to tears. But that was the dynamic of most Saturday night gatherings and they christened, if that was the right word, such people as the Two O'clock Neurotic.

By midnight as in all the fairy tales, the crowd would always thin out. People who had arrived as couples went home, their entertainment completed; they were out of the sexual hunt after all. Home, with something to talk about and after a cheap night out too. Those who had linked up, fallen in love or lust, crashed in immediate attraction, dashed off to fornicate in joy and delight. By two o'clock, all the interesting people had left and only two types remained - the energetic dancing crowd and the absolute dross.

Just as Stella used the usual rigmarole of avoiding grasping men at a party and tried to remember it forever, it was a blur how she began talking to a fair-haired man named Doug. Or even when she had learned his name, for they did not mention names in the beginning. So often events while they are happening are quite blank as if made of large blocks of colour and sound. Later, rethinking it, names and reasons and other peoples' motives and results crowd into what had seemed a plain moment at the time.

So that a week later, when Stella thought of meeting him that Friday night she met him already knowing his name, Doug, his age, 23, his broken marriage, his silly wife bringing up his child, while he was not allowed to have him ("I could look after him. We get along together, but it's not allowed. She's got him and I can't do anything to stop her. And she's a right cow at times,") his studying at Woolwich Polytechnic, his ghost hunting, his sunburnt back, his last job as a paving stone-layer, his mother who he had recently attacked,

("She got on my nerves about the kid. It wasn't my fault, but they won't take it from its mother and I won't let my ma bring it up either. She's just as bad. So I went for her,") his bottle of neat alcohol ("Have some, here,") and his often sharp comments to her, (You don't want to waste any more time here, do you? You want us to get back to your place as quickly as possible. Come on then!")

Doug contradicted himself here because they were sliding in a heap of coats and cloaks and it seemed he would stay where he was and settle down, dragging her into the sea of clothing with him. He kissed her as she fell against a fur coat and more jackets and coats fell over onto the floor.

"We can't stay here, it wouldn't be right to do anything here," she tried to sound enthusiastic and cautious at once. Doug briskly changed mood, became clear and stood up,

"Let's go!" Out of the party, in the navy blue road, their drunkenness doubled, as if the silence around made new complications and threw more back into their inner havoc. "Look! There's a motorbike along here, we could get home on it." He went up to it, tried to kick-start it, while Stella quietly panicked, a) the police might stop them b) Doug was drunk c) so was she d) she might fall off e) they might crash f) the owner might catch them g) they had no crash helmets h)Doug did not know where she lived i) She did not know the way home from here j) she might lose her job if there was a scandal. It became quite crucial. While appearing to egg him on, Stella listened doubly-hard for any stray taxi wandering round Wood Green at this hour. One appeared in the distance just as Doug was beginning to lose patience with the non-starting motorbike and was kicking it randomly. Its unmistakeable thrum sounded louder in the empty street.

"Oh look, here's a taxi, we could get in that," she made it sound as though a surprise circus was marching into Wood Green High Road. He weakened or changed moods and lumped into the taxi with her. In the comfort of the deep seat he kissed her, or she kissed him, or they met somewhere in the middle of both these decisions. Warm alcohol-filled mouths and subtle lickings of smooth sides of teeth. Their tongues lay side by side resting, a language of liquids and moist spaces. She had wanted him for at least an hour; or all of her life that had led up to that hour was now being spent rapidly. And he felt her welcome, softness and harsh eagerness combined, another home to go to. The tight black-lace streets pulled along intensifying their awareness of each other. The taxi driver was used to such things.

Stella paid the fare. It was worth the luxury. On the other hand, the best things in life are free. Because she half expected it, it was obvious that Doug had no money (The wife, the child, the course at the Poly) so she paid for the taxi as if removing some weight from his obligations.

He sat on the edge of the bed as soon as she opened the door and looked around it. He did not walk round it as most people would the first time. They would look at any books look at any paintings, the washing drying on the rack, magazines on the table, the necklaces, never worn, hanging from a nail, (Ostentatious, said one critical visitor.) Then they usually looked in the mirror as if to finish by setting their own reflection also in the room.

Then they usually sat down on the bed, and some time later (blur, blurred) they would kiss her. All this time Stella would have been pirouetting around making coffee as some excuse for conversation, to show him (and convince herself for one more time) how interesting a person she was for all occasions.

The prince and princess fall in love and dance a typical pas de deux.

In the morning he looked at the latest painting on the mantelpiece. It was about mornings in a park, all blues, turquoises and greenish tints. After staring at it for a bit, Doug said caustically,

"You take one colour and flog it to death"

"But if you have made it, then you can hack it about. If you haven't made it, it doesn't exist. That's my motto," she said. But that was more or less true. Taking a chord of colours made a picture flow. Too much contrast, like orange versus lilac seemed to shout or even clash. The paintings were mostly aimed at harmony – blue to green to turquoise, yellow to orange to red. Always only half the rainbow, not the full paintbox fighting it out, each colour against another. Each painting held its own world inside its edges.

Stella produced another party for them to go to for Saturday night, at the poets' house yet again. He strode round the basement rooms having a couple of words with everyone as though he was conducting a survey. She was dancing with various friends to loud Tamla Motown records, a contrast with their daytime intellectual image. People were already keeling over and going off into the garden to be sick, but the atmosphere was bright, in contrast with what was actually going on. Every now and then Doug would give her a swig of the bottle of neat alcohol in his pocket. In a strange demarcation line, he disapproved of those who were smoking dope as the heavy smell grew around them all.

Doug was suddenly excessively moral as though he was a grandparent. He told her,

"I'm not going to stay here and watch these people destroy themselves. Give me the key if you want to stay here, then." Unusually, Stella was determined to remain, some mix of group loyalty and curiosity. She gave him the keys for the front door and room door and off he went back to her place. Luckily he remembered the way and the timing was not too bad; Stella was soon back.

"It got boring. They all started to look silly, you were right." After drinking the neat alcohol on Saturday night they woke up to green ceilings and jigsaw selves. After a bath each and Doug going out to buy a razor because she had none -

"You ought to have them."

"I'd have to buy one for each man and they might get suspicious" – they went out into a piercing green sun. Or so it appeared to them both.

The house at the end of the street had just been repainted a bright white that week, the scaffolding had gone and they both walked gingerly past it, shielding their eyes from the zigzags of red and purple it was shooting out at them. The paving stones were light pink, which hurt also. It was mid-afternoon

In a bright shock therapy idea they both agreed to go for a curry. In the quiet Indian café with its immaculate tablecloths they were politely handed the usual numbered menu, where the curries were ranked according to strength. So far Stella had only got as far as stage 4, but today they both went for number 12 to counteract the neat alcohol hangover. The two fires would defeat each other.

Doug went off after pub closing on Sunday night. She did not see him to the bus stop nor walk down to the tube station. They merely walked up to the corner of the hill and said goodnight. Or he said "So long" and she said "Goodnight" or something. No arrangements, no catching, phone numbers, a friend's name, an address, a pub name, somewhere to go, a film, a time. They never saw each other again – which was what they were both saying, accepting, without explaining to each other any of the reasons why.

Once, when he had gone to phone in the hall she had gone (dangerously) through his jacket pockets and found an envelope addressed to his parents' house. Stella copied it down in her diary, knowing she would never use it. It was in her handbag then, as they said goodbye on the hill, without any kissing.

"I have to call into college today anyway and feed the mice and rats. The poor things have to be fattened up, or at least have sleek coats, ready for experiments. And it's where I got the neat alcohol from"

Months later, even, when viewpoint usually change she still accepted that minute as it was: an ending. Nothing could have been changed; they would not have continued to be alive to each other over a longer time, although they had connected as much as each other was able to; they both knew that. It was as if what most people spend slowly across a lifetime, they had recklessly blued in a single weekend, with none left over. Of course she cried, some time on Tuesday night.

Back at work at Senate House she was told by Theresa as they sorted through the batch of maths scripts that no one else wanted to do,

"You could have gone blind." Getting back from work, the white wall diminished into ordinary white spruceness as she walked round the corner, all its neon lighting gone.

35

A few weeks later, a phone call, Sunday morning. It was Stu, he had bought some food, could he come round and cook breakfast at her place? The party at Matt's place had left many surplus people still in various states all over the floor and Matt had suggested he went off to Stella's for a bit of peace. Was that all right?

Stella was intrigued and bored at the same time and agreed, could he get some milk on the way. He arrived looking quite bright and perky, considering the circumstances. They sat and ate a mixture of classical English breakfast and total invention. As there was no marmalade, they had Branston Pickle on toast with lashings of tea piled up with sugar and of course the bacon in thick white bread sandwiches. It was interesting to see him here in the daylight; they had met in deep gloom, stuck together on a striped mattress in a room in Matt's basement.

She could not remember what they talked about then, as most of her attention was still focused on wherever Matt and Sally could have got to and what a predatory bitch Sally was. Plus of course what a careless slipshod Matt was, never able to be loyal to any woman for long enough for anything to gel.

Stu changed the atmosphere. He was going to do a reading in the West End that evening and she could come with him if she wanted. The translation was that she would be paying the tube fares of course. Some months later Stella met a poet musician who was amused to find she had been putting Stu up on his visits to London.

"Oh, he used to stay in my place, I wondered where he'd managed to move on to. Well, you have two advantages – yourself and being in Hampstead, he'd like that. But I found that under that image of the little-boy-lost and those old jumpers with the elbows worn out, there beats an adding machine. Look out." Ken was off to a gig in Birmingham himself just then.

By six thirty that evening Stella and Stu were sitting on a bench in Soho Square going over Stu's poems. It was a warm summer July evening with an almost countryside atmosphere. It was probably the same bench that Stella, Sue and Sally had met Rutger when they had visited London to see the Picasso exhibition in September.

"Should I take out this line? Does this sound right?" The poetry reading was going to be at an art gallery nearby. Lionel had arranged it, they had secret links of power here and there, contacts never explained. Matt looked a bit sheepish about the events of last night.

"You sent me someone nice, so I thought of sending you someone as well," he translated the night's betrayal. Stella gave him a cold look and moved away. Again, trying to paper over the cracks, Matt politely introduced her to Lionel, the great fixer, as an artist. Lionel immediately asked her if she had held an exhibition and when she, being honest said no, he rapidly turned his back on her. Stu did not notice.

The reading was a great success. At the end, women of all ages clustered round Stu, wanting any contact, like asking for a relic. Stella could hear offers of hospitality of various kinds being promised. She was surplus to requirements already. But for some reason, Stu caught up with her when the group went on for a drink and continued home with her. She was frozen but it did not show.

The next Saturday night Stu surprisingly appeared again and they spent it going round her favourite pubs selling the latest issue of Stu's poetry magazine. People bought it because they knew her, not because of any interest in the writing. At two shillings, it was quite pricey, as much almost as twenty cigarettes. Stu was delighted and left her with another dozen to sell by herself when he was gone off hitching north again on Monday.

"You can easily get rid of these, just going round the pubs on any evening yourself," he airily declared. But once was enough; she realised people could not be pestered week after week. On her own, the confidence drained away. The magazines stayed piled under the bed next to her paintings and she gave him some money later on when he turned up again. She was the only one with a job after all; the rest of them were intellectual hustlers. The magazines became a way of paying small debts and became expensive calling cards. One of the poems was by Robert Creeley, a favourite voice that called out clearly amongst the others.

36
Sunday afternoon was like an arty Hancock's Half Hour   "It's all right for you painters."

"It's all right for you poets."

"Have you got any paper to write on?" Stu asked. Stella gave him a couple of sheets of semi-tracing paper. After a 's pause he wrote a poem about the stables that could be seen out of the window and gave it to her. Years later she saw it published in a book, the exact same poem, dedicated to another woman. He either wrote out a poem he had already finished, and knew it off by heart or did a copy when she was not looking. He mentioned that he would be going off to Cornwall for a while.

"Oh, why go that far away?" He had no money for travel, that was obvious. It was quite a distance to hitch all the way to Cornwall and so far it was not a centre of poetry functions.

"Oh, I've got to go and visit some girl. She's having my baby. I said I'd turn up when it was due. It's going to be adopted, though, so I won't be moving there, it's just a visit. I'll start hitching there after seeing Barry about another poetry-reading gig." Stella was shocked at this disclosure and his coolness about the pregnant girl, but it got worse. She wanted to know more about all this.

"So what is going to happen after the baby's born and adopted? What's going to happen then?" He, however, was completely unfazed about the future. He knew what was going to happen, he contained it already like a fortune teller.

"She'll go to parties, get drunk, get all emotional and end up crying on some guy's shoulder about how bad it all is and there's a baby somewhere that she'll never see." This was even worse. He had already predicted the unnamed girl's every move, as though she was some puppet he could control the strings of, even at a distance, even in the future. He possessed her future, according to this account. No way was he going to play at happy families in the wilds of Cornwall, so far away from the bright lights of London and all its opportunities.

Stu said he was now a leading lyric love poet. He said this with pompous dignity. They gave themselves labels like this and no one ever challenged them. Men put on these labels themselves. No one ever peeled them off.

She was disgusted with him and also with herself as though she, too, had deceived the unknown girl. This was no way to treat anyone and she definitely did not want to be involved with Stu any more. The unsold poetry magazines rankled too, as he expected payment and she had given him the full price on his previous visit.

"I'm always needing money, you know how difficult it is."

A bath would be a good idea now, the ideal way to start anew. It was drifting towards a quiet Sunday evening now and it would do her good as well as being necessary. After any weekend Monday was always the worst day to get through, though Wednesdays were as bad, dead centre.

Because the bathroom upstairs was never clean enough to scatter underclothes around, as in the best adverts, Stella had taken to undressing in her own room first and going upstairs wearing the throw-over dressing gown. Its orange and purple flowers always made her feel carefree the first second on; then the towelling edges always rubbed annoyingly. It was yet another cast-off, a present given by one of her employers.

So, sitting on the edge of the bed she took off all her clothes and sat looking down. Big toe, left foot, getting squashed by shoes so often it had begun to hide behind the second toe. She brought it out, wriggling all the toes. Knees not too coarse now as she did not kneel to clean so often any more. Legs too short for fashion, sturdy with beginnings of fat on the inner side. Hairs beginning to grow again, must get some new razor blades. (All that fuss Dan made about getting a razor. How daft she'd been to run out and get one. Unnecessary expense too.) Pubic hair spreading annoyingly off-course, over onto sides of legs. No brief swimming costumes without drastic mowing. Not the sort of thing you could discuss with other women somehow, not even these days. Obvious why men preferred blondes, they would not have the same problems, any stray hair anywhere being almost invisible.

And suddenly she was back at childhood holidays and the beach at Heswall. Off the light blue one-decker bus, with the essential tomato sandwiches and orange juice. Down past the lower village and the lanes to the field with the white horse, old and tolerant now, the River Dee and the Welsh Hills behind him. From there they could see if the tide was in or out. He was like an earth-bound weather-vane because the scene behind him always changed, always foretold how their day was going to be – yet he himself was also part of that weather, its guardian.

Down more side-tracks, Mother and Aunt Marie and often Nana carrying the cardigans by now, Stella and Anne slowing down more and more until it became almost unpleasant, an endurance a test of who would give up first. Grit got into every shoe as the roads were literally home-made. Whenever a larger pothole than usual appeared, someone from the bungalows would contribute a bucketful of cinders, or throw a couple of bricks into the hollows if it was really drastic. So the random mendings were as uncomfortable and often as dangerous as the original breaks and potholes. The cinder particles, on hot days, flew through the holes in sandals and penetrated through socks. Yet in the evenings after summer rain those same lanes were gentle with water, graced with puddles and little frogs would be passing across the narrow lane from one ditch to another in the green dankness just before sunset.

On one of the afternoons they would go to Padgate with Nana and Aunty Kay and buy cockles and crabs from the always-deserted café and eat them on the terrace with the beach nearby, washed down with pots of tea and white bread. The swimming pool was not in use yet and stayed empty, with only autumn leaves and rubbish collected into its corners.

On the seashore there were still gigantic blocks of concrete placed strategically along the sands in case Germans tried to bring their invasion nearer by sailing up to the beaches, even this far up on the Wirral. Stella had already scratched her leg as the kids jumped from one block to another. Nana warned them about the barbed wire which was still wreathed about here and there, already going rusty and growing even more lethal.

And there, right across her pubic hair, was a crab, exactly the same, wandering about. Its little legs navigated around the pubic hairs with effort. The past and the present clashed and she grabbed a piece of paper and squashed it to death. Then reaching for the scissors she got all the hairs trimmed down to almost nil and dropped the lot onto last week's New Statesman spread on the floor. Discarding clothes, getting the dressing gown and shampoo bottle, Stella dashed upstairs with the usual four pennies to have as hot a bath as she could muster.

And coming back to her room, ripping all the sheets off the bed and throwing in last week's underclothes, she hurried down to the launderette as soon as her hair was dry, to remove any burgeoning crabs, taking a book of poems to read while the washing whirled round.

So much for Stu and his lyric love poetry. He must be crawling with them.

That Saturday afternoon, Stuart phoned that he was going off to meet a girl who was going to give him some mescaline smuggled back from her travels in Mexico. He was overjoyed to get his hands on it, or to be able to boast around that he had undergone the experience. There were all these interesting people he mixed with now. Last time he had taken some LSD, but this pure mescaline was supposed to be different.

"What happens, what do you see?" Stella asked him.

"Oh, there are details of colours wherever you look, like on the pavement, for instance. You see things that aren't really there, it's like space travel."

She often saw pictures on the paving stones going up Pond Street after rainfall, when each flagstone had a different puddle reflecting the light. It was like walking on top of an exhibition itself. How sad that Stu had to take drugs to get what was freely available if only you looked properly at the surroundings. He said he would ring her up on Sunday evening afterwards. As if.

Stella did not want to be in the house if he did ring up and at the same time she did not want to be in the house if the phone did not ring. She could leave Miss Spedding to deal with him whatever state he might be in. She would dash round to Fred's right that afternoon to see if there was still a chance of a room going. She had kept in touch with the house after cleaning there. It had quietened down with a change of tenants, Fred had seen to that. No, phoning up would be quicker. Fred had mentioned Luke was moving out and as an ex-tenant had she ever thought of moving back in? He said what a coincidence, that he had the top front room free right now, could she afford it? The new office wage made it possible. Could she come round right now? He was going out soon, but they could settle it all quickly. One week's rent was the usual deposit, she knew that.

Rapidly she rummaged out all her paintings together from under the bed, collected clothes, crockery, books and the frying-pan, all ending jumbled together in the back of a taxi, leaving a week's rent in the old rent-book pushed through Laurence's office door, with a note of apology, and sailed off down towards the Heath.

The large ultramarine blue painting of the Empty Cathedral just fitted right across the entire back seat of the taxi and Stella squashed beside it clutching the old hatbox and two bin bags of clattering crockery, clothing and books. Two binbags were progress of a sort; it had always been one bag before. And the clutch of paintings showed the time well spent since she had first moved in.

"It's all right!" She reassured the bemused taxi driver. "It's not a moonlight flit. It's the middle of the afternoon after all and the rent's left there in the rent book, it's all properly done, honestly." Summer Sunday afternoon. A sharp razor cut.

"I'm on the way with what I've got here." Originally meant to be the 36 views, many of the pictures had strayed into entirely different subjects. The frying pan rattled against the painting of Notre Dame Cathedral stretching across the taxi, a field of voluminous blue and imitation stained glass as the taxi sped off round the corner towards the Heath. She was going to start all over again, this time in a larger room. Space was essential, more and more of it. Space was wonderful stuff. The bigger room would easily house the new paintings, all 36 of them in its fitted wardrobe.

Clouds need clean brushes, the leaflet from the art shop said. You created your own skies and kept them clear and bright, or made them deep and dramatic. It depended on what you were feeling at the time.

Printed in Great Britain
by Amazon